ALSO BY INGO SCHULZE

New Lives

Simple Stories

33 Moments of Happiness

One More Story

ONE MORE STORY

Thirteen Stories in the Time-Honored Mode

Ingo Schulze

Translated from the German by
John E. Woods

Alfred A. Knopf
New York
2010

For Natalia

Then one day followed the next without the basic questions of life ever being solved.

—*Friederike Mayröcker*

Contents

Cell Phone

They came during the night of July 20–21, between twelve and twelve thirty. There couldn't have been many of them, five, six guys maybe. I just heard voices and the racket. They probably hadn't even noticed light burning in the bungalow. The sleeping area is at the back, and the curtains were drawn. The first sultry night in a good while and the start of our last week of vacation. I was still reading—Stifter, *Great-Grandfather's Satchel*.

Constanze had received a telegram from the newspaper in Berlin, telling her to report for work at seven thirty on Tuesday morning. Evidently her secretary had coughed up our address. The series about Fontane's favorite places was getting bogged down because commissioned articles weren't coming in on deadline. That's the problem when you don't go far away. We're both on the road all year more or less—I work for the sports section, Constanze for the feuilleton—and neither of us has any desire to spend our vacation sitting around in airports too. We rented the bungalow for the first time last summer—twenty marks a day for twenty by twenty feet—in Prieros, southeast of

Berlin, exactly forty-six kilometers from our front door, a corner lot with pine woods all around, perfect when it's hot.

It was odd being there alone. Not that I was afraid, but I heard every falling branch, every bird hopping across the roof, every little rustle.

It sounded like gunshots when they kicked in the fence boards. And then the whooping! I turned off the light, pulled on a pair of pants, went to the front—we always keep the roll-down shutters open at night. But I still couldn't see a thing. Suddenly there was a hollow thud. Something heavy had been upended. They yowled. My first thought was to turn on the outside light, just to show that somebody was home and the idiots wouldn't think nobody would spot them. There were a couple more loud noises—then they moved on.

I could feel sweat beading even on my legs. I washed my face. I could open the window from the bed. It had cooled off a little outside. You could just barely hear those guys now. Finally everything was quiet again.

My cell phone rang at seven on the dot. "Rang" is actually the wrong word, it was more like a "tootle-toot" that kept getting louder, but I liked its familiar sound because it meant Constanze. She was the only person who had the number.

While Constanze talked about how unbearably hot Berlin was and wanted to know why I hadn't stopped her from driving back into the brutal city, I took the cell phone with me out into the sunny quiet morning and surveyed the damage. Three sections of fence were lying in the path. The concrete post between them had been broken off just above the ground and tipped over. Two twisted steel rods stuck up out of the stump. Out by the gate the rowdies had turned the newspaper tube on its head. Just underneath it I discovered the roof and back wall of the

4

birdhouse. I counted seven fence slats that had been kicked in, plus four ripped loose entirely. Constanze said that she hadn't realized what a dirty trick that telegram was until now. I really shouldn't have let her drive back.

I didn't want to worry Constanze—she's always quick to get the feeling that something is a bad omen—so I didn't mention last night's visitors. It would have been hard to interrupt her anyway. She had already laid into the people who had rented the bungalow before us for turning the power off and leaving a half-full fridge. Suddenly Constanze cried that she had to go, kiss-kiss, and hung up.

I crawled back into bed. The damage was nothing I needed to take personally, of course, and there was a relatively simple explanation, too. The half acre of land that goes with the bungalow is only leased. That will end in 2001, or 2004 at the latest, when the transitional period will be over and our acquaintances will have to leave. That's why they haven't invested anything for several years now. The fence is held together by wire in places where the wood is too rotten for nails.

Last fall Constanze wrote an article about the New York police and their new philosophy. I remembered an example about a car abandoned on the street for weeks. Trash collects around it, yellowed fliers are wedged under the wipers. One morning a wheel is missing, two days later the license plates are gone, and soon the other three wheels. A rock is thrown through a window, and then there is no stopping it. The car goes up in flames. Conclusion: You don't let junk even start to collect.

At least Constanze had been spared this incident. Together we would probably have done something reckless, or Constanze would have been depressed for days because we'd turned chicken and taken cover. But now I had to do something, otherwise next thing you know they'll be throwing rocks through our window.

I got up to clear the sections of fence from the path. The first slat I picked up broke apart. With its protruding nails it reminded me of a weapon from the arsenal of Thomas Müntzer. First I threw all the slats in a pile. Then I began dragging them to the shed. To leave them lying out where anyone could get at them seemed too dangerous. Maybe I was exaggerating. But the fact was that not even a symbolic barrier protected the bungalow now.

Given the situation it was good to have a cell phone. I'd brought the envelope containing all the instructions—which Constanze had jealously guarded—along with me to Prieros and had finally learned how to activate the mailbox. It was my surprise for Constanze.

The "Hello!" of a man's voice startled me. Medium build, dressed in flip-flops and a sweatshirt, he was standing at the gate and asked what damage the rowdies had done at our place.

His fence was missing two slats. "A latticework fence," he said. "Do you know what kind of strength that takes?" The worst thing for him was the dent in the hood of his Fiat Punto. He'd searched a long time for whatever it was they'd thrown, but had found nothing. His crew cut looked like a fur hat set across his brow.

"It always happens during summer vacation," he said. "All young kids. Always during vacation."

I led him around. He took the inspection tour very seriously, squatting down a couple of times as if searching for clues. He found more pieces of birdhouse, turned the newspaper tube back to horizontal, and helped me with the rest of the fence slats. He had notified the police last night and evidently hadn't let them off the hook until they had promised to send someone. "You need to know," he said, "that this is small potatoes to them. Undermanned like they are, totally undermanned."

He was interested in what I had to say about the New York police, and I promised to send him Constanze's article.

"Can you give me your cell phone number?" he suddenly asked.

"My cell phone number? I don't even know it."

His frown pulled his bristly hair so deep that its leading edge pointed straight at me.

"I'll have to check," I said, and asked what he planned to do in case these guys came back.

"First off, get in touch," he replied curtly.

"That can't hurt," I said.

Inside I sat down on the bed with the envelope in hand. All my colleagues had cell phones. I never understood why they put up with them. I'd never wanted a cell phone, until Constanze came up with the idea of a one-way phone. To make calls, yes— to be called, no, with the exception of her, of course.

As I copied our number I noticed that it ended in 007.

"My name's Neumann, by the way," he said, holding out a store receipt on which he had scribbled his own number. In the same moment the phone rang. With a hasty good-bye he headed off.

Pretty much everything had gone wrong at the office. Constanze would have to stay in Berlin, at least until the day after tomorrow. She said that the latest deportations had also set off a row within the feuilleton staff itself. I had no idea what deportations she was talking about. We didn't listen to the radio because the FM button was missing.

Constanze was still angry and claimed that those guys just hadn't been able to deal with losing to Croatia in the World Cup soccer match. That was why they were carrying on like this.

I told her about last night. She just said, "Well then, come home."

"Yes," I replied. "I will, tomorrow." I didn't want to look like a coward. Besides, it was easier to deal with the heat here.

I tidied up. In case the police actually did show, I didn't want them to think it made no difference if something got kicked in here or not. I was also going to tell them that our landlord had only leased the lot, since it was now the property of a Westi. As a final touch I swept the terrace.

That afternoon I spoke with some of the other neighbors as well. We agreed to leave on all the lights we could at night. We parked our cars with the headlights directed at the fences, so that we could suddenly blind these guys and maybe even get a picture of them. Our motto was: People, noise, light. We bungalow dwellers developed a kind of Wild West solidarity. No policeman ever showed his face, but we didn't waste words talking about that.

Out of a kind of gratitude I dialed Neumann's number. I had at times found it intoxicating to be connected by satellite with people anywhere in the world. That we were neighbors, not three hundred yards apart, made the idea seem even more fantastic. But instead of Neumann himself, I heard a woman say: "This is the voice mail of . . ." followed by a pause, and then out of a galactic void I heard the words: "Harald Neumann." I felt goose bumps creep up my arms, clear to my shoulders. Of course even friends often sound distracted or depressed on their answering machines. But Neumann didn't just sound downhearted—it was as if he were ashamed even to have a name.

A little later there was a brief thunderstorm. I saw Neumann coming out of the woods with a basket full of mushrooms. He called to me from a good distance, "Like turnips!" He probably meant that in this weather you could gather mushrooms the way you could harvest turnips, or that they were as big as turnips. He invited me to help him eat them.

In comparison with our little shack, his bungalow was a small palace, with a television and stereo, leather chairs, and two bar stools. Neumann served red wine and French bread with the mushrooms. After that we played chess and smoked a whole pack of Clubs between us. There seemed to be no connection between the Neumann here before me and the man who spoke his name for his voice mail. All the same I felt shy about asking him about his family or occupation.

Toward evening the clouds above the lake turned pink. I laid my big flashlight and Neumann's number where they were handy. By ten o'clock the lightning was flashing with the regularity of a warning light. A cloudburst followed. By then it was clear to me that no one would be coming that night.

The next morning I packed everything up, did a last dusting, and said good-bye to my neighbors. I didn't find Neumann at home. Presumably he was in the woods again. I don't think people got the idea that I was a coward. They realized that Constanze was no longer here. The telephone call with our acquaintances—our landlords—proved more difficult. I was supposed to take care of the fence. There were still some posts in the shed. But the refrigerator alone had cost us a whole morning—that was quite enough.

In late September the cell phone rang in the middle of the night. In the first moment I thought it was the peep it makes when the battery is low. But the tootle-toot got louder each time. I got up, groped in the dark for my shoulder bag, and rummaged in it. I traced the tip of my forefinger across the keys—I needed the middle one in the second row from the top. The signal was now insufferably loud.

"Those guys are back again. They're really raising a racket!" And then after a brief pause: "Hello! This is Neumann! What a racket! Do you hear it?"

"But I'm not there anymore," I finally said.

"They're really raising a racket!"

The light on Constanze's side went on. She was sitting on the edge of the bed, shaking her head.

With my free hand I covered the mouthpiece. "A neighbor from Prieros." I could feel myself breaking into a sweat. I had never mentioned exchanging phone numbers—we wouldn't be going to Prieros again anyway.

"Are you alone?"

"Somebody has to hold down the fort," Neumann cried.

"Are you alone?"

"They're breaking down my fence, the bastards."

"Have you called the police?"

Neumann gave a laugh, then had to cough. "That's funny . . ." It sounded as if he'd been drinking. I had never sent him Constanze's article about New York.

"What is it you want?" I asked.

"Just listen to that racket!"

I pressed the phone tight to my ear, but it made no difference.

"Now they're at the mailbox!" he shouted. "They'll have to sweat and strain at that. Not even two of those lunkheads can manage that. They've gone too far. . . . Enough is enough!"

"Stay where you are!" I shouted.

Constanze was standing in the door, tapping a finger at her forehead. She said something from the hallway that I didn't understand.

"Hello?" Neumann called out.

"Yes," I said. Or did he mean those guys at the fence. "Stay inside!" I shouted. "Don't try to be a hero."

"They're gone," he said, and laughed. "Nobody in sight, they've taken off, scared shitless. . . ." I distinctly heard Neumann take a drink and set the bottle back down. "These lunkheads," he gasped.

"You shouldn't be there all by yourself."

"So how are you doing?" he interrupted me in an almost hoarse voice.

"Stay in the house," I said. "You shouldn't even be out at the lake, or just on weekends maybe, but not during the week."

"When are you coming back? We still have a game we haven't finished. Or would you like to play by mail? You want to give me your address? I've got some dried mushrooms, a whole sack full."

"Herr Neumann," I said, and didn't know what else to say.

"The garbage can!" he suddenly bellowed. "My garbage can!"

"Forget about the garbage can," I said. "It's not important." I called out, "Hello?" and "Herr Neumann" a few more times. Then there was only a dial tone, and the display read: "Call ended."

Constanze came back into the room, lay down on her side,

facing the wall and pulling the blanket up over her shoulders. I tried to explain the whole thing to her—how I'd hesitated at first, but that in the end I'd been glad I could call a neighbor for help in an emergency. Constanze didn't stir. I said I was worried about Neumann.

"Maybe he'll call back," she replied. "This will be happening fairly often now. But of course you never give the number to anybody."

I think at moments like this we're both so disappointed with ourselves that we hate each other. I went to my study to fetch the charger for the cell phone.

"And what if he passes your number on?" Constanze turned over and propped herself up.

"Why would he do that?"

"But just imagine if he does!"

"Constanze," I said. "That's silly."

"You need to think about it!" The strap of her nightgown had slipped off her shoulder, and she pulled it back up. But it didn't stay. "Think of all those people who could call now," she said. "All those neighbors."

"Our number's in the book, a perfectly normal number. Anybody can call us."

"That's not what I mean. If a building is on fire or gets bombed and somebody runs out with nothing but his cell phone, because it happens to be in his pocket. You'll be able to talk with him now."

I plugged the charger into the extension socket beside the bed.

"It can very well happen," Constanze said. Her voice now had that "governess" tone of hers. "Somebody calls you up from Kosovo or Chechnya or from wherever that tsunami was. Or one of those guys that froze up on Mount Everest. Now you can talk with him to the bitter end, until it's all over."

Braced on her elbow, one shoulder still bare, she went on talking while she stared at the tip of her pillow, which was propped up a little. "Just imagine all the people you'll be dealing with now. Nobody has to be alone anymore."

It was pointless to call information, because it was pointless to call Neumann. I don't know which would have been more unpleasant, to have him answer or to have to listen to the way he pronounced his name on his mailbox.

The display showed the symbol for recharging: the outline of a little battery, with a slanted bar marching across three positions. It was the last thing I saw before I turned out the light. In the dark Constanze said, "I think I'm going to file for divorce."

I listened to her breathing, her moving, and waited for the tootle-toot.

The shutters on the newspaper kiosk had already rattled when our hands accidentally touched. It took another eternity before we risked moving closer to each other. Then we started to devour each other in a way we hadn't done for ages, as if lack of sleep had made us crazy.

At some point the tootle-toot began. It came from somewhere far away, like the signal of a spaceship maybe, soft and indistinct at first, gradually pressing closer, growing louder and louder, and finally drowning out everything else, until it seemed as if Constanze and I were moving without making any sound at all. The only thing we could hear was that tootle-toot—until it suddenly stopped, left us in peace, and was as silent as we were.

Berlin Bolero

"What a slime bag!" She pressed her glass to her cheek again. "And you played right into his hand. Kept your mouth shut the whole time. And he's such a . . . I just don't get it."

Robert spread his fingers wide. He wanted to know if he could feel the wart if it didn't rub against his middle finger. It had first felt like a scab, then like a crumb of toast.

"Four weeks at the outside," he said, and looked up briefly. She was still leaning against the windowsill, in her dark blue bathrobe, her right arm under her breasts, her left elbow cupped in her hand. "If they hold to their plan, at most two, two more weeks."

"It leaves such a nasty taste." She sipped at her brandy. The red streaks across her cheek were gradually fading. "I don't understand how you could do it, I just don't get it."

The rest of her brandy sloshed back and forth like the waves in the cube that he always picked up from the counter whenever he handed over his insurance card at the dentist's: a little white sailboat on towering blue waves, always staying afloat, its sail to the wind, even when he upended the cube. His fingers slid into dovetail position. "We've made it through ninety-six weeks. And now it's just two more—"

"Ninety-six shitty weeks!" She squinted and opened her mouth. The glass was empty. "All down the tubes—"

"Those ninety-six weeks weren't *shitty*, Doro, not—"

"More than just shitty, it's been . . . What do *you* call it when winos hold their clambakes in the entrance to your building, don't even look the other way to take a piss. Or when your underwear in the drawer is filthy because somebody's constantly drilling into a wall on one side or the other. And never a ray of daylight, with the fucking plastic sheeting over the windows, and then I'm supposed to be happy it's just the sheeting and not some fucking asshole squatting at the window giving me the fucking finger."

"What?"

"Oh Robert, what planet do you live on?"

"Who did that? Would you recognize him again?"

"Don't give me that crap. . . ."

"I'm serious." He had stood up. But then she gave him that look—he didn't want to stand in front of her without being able to touch her. The muddy yellow light of the CD player surprised him.

"You think you're serious, but you don't know what you're talking about. You're usually more imaginative." She rolled the empty glass between her palms as she moved toward him.

"Doro," he said.

She poured herself another.

"That's rotgut. . . ." He had been keeping count and remembered to include this one. This last glass, filled to the brim, was as good as two.

She knelt down, bracing her hands on the coffee table, and slurped at the brandy. A strand of hair fell across the rim of the glass. "It's not all that bad, your friend's rotgut, your bud . . . dy's rotgut." To get to her feet she held on to the armchair. He didn't want to scold her. What he wanted was for these minutes in their life to match all the others. They ought to be able to remember every hour of their lives without regrets.

"Bud . . . dy," she repeated, and tried to drink as she took a step.

The one thing Robert felt he could hold against the man was that he'd lugged this booze along. Neither of them drank the hard stuff. Doro even had friends who never drank. You really had to keep that sort of thing in mind.

"Your bud . . . dy."

"Two more weeks," Robert said, looking at his hands and naked toes. Would he recognize them among a bunch of others? His hands, yes. They'd grown familiar now that he'd been regularly trimming cuticles. "But it's all been crystal clear, from the start."

"From the start!" She whirled around. Then she calmly said, "Those construction heinies have had to shell out week after week. They promised buyers vacant apartments, vacant, not occupied. So they just keep upping the ante, week after week. . . ."

"As if I didn't know that—"

"And they've gone way up by now, I mean sky high. And you claim we've discussed this. You guys'll never get it."

"What's with 'you guys'?"

"I mean you guys, the whole pack of you—"

"Just sit down, okay?"

"I thought you were being clever, letting them dangle out

there, and then right before the end . . ." She briefly balled a fist. Sweat was beading on her forehead, and her upper lip too. "We'll never get an offer like that again, never!"

"When it's all over and done with . . ." He looked at her, he wanted to go on talking. Once they could see the TV tower again, its flashing light, their star, and the magpies on the antenna during the day, and the chimney across the street, and the shadows creeping down the facade in the morning, until the balconies just cast little banners, pennants, as if the wind had picked up, blowing in from Friedrichshain. Robert stared at the ivy with its squidlike arms, at the bicycles in the courtyard.

She laughed.

"I don't put up with it for two whole years and then say, Thanks a lot. It's really been renovated nicely, lovely stairwell, good paint job."

"Not so loud!"

"You're such a dolt. How do you suppose he comes up with a number like that—one hundred eighty thousand, that's exactly twenty thousand more. You could have demanded two hundred. Two . . ." With her free hand she traced the numbers in the air. "And five zeros. Did he show you anything? Some scrap of paper that says the apartment belongs to him?"

The CD player light bothered him, it was like somebody lurking behind the armchair. Every week he pulled out the blue ten-pack of classical music that Dorothea had given him—ten CDs for eighty-eight marks—and selected one. He knew the names of most of the composers, but memorizing titles and conductors and orchestras was like learning Russian vocabulary words in the old days. He couldn't recall which CD he had heard last.

"You could've at least asked, before waiving our claims—as if I didn't even exist, as if I were just air, thin air. . . ." She turned around, went out into the hallway, holding the glass with just her fingertips and then slamming it down on the telephone stand. With a few strides he was right behind her.

"I'm not running away," she cried without looking around. "You blockhead, what a damn blockhead you are!"

"Doro," he whispered. "The kids."

"I've got to go!" She pulled the bathroom door behind her. He let his arms droop.

He sat down on the living-room sofa, right on the spot where a semicircular crease marked the spot he had just left.

By the time she stepped over the threshold again, he had to know how the evening was to proceed, how they would get to bed and fall asleep. Once they were in bed, the worst was over.

He followed the advice from a book he'd been reading during breaks at work: "Live in distinct units of time." He just had to get Dorothea and himself through the evening, through the night.

He trusted mornings, the half hour in the kitchen when the kids had dressed and Dorothea came in and he poured the milk into her coffee. When he left the house with the kids, the dishes were already in the dishwasher.

He had been working on the apartment for two and a half years now, first the central heating and electricity, then sanding and sealing the floors room by room, repairing the windows. Every screw anchor, every bracket, every newly painted doorframe, gave him a greater sense of security. It was the boys, however, who gave him real security. When Dorothea would invite her university crowd over and show them the apartment, and he would appear in the living room with the two boys in his arms for a good-night kiss, and Dorothea would say: "Here they are, my three men!"—then no one had it better than he did, at least no one he knew.

Suddenly there was that melody again. It was coming from her purse. Robert knew the classical piece, knew the composer's first and last names, even knew what name would be blinking on the display of her cell phone. He tossed the purse on the sofa, picked up a pillow, and pressed it down on the purse until the classical melody finally died away.

Robert had trained as a carpenter and switched from construction site to construction site for almost ten years. For three years he did heating installation, for eighteen months he delivered office furniture, hauling and assembling it. For two and a half years now he had been working for Magnum, a catering service. He had never been fired. The companies had all gone bankrupt. Nobody fired a man like him—he would bet you anything on that. There's always enough work to be done. So there. And Dorothea? He'd never really counted on her, which was why he had been so nonchalant about things. She was already thirty-one when she got pregnant the first time. He had never known you could study that long. Whenever Dorothea got work for a couple of weeks, it was always without pay. She would be so happy to find work that each time he assumed it was permanent. But she didn't really have to work. He took care of his family, he knew what was good for them. He didn't need any advice, certainly not from these construction heinies.

The construction heinies had invited them to a renters' meeting, kept staring at Dorothea, and had gone absolutely nuts when they heard Dorothea's dialect. A southern German, a woman from their part of the country, evidently they hadn't expected that, not in an apartment like theirs. But he had decided to put up a fight.

He had removed the lease from its folder only once—for thirty minutes. He had to take it to the copy shop on Wins Strasse, where he could get a discount on Dorothea's student card. He wasn't about to let the original get lost—or for that matter even get dog-eared—being shunted around in the mail.

He heard the toilet flush and didn't know if he should stand up or stay put. Dorothea was well prepared now, had armed herself with complete sentences. He would only be able to repeat how in two weeks . . . once the plastic sheeting was down, and the scaffolding . . . after ninety-eight weeks, there'd be sky again, a day of celebration, of victory. . . . And for the first time that idea didn't make him happy.

For the first six months nothing happened. Then came the notice about the scaffolding: Beware of Burglars! He bought mace and deposited a can in each room. And then the sheeting. Not one word had been said about sheeting. They had sweltered behind it for ten months before a single construction worker ever appeared. "We're being pargrilled," Dorothea had said. He told everyone, "If nobody moves out, they can't do a damn thing."

Once things got rolling the construction heinies rang the bell every week, and finally were at the door every day. He didn't want any renovations. He didn't have to go through bad experiences to know what was good for him. He had found his spot, and he wasn't about to leave again.

"Shouldn't we at least look at another apartment? Just look,

I mean." And he had simply asked Dorothea: "What don't you like about our place? What does it still need? What did I forget to do? What you would have different? So there."

The construction heinies crept through cracks just like the dust, and wet towels didn't help either. He didn't want the water heater removed from the bathroom, he didn't want central hot water, he heated with coal, you could depend on coal—even in a power failure, or a war. He had rented a second cellar storage space and had briquettes delivered, as a backup. And bought candles, so many they haggled for a discount.

All these types of guys knew how to do was throw money around, and if that didn't work, more money, and then some more. He could handle himself. They were the ones behaving badly, losing their patience and accusing him of all sorts of stuff. He didn't care where they came from or whether the construction foreman lived in Neukölln or Hellersdorf. He knew just one thing—that much money would wreck his family, that they dared not let themselves be softened up and abandon their apartment. They had to survive the ordeal. And he would help Dorothea to be strong.

This fellow had caught on, and so slipped his business card under the door this evening. He was in his midthirties at most, even though he had so little hair left there was no part, even from up close. The skin on his head was shiny. "Anybody who toughs it out this long ain't about to move out, right? They keep pushin' their luck. And puttin' me off till the bitter end." Robert liked the guy's Upper Lausatian accent and let him explain.

"I bought the apartment, this place, but vacant. Those guys in the West"—he meant the construction heinies—"say it's just a matter of money, right, as to when you'll move out. But I don't believe that anymore. I want my money back, yeah, want out from under the contract, see? I've waited two years. They'll keep on puttin' me off to the bitter end."

Finally somebody had caught on. They were never going to move out, not even for a hundred and eighty thousand. Why shouldn't Robert sign? The construction heinies would have it in writing, all nice and official, so to speak.

Dorothea got home just as his visitor was about to leave.

"Have you ever stopped to consider"—setting Robert back on his heels—"how long you'd have to work for that kind of money? Six years, seven years." She wouldn't look at him, not even when she was speaking, and tugged the collar of her bathrobe tight, as if she were freezing. "Two hundred thousand, a two and five zeros, we've never discussed that, never."

He could feel his eyes twitching, but he didn't reply. He knew that—even if he was a blockhead—knew it only too well.

"I thought you guys had finally figured out how it works," she said. "But you don't have a clue."

He looked up. Dorothea was bracing herself with one shoulder against the wall.

"You know . . ." Her head was swaying as if to some melody. Robert had seen her drunk only once before, before the boys were born. The whole way home she had sobbed and kept kicking at him. He had to drag her along behind him, like a stubborn dog. They hadn't encountered anyone else. If he had left her on her own, she might have frozen to death. She shouldn't ever forget that. She often came home late, sometimes very late. But the next morning, in the kitchen, everything was fine again.

"You know . . ." She let go of her bathrobe, edged her way along the wall to the door, and staggered out.

He followed her to the hall. The toilet door banged shut, the light went on, the toilet seat clattered against the water pipe. She retched and immediately flushed.

It was like a scene in a sitcom, when people suddenly appear, make some remark, and vanish again, leaving the others staring helplessly at one another to the sound of a laugh track.

He could hear her again now. She hadn't locked the door behind her.

He paid no attention to Dorothea's shriek or to the hand that waved him off, trying to shoo him away. She had to know that sort of thing wouldn't work with him. He pushed her aside just a little, grabbed her left hand, and pressed against her hips. She bent down over the toilet bowl again, retched, coughed, spat. He held her forehead with his right hand. Her bathrobe was wide open, its long belt now brushing his toes. A thread of saliva dangled into the toilet bowl, where brownish yellow phlegm was floating.

He spoke calm, yes, comforting words to her, while she plucked at the thread of saliva as if it were a harp string. He raised her forehead a little and pulled the toilet chain. "Don't worry," he said. "Just take it easy, Doro, nice and easy."

Gradually the world settled back into place. If he had to he could hold out till tomorrow morning, no question of that. As long as he felt her forehead resting in his hand nothing bad could happen.

Actually things had turned out just as they should have. His decision was final. He had done everything right. He felt like that ship on the blue waves, its sail to the wind. And even this high-proof stuff, this ill-considered gift, had served a function. How could they otherwise have made it through till tomorrow without brandy, without Dorothea's forehead in his hand? He was grateful to him, to the fellow with the shiny skull, truly grateful.

Robert now knew how he would get Dorothea through the evening, through the night, no matter what she might have to say.

Once this part was over, he didn't dare forget to turn off the CD player. Then he could check the CD he had played last, and remember the name of the composer. The alarm clock was set. He let Dorothea go on and on.

With his left hand he brushed the hair from the nape of her neck. That had to feel like a caress. Except she could no longer stay on her feet. Her forehead was damp and warm. Or was that his hand? He pushed in closer, so that he could prop his elbows against his ribs. He would make it through this. He just wanted to switch sides, hold her forehead in his other hand. "You've got to bring it all up," he interrupted. "All of it." Why wouldn't she finally just shut up?

It turned out to be no more than a twist of his left wrist, just like a familiar gesture of Dorothea's when she would tuck up her hair. For a moment he sensed the full weight of her head. His right arm dangled there as if it had fallen asleep.

Robert surprised himself with the deftness of his move, as if he had practiced it. He could feel that crumb of bread between his fingers. Her hair wrapped around his hand was wonderfully soft. He pulled Dorothea's head back farther and farther. Her face was now directly below his. They stared at each other, watching each other, until he realized that it was too late, that he could no longer simply let go. And so, when she closed her eyes for a moment, he saw no way out except to kiss her open mouth.

Milva, When She Was Still Quite Young

To this day I don't know what I should make of it. Was it a catastrophe? No big deal? Or merely something a little unusual? For me the worst part was those few minutes immediately afterward, that half hour in the car with Harry and Reiner. Harry was driving fast, though the dust kicked up by the redhead in the VW Passat still hung like fog over the country lane. "Gonna be fun," Harry kept muttering. "Gonna be great fun." The windshield wipers went on and water spurted up. Reiner—a cigarette in the corner of his mouth, the crushed pack still in his left hand—was clutching the grip above the door. A stone banged against the undercarriage. I could taste the dust on my tongue.

Before we picked up our wives in Perugia we had to get the story we were going to tell them straight. Even though we ourselves didn't really understand what role the redhead had played. Was she the guy's girlfriend, fiancée, a prostitute? Or a sharp-witted wife or daughter or, as Reiner suddenly claimed, a killer, whose plans we had just screwed up—or had we done her a favor?

Without even braking, Harry turned onto the road to Città della Pieve. Should we try to make it back over the border today, or would making it to another region suffice? Or was it totally unnecessary for us to take any special precautions?

Harry and Reiner were arguing. I interrupted them just once to say that it was an absurd idea to try to hide our VW Sharan or let it roll down a slope somewhere—in the valley to our left was the autostrada from Orvieto to Rome. Harry told me not to get involved. "You don't have to worry your little head, not you, you're free and clear, you restrained yourself oh so nobly." As he said it he glanced briefly in the rearview mirror.

My one big worry was that sooner or later my wife, Doreen, would figure things out, no matter what sort of story we dished up.

Until that day I had lied to Doreen more out of laziness, and not because I had ever had anything to hide. But for her there's nothing worse than a lie. That's why I wanted us to tell the truth, simply tell how it had all come about.

"Go right ahead, just say what happened!" Harry exclaimed. "Explain that to them."

I was sitting behind Harry and Reiner and had visions of having to move out, of all the thousand chores, all the running around to be done. Although over the last few years things had actually become easier, it was costing more and more effort to deal with the details of an orderly life. That's what I was thinking about, and how risky it was to be having such thoughts now.

Reiner and Sabine, Harry and Cynthia—we used to camp out together on the shores of the Baltic, later then on Lake Balaton and, when that got too expensive, in the Tatras. Over the last few years we had all moved several times. Harry and Cynthia had even spent two years in Holland. None of us was still working their old jobs. We called one another on birthdays.

I no longer know which of us came up with the idea of Italy, of Umbria. Two years after the earthquake of '97, there were still bargain-basement prices, and the photos of vacation houses were a promise of paradise.

I had come to realize over the last few years that I needed to work at my friendships if I didn't want to be all alone someday. Besides, Doreen and I had never gone on a trip with just the two of us. Until last year Ulrike, our daughter, had always come along.

In April I got hold of a map of Italy, located Umbria, and checked how far apart Aviano and Piacenza were. Those names don't mean much nowadays, but in the spring of '99 you heard them daily on the radio, because it was from there that NATO aircraft took off headed for Kosovo and Serbia. Not that I would have been afraid, there were hardly any missions by then. But it seemed a bit odd to willingly get too close to such places.

When we left on May 10 it felt like I was taking off for a class reunion. The fact that we were using three cars had a calming effect. Besides we all still got along fine. You could tell that right off.

We spent the first week near Gubbio. We slept late, ate big breakfasts, took occasional long walks, sunned ourselves for hours on the lawn behind the house, and went on an excursion to Assisi.

Sometimes we watched CNN but avoided talking about the details. Reiner said that words like "airbase," "air strikes," and "Serbs" already seemed more familiar, more appropriate to him than the German terms, which really just sounded like translations. It was much the same for me. If I read the word *Katastrophe* somewhere, it immediately became "catastrophe," whether it was about a flood in Bavaria, pollution in the Danube, or Albanians.

After four days Doreen remarked in the car that she felt like it was high time we went on a real vacation. I asked her what she meant. Was I supposed to pack our bags and declare: "My dear friends, we've had enough of you"? "Why not?" she said with a shrug.

On May 15 we went to see the "crazies" of Gubbio. Three teams run through the narrow streets carrying massive heavy candles and figures of saints on their shoulders. What an incredible hoot! The festive atmosphere was infectious. That evening Reiner, Harry, and I stayed on in the kitchen and polished off two bottles of Campari and the rest of our beer. When Sabine arrived to drag Reiner off to bed, he poured beer into her cleavage, which was a really stupid thing to do.

Cynthia demanded a ladies' shopping trip to Perugia in compensation, while we men would be sent to set up house in our new quarters in Città della Pieve. Doreen's private response to me was in terms of "treason"—she used that very word—as if I had been guilty of God knows what.

We packed everything into Cynthia and Harry's Sharan and drove past Lago Trasimena and Chiusi with its Etruscan graves, but didn't find the turnoff right after Città della Pieve—it's easy to miscalculate distances—came through a little oak woods, spotted a lovely ruin that evidently now served as a quarry, and suddenly found ourselves in an open field. Straight ahead, glistening in the sun, at the end of the chain of mountains, was our country house, nestled among slopes of green woodlands.

"They'll all just melt," Harry said.

Halfway there—with the ruts in the road getting deeper and deeper—he gave a yell and hit the brakes. "A snake," he said.

Actually we should have been on our guard when we saw a woman emerge from the swimming pool next to the house. She picked up a green towel, shook it out with one hand, and began drying her hair.

There was a large parking area, and we pulled in beside a new Passat with Berlin plates. Our landlord was, we'd been told, a German who owned a horse farm nearby.

We knocked at the door, walked around the house and swimming pool—the water was ice cold—took turns stretching out at poolside on the white plastic deck chair, and took in the view. "Pure luxury," Reiner said and between two fingers held up a bikini top he'd evidently found in the grass. We knocked again, but nothing stirred inside the house.

Harry pulled out a folded piece of paper. Glued to it was a photograph—tinged a bit too blue—clearly showing this house with this swimming pool in front. I was trying to make out the message scrawled on the back when Reiner gave me a nudge.

An older man was looking down at us from a window upstairs. He had a deep tan, a jutting chin, and gray hair combed front to back.

I called up to him that we were the people who had rented the house for the coming week. "Are we too early?"

At first I thought he didn't understand German, and tried again in English. He interrupted me, however. "Shitheads," he shouted. "Beat it, get your asses out of here!" He pushed back from the windowsill and vanished into the room.

"What was that about?" Reiner asked.

"He signed right here," Harry said, holding the piece of paper up to me. "He signed it, it's his signature."

"Herr Schröder," Reiner called up, "Signor Schröder!" I rapped at the door several more times and finally banged it with my fist.

Harry stepped back a bit and gave the lock a kick. The door sprang open, and a few seconds later Signor Schröder came stomping out.

"Scram!" he shouted. "Scram!" We backed away from his wide-flailing arms. For a moment I was afraid he would set dogs on us.

Schröder reeked of perfume, had strikingly blue eyes, and was shorter than I expected. His Bermuda shorts were hiked almost up to his old-man breasts, which like his shoulders, arms, and legs were covered with gray hair.

We three remained calm. We wanted to talk with him. We were three men, all around forty years old, and were not about to have a doddering loudmouth from Berlin spoil our vacation. We wanted to come to some agreement. We had shelled out a deposit of a hundred marks apiece, after all. But Schröder just kept on yelling "Scram, scram!" and flapping his hands as if we were flies.

Harry showed him the contract. Schröder made a grab for it, and as Harry tried to pull it away it got torn. Schröder wadded up his piece, dropped it, and turned away.

Harry took hold of Schröder's upper arm. They stood there frozen like that for a moment. Then Schröder whirled around and boxed Harry on the ear. Harry stumbled, fell to the gravel, but was back on his feet at once and hurled himself at Schröder—or better, Schröder had reeled back a few steps after Reiner gave his chest a shove. Harry threw him to the ground.

My friends bent down over him. All I could see was their backs. I had the impression that they were speaking with

Schröder in low tones, threatening him. After that it looked as if they were stuffing something into a gunnysack.

I failed to hear the woman's shouts. They didn't include a word of German anyway. I just kept staring at Reiner and Harry. They were my friends, and they were in the right. Schröder had earned his little object lesson. And then—you think you know all about it, but in fact the crack of a real gunshot sounds a lot louder and more brittle.

The redhead was aiming at me. I waited for that famous film of my entire life to start fast-forwarding. I also realized it was actually illogical to start with me.

Harry and Reiner stopped working Schröder over and stepped back, back from the door where the redhead stood. She had a yellow purse slung over her shoulder and was dressed in a black pants suit. She aimed the pistol now at Harry, then at Reiner, then at Harry again. I can't say much more than that.

The old man was lying between them like a big gym bag. I figured the redhead would kneel down to look after Schröder, or maybe even press the pistol into his hand, because suddenly, like a soccer player signaling an injury, he thrust his arm up and snatched at the air a few times.

Without taking her eyes off us, the redhead hissed something at him. I don't know where she got the green towel that she tossed to him. It landed across his knees. Then she ran along the wall of the house to the parking area, to the new Passat. She must have been familiar with the car, for in no time she was gone, tearing across the field.

I gave the old man a once-over. He was breathing heavily and constantly seemed on the verge of wanting to cough, but evidently lacked the strength even for that. He tried to look at me but kept wincing the whole time, as if in great pain.

Although he apparently had come away with just some scratches and abrasions, his chest hair was smeared with blood. Through the front door I could make out large white floor tiles and a huge exhaust hood.

We three were still at odds in Perugia. But it felt good to be among people again. If I ever have to go into hiding, I'd much rather do it in a city than in a forest or mountains.

I suggested we look for a hotel for the night and then inquire at the tourist office tomorrow about a new rental. Reiner and Harry agreed.

Harry said we should nip any stupid ideas in the bud, and Reiner threw an arm across my shoulder. "Let's be nice to us for a change," he said.

The women appeared marching at double time, large paper bags slapping at their calves and knees. They had hung their purses around their necks. Doreen's face and arms were flecked with red spots. Cynthia was crying. This of course worked to our advantage.

Some beggar women with babies at their breasts had followed them. "We didn't pay them much attention, we ignored them," Sabine exclaimed. The beggars weren't about to be shaken off, became more and more brazen, and had finally grabbed hold of Cynthia and Sabine by the arm. "I tried to break it up," Doreen said. "But they started scratching at me, really sinking their nails in." And Cynthia said that they couldn't take their eyes off her new watch, a present from her parents.

Reiner then told our wives our story about a petty crook from Berlin and an Italian whore, adding that at least we'd been able to get our money back and weren't going to let lowlifes like that ruin our vacation. And that I'd made a marvelous suggestion.

"That's the best idea of the whole vacation," Sabine said.

Harry went to arrange for a hotel, while we sat on a terrace directly next to where we had met and ordered mineral water and Campari-orange.

"The awful thing is," Sabine said, "that you've constantly got to keep your eyes peeled in case those women show up again."

Our hotel was the Fortuna, had four stars, and in front of its glass entrance doors was a thick red carpet with gold stripes at the edges and a coat of arms in the middle.

It turned out to be a very lovely evening. The women modeled their new frocks, and I had a sense that Doreen regretted her charge of treason. She drank at least as much as I did.

Harry whispered to me that I should just hold in there and had no reason whatever to hang my head. The moron had no one to blame but himself, and had collected more than enough for his pain and suffering. "He started it," Harry said. "He wanted it that way."

The redhead kept running through my mind, over and over. It's hard to describe her. She looked like the chanteuse Milva when she was still quite young.

At the breakfast buffet Reiner grinned at me. The hotel bill, he said, had been taken care of.

We found a nice place in Passignano on Lago Trasimena. This was pretty significant territory. Hannibal had won a battle against the Romans here in 217 B.C., but except for a marked trail and a few excavated cremation graves there's nothing left to see.

Lago Trasimena isn't very big, and above all it's shallow. That eased my mind, because news reports that planes unable to get rid of all their bombs over Yugoslavia were dropping them in the Adriatic near Venice were apparently no joke.

Except for an excursion to Orvieto we stuck to Passignano. I wasn't about to have the redhead recognize us in a restaurant somewhere. Maybe they were looking for us.

But nothing ever came of it. Neither at the border—not a soul there anyway—nor back at home. Several weeks later I received a police notice—a speeding ticket. And at one point Doreen wanted to know what had really happened with the guy from Berlin. I had been expecting the question.

Apparently my answer was so convincing that Doreen didn't pursue it. Hasn't to this day. I think she's forgotten about it. Everything seems okay with Reiner and Harry, too. We are back to calling one another on birthdays. I always intend to bring up what they did to Schröder. But that's not easy on the telephone.

I know that things have changed somewhat since then, but I can't put my finger on it. I've lost friends before Reiner and Harry, but that's not it. We might even set things right again. It's more as if I've crossed a threshold, as if my brain shifts automatically to memory—or at least is testing what that might be like someday, when old age really sets in.

I still think about the redhead a lot. Because as things are, she surely is and remains the only person who has ever seriously considered knocking me off. If a woman I don't know at all decides I shouldn't die, isn't it within the realm of possibility that she could just as well have decided to have a go at it with me, maybe a life-long go? I would have climbed into her Passat as a hostage and never surfaced again. I know that sounds odd. But I increasingly find myself considering such notions, and it costs me more and more effort to find my way back to everyday life.

Sometimes, however, I give myself over to the most routine memories, our arrival at the place near Gubbio for instance. I see us unpacking the car that evening. Harry uncorks a bottle. We take a short walk in the meadow behind the house, looking across the hills and up at the towering snowcapped Apennines, each of us with a glass in hand. Nobody says a word, not even when we find ourselves in a circle as if by chance and clink glasses. At this point I never fail to get goose bumps and can think of nothing better than breaking into song.

Calcutta

For Günther Grass

This was three weeks ago, on a Tuesday. The forecast had been for rain, but it was clear and sunny all day. After putting in my two hours of practice, I ate an early lunch and set to work mowing the lawn. The plan was yard work for this week, the garage and the snow tires the week after—dealing with the car just in general—then came cleaning out gutters and another go at the yard, and finally, as my last outdoor chore before snow set in, the graves. If you wait until the week before Remembrance Sunday, the cemetery parking lot is full.

I first noticed her standing at the threshold of her back door and gazing my way. By "her" I mean Becker's wife. We generally refer to our neighbors only in the plural, the Beckers—him, her, and their three kids, Sandra, Nancy, and Kevin.

Becker's wife didn't respond when I called over. I repeated my "Hello, hello!" and waved. She kept on looking in my direction but didn't react. On Sunday, that is two days before, she had brought us the mousetrap, and we'd thanked her with a jar of quince jelly.

I didn't have a clue what could have got her ticked off at us over the course of the previous forty-eight hours. I detached the half-full basket from the mower. But instead of emptying it into the blue plastic bag—which would have meant turning my back to her—I carried it to the compost heap behind the garage. I'm always amazed at how fast grass and our little hard apples are transformed into a kind of glop. The stupid thing is we have no real use for it. What we need is mulch to keep the weeds from shooting up over our heads, and good mulch is expensive.

I reattached the basket to the mower. When I straightened up I automatically looked in her direction, gave another wave, shouted, "The last time!"—I meant mowing the lawn—and attempted a smile. She stood there like a figure in a wax museum.

I went back to work and the pace picked up, since there were no apples lying in the grass and only a few drifted leaves.

Maybe I should say something about the mouse, about the mouse and the mosquitoes. Saturday night Martina had woken me up. "Do you hear that? Don't you hear it?" She sounded just a little hysterical. "A mouse! Don't you hear it?" The mouse must have scampered in at the window. There had been frost the past few mornings. Martina claimed mice had no trouble clambering up a stucco wall, especially if it was overgrown with a grapevine.

A mousetrap didn't even occur to us, as if that was old-fashioned, obsolete. Martina's plan was to lure the Findeisens' cat over, and I was supposed to move one cabinet after the other away from the wall. There was no mention of a mousetrap until noon, when she was hanging up the wash and told Becker's wife all about it.

The two green interlocking boxes looked more like a home-made telescope. Inside was a triggered pedal, so that when the mouse ran over it the door slammed shut behind. Becker's wife had recommended using sponge cake. Sponge cake was sure to catch any mouse. As I said, that had been two days ago, and I knew of no reason to feel guilty.

And then I just couldn't take it anymore. I left the mower standing in the middle of the lawn and walked over to her.

"I bought a sponge cake," I said. "Would you like a piece?" I wanted to add that even stale sponge cake tasted good with Martina's jelly. But she interrupted me.

"Keep your fingers crossed for us," she repeated more loudly. With every step she took the legs of her black leather pants rubbed together—a sound somewhere between a squeak and a crunch. "If you want to do something for us, cross your fingers."

As she spoke Becker's wife braced herself against the clothes pole and stared at me almost savagely.

Standing between the fence and the quince tree, I listened to her and had no idea how I would ever be able to make my retreat.

Kevin was in a coma. It had happened in front of the theater, between the two construction sites.

She described it all in great detail. I might even say she got caught up in it, pressing both hands to her ribs and pelvis, slapping her thighs, only to begin squeezing her temples between the heels of both hands and attempting to turn her head, but holding it in place as if caught in a vise. Her sweater had inched up to her navel.

Becker's wife began to weep. I was about to scale the fence and take her hand in mine when their telephone rang.

She left the back door ajar. So I waited. After a few minutes I pushed the mower over to the fence, dragged the extension cord over, and set to work again in view of her back door, never letting it out of my sight. I assumed Becker's wife was telling somebody what she had just told me, and wondered if she was making the same gestures as she held the phone, but with only one hand touching her body.

Instead of bothering to bend over to empty the mower basket, I went into a squat and, slipping the plastic bag around it, upended it all at once. I worked as if under the watchful eye of a supervisor.

To be honest I was relieved that the reason for her strange behavior wasn't because of some misunderstanding between us—if there has to be a dispute, better one with your colleagues than your neighbors. At home you need your peace and quiet.

Neighborliness requires nothing more than a greeting and a few extra words. That's no problem in summer. And when there's nothing more to do in the yard, you don't see much of one another, even if your back doors are only forty feet apart.

I rang the doorbell at the Beckers' and the Findeisens' just once all last winter, under the pretext of needing a couple of onions and a lemon. You have to do that sort of thing on weekends, of course. And bring back at least twice as much on Monday. You want them to know they can depend on you. Moreover, hardly a week goes by that I don't accept a package for somebody on the block. And I'm willing to do other favors as well, all anybody needs to do is ask.

And so I kept my eye on her back door, but somehow missed the moment when she closed it. Had Becker's wife noticed that I had long since finished mowing around the quince tree? Had I looked ridiculous?

It was on the little strip of grass between the street and the house that I found the schnapps bottles. There was always at least one, but this time there were three: two bottles of Golden Meadow and one of Little Coward. A fourth one missing its label had been set upside down on the narrow brick border around our herb bed. Evidently street people had taken a break at our place on their way to the shelter. That also explained the dog shit, which luckily the mower cleared as it passed over.

I always assumed we had come to some tacit agreement with the street people: They were to screw the tops back on the bottles and not fling them into the street or against the wall of the house. Most of the time I just tossed these wino bottles into the garbage, although normally we carefully separate metal caps from glass. But tossing four of them into the container at once—no, I couldn't do it. On the other hand, the idea of screwing off the caps disgusted me—those belong in the yellow bag—plus having to rinse out the bottles before putting them in the bin for throwaway glass. I propped all four against the garbage can. Maybe Martina would come up with a solution.

That particular afternoon the grass smelled at times like sorrel, then like fish, and then again like it had in the spring. It even left a taste like sliced cucumbers in my mouth.

Around five o'clock Becker himself came home and vanished into the house. He works in a computer store. At one time he had been part of the cadre responsible for selling Planeta printing presses worldwide. Martina always holds up his example to me—he had just rolled up his sleeves. Because he, or so she claimed, didn't think he was too good for any job.

He's one of those people who can eat whatever they want and never get fat—and pride themselves on the fact. He almost always wears faded blue jeans, with a big bunch of keys hanging from one belt loop to announce his comings and goings like a cowbell.

Ten minutes later the Beckers drove off with the two girls.

Although it was almost dark and I had done more than enough for one day, I went on working. I prefer to go back into the house along with Martina, or after her on those rare occasions when she fixes supper. Nowadays she's frequently late, a whole hour on that particular Tuesday. I waited to tell her the news until she was sitting in the kitchen.

I had taken note of every detail—from the broken cheekbones, collarbones, and ribs, to the pelvis and legs, down to the decrease in cerebral pressure, and how Nancy, who had witnessed the whole thing, was getting psychological counseling.

Holding her head between her hands, Martina looked as if she were covering her ears. She often sits there like that when she's tired. I think we were both relieved to find Felix at the door.

In May he had joined a group of fellow students in a shared apartment not far from Market Square, a real tumbledown dump. He's been paying the fifty marks' rent himself. I don't know where he's getting the money from.

Martina told him about the Beckers. I was hoping she would forget some detail so I could chime in. She asked me how the driver was doing. I shrugged.

"Close call," was all that Felix managed to come up with in reply to Martina's report. She wanted to know what he meant by that. Felix had his mouth full and chopped at the air with the edge of his hand. "It happened to our neighbors, that's a close call."

I waited for Martina to say something. But nothing apt came to her either.

Ever since he moved out, Felix and I are getting along better again. We both think Martina's new hairdo is silly. From a distance it looks like she's wearing a beret.

Felix was still eating when Martina stood up with a start. She ran upstairs ahead of us. "Nothing this time either," she said, eyeing me.

It was only then I realized how much I hated having a mousetrap in the house. At that moment—I'm certain of it—the feeling crept over me that those interlocked metal boxes were like bad-luck magnets. We placed the trap closer to the window and crumbled more sponge cake.

It stayed sunny all week. I practiced every day from nine to eleven. I think my playing is pretty good, even if of late there is nobody to hear me. My bow technique especially has improved quite a bit. Bow technique and etudes. I had never really had the time before. Bach and Mozart as my reward. Afterward I concentrate on housework.

When I'm not in the mood for practicing, I listen to music. All I ever ask for are CDs. The public library doesn't have many to lend out. Of late I've been listening to our records again. What a feeling to lift the tone arm to the edge and slowly shift the lever and watch the stylus make contact! The complete Beethoven with Masur, Schumann with Sawallisch. I've listened to them since I was fifteen, sixteen. I could conduct them. I could direct it all by heart. I've always worked as a construction engineer, usually as project manager. But deep down I'm a musician.

Becker's wife had taken sick leave. I watched her open the door for her kids. Their front door doesn't open onto the street but is at the side, directly opposite our bathroom window.

As soon as her husband came home, they would drive off,

with Sandra and Nancy usually along. They'd come back after two or three hours.

That Friday Becker's wife was just returning from shopping when I went to check the mail. She had lost weight. She looked good. I nodded to her but then turned back as if I had the wrong key.

"We're keeping our fingers crossed," was the statement I had prepared for any eventuality. She would hardly have been interested in news about the mouse. Not that there was any, although the first thing Martina did when she got home from work was to run upstairs. "Nothing this time either," she'd say.

I added a piece of ham to the sponge cake. Normally our eyes take only a few days to integrate a strange object into a larger familiar image. But I found the thing more and more disgusting—the very idea of having to hold both boxes in my hands with a mouse running back and forth inside. Or would it play dead? Once we got to that point I wanted to call the Becker kids over. It would add some variety to their lives. And they could take the trap with them.

It was always Martina who heard the mouse. I wouldn't even have noticed a mouse without her. What plagued me at night were the mosquitoes. I always thought mosquitoes die in the fall. This year it looked as if they were going to spend the winter with us. At first I thought they were biting just me—one even managed to creep up inside a nostril. But come morning I saw that Martina had more bites than me—so I had no reason to complain.

Last year around the same time when I was tidying up the attic, I discovered that a whole army of spiders had marched through the skylight. But mosquitoes in November is an entirely different matter, wouldn't you say?

That last week in October I had also taken care of the gutters and had cut back the grapevine. Of course I take care of the chores too—from shopping to cleaning house. I like doing it.

If Martina were the one to stay at home, the world would find that perfectly normal. Men, however, are always telling me how much they have to do. And if I say that I'm up to my ears in work too, they grin and give me a dumb look.

You automatically take a backseat of course. I never sit up watching television longer than Martina. When she gets up in the morning I head for the kitchen to make breakfast. As long as Felix was still living here, it was me who woke him up and chased him out of bed.

I think Martina likes having hardly any housework to do and always having somebody who's there to greet her, who sets the table for her. Everything has its good side. And as long as the money covers expenses . . . It used to be perfectly normal for somebody to stay at home full-time.

The thing is, once Lippendorf was finished, I put in an application with every department, even PR work. Who should know a project better than somebody who helped build it? After all, I knew that box inside and out. Do you suppose they gave me a chance? They didn't even call me in for an interview. It's all a matter of cliques, whether old or new. You side with either one bunch or the other. Otherwise you're just out of luck. The unemployment office had the bright idea of sending me to a free newspaper. I was supposed to polish doorknobs looking for advertisers. "I built a power plant," I said, and was out the door. If I ever take on something like that, it's all over, I'm washed up. I don't need to explain that, do I?

Early in the second week with the mouse, I had just come in

from the yard and was about to take a shower when I heard our car in the driveway, and seconds later Martina's footsteps. Just as you can automatically hum the rest of a familiar melody, I waited for the sound of her key in the front door. I stepped into the tub, but then turned the tap off again when nothing more happened. I interrupted my shower a couple of times to call Martina's name. Finally, my hair still wet, I walked out into the yard. Martina and Becker's wife were standing at the fence. Martina had done some grocery shopping. So I had the excuse of offering to take both bags into the house. I unpacked it all, made some tea, set the table, and thumbed through the newspaper inserts.

"Makes a person feel truly sorry for them," Martina said after having drunk a glass of apple juice. I was annoyed that she took it for granted that I had once again put together a nice meal and then had to wait for her.

From then on they stood there every evening. Becker's wife would even come outside in the dark just so she could talk with Martina.

So we were kept well posted. Martina talked about how much Andrea, Becker's wife, missed her Kevin every time she turned around. "An adult," Martina said, "would no longer be alive. But with children there's still hope even when doctors are at the end of their tether."

I thought about how even in cases like this a certain kind of routine sets in. You drive to the hospital, hold your child's hand for a few hours, convince yourself he's just sleeping, talk with the doctors, have them explain what they'll be trying to accomplish with the next operation, and cry a little before you leave. The garage door signals that they're back home. Evidently you have to give it a kick to open or close it. One after the other, three motion-sensitive lights go on, and the four Beckers march into the house Indian file as if moving across a stage.

Until yesterday at any rate there was nothing new in the mouse department. I was constantly greeted with Martina's message of "Nothing this time either." I was told I ought to pull the furniture out from the wall a little more at least. The back of one cabinet had been nibbled at. "You see!" Martina exclaimed. "Just look at that!"

How was the mouse my fault? Can you tell me that?

I went out into the yard and set to work weeding. The best time for pulling weeds from between the walkway cracks is when everything is damp and nothing is growing anymore.

Suddenly somebody said, "You've just about got it licked," or something like that. Even though he was wearing his bunch of keys as always, I hadn't noticed the head of the Becker household.

Becker was resting his hands on the fence, and it was obvious this was going to be awkward and I couldn't just keep on squatting there.

"Well?" I said, "How's it going?"

"You ever been to Calcutta?"

I thought maybe he had misspoken and meant the Indian restaurant that had just opened up on the grounds of the old Russian barracks. Luckily I just said no.

"That's a city you've got to see!" he exclaimed. "You don't understand one thing about this world if you haven't experienced Calcutta."

He started in and there seemed to be no end to his tale. The whole thing sounded a little odd to me, but I listened all the same. At first I was still thinking about Martina—about me and

Martina—but then I just listened to what the head of the Becker household had to say.

"You planning to go back?" I asked when he paused to blow his nose.

"Wait just a sec," he said, turned around, and went back into the house. He returned with a heavy necklace, corals alternating with silver balls.

"Here, have a look. Stuff like this goes for a song there."

I raised my dirty hands. He misunderstood and hung the necklace over my right forearm.

It was really heavy. I examined it while he went on talking. After ten minutes he took the necklace back and wrapped it around his wrist. It was already dark when he stuck out his hand to say good-bye.

I called my mother that same evening. Sometime I'd like to actually ask her why she hadn't let me enroll in the high school that focuses on music. Have you ever heard of a musician getting fired? I haven't.

Lately my mother always wants to know if I'm sleeping okay. That's become her criterion for general well-being. I told her I'd be sleeping well enough if weren't for the damned mosquitoes.

"That's funny!" she exclaimed. "I've got bites every morning, regular mosquito bites." Now that was eerie, I thought, right out of Hitchcock. If those little beasts were suddenly going crazy at the end of the millennium, that meant something. On the other hand that might get things moving, there might be a lot of new jobs, cram courses for trained exterminators.

Last night I left the window wide open—that way it wouldn't be so cozy for mosquitoes.

I assume it was the Beckers' garage door that woke me up. I heard their car start and back out onto the driveway. I recognized Becker's voice. He was talking to his wife. Then the girls came trotting out. He told them both to go back to bed. All I heard from her was a kind of a clucking and that sound her leather pants make when she walks. Both car doors slammed shut almost simultaneously. I didn't get up. The girls stayed outside for a while. I could only make out individual words.

I was surprised that they left the garage door open. Maybe they thought they'd be back soon. It was a foolish thing to do, though—an open garage with bikes, tires, and all sorts of tools.

Farther off in town I could hear a few cars and a freight train approaching. We've lived here long enough to recognize all the sounds. But they travel this well only on November nights.

Gradually I could make out the stems of the leafless grapevines framing the window. They looked like the feelers of giant snails or like Vs for victory, or like the feet of animals you might assemble out of matchsticks. As it grew lighter and the Findeisens' car drove off, the stems seemed to turn reddish. Where they thicken at the end they look like Q-tips. For a moment I thought I smelled alcohol, and thought of the street people and their bottles. I had no idea what Martina had done with those.

She slept until the alarm went off, threw me a quick glance, and sat up on the edge of the bed. Before getting up she stretched her arms above her head. I used to pull her back into bed sometimes.

I could sense that it wouldn't even take her asking me a question—just one single word, something totally trivial—and I'd lose it. I've slowly learned to live with the feeling. It hardly scares me anymore. It comes over me with almost soothing regularity. And I give in to it—but of course only when I'm alone. Other people, especially those who think they know me, would find it upsetting. Basically it's nothing more than bleeding radiators. That has to be done every now and then.

Of course it was clear to me that I had to get up. The timing was tight, and if nothing had been done when Martina emerged from the bathroom, she'd have to leave without breakfast. Pulling the car out and sitting there waiting at the front gate wouldn't help either.

I thought I heard the Beckers' car. I raised my head from the pillow and listened. From that position I could see the mousetrap. It was still wide open.

And then I heard the bathroom door and Martina going downstairs. Step by step, stair by stair, finally her heels striking the kitchen tiles and the squeak—or more like the whinny—of the refrigerator door.

Suddenly it was clear to me that the mouse—presuming it was still alive—had been listening to these same sounds and noises, although maybe somewhat muted by the cabinet. And that it probably could tell whether somebody was going up or down the stairs, and that it felt frightened when steps approached, and maybe even joy or at least relief when they moved away again, though that didn't change its situation. And I understood that all I needed to do was close the trap, carry it out into the yard, and come evening tell Martina that the mouse had shot away like an arrow. I was sorry I hadn't thought of that earlier, and how this was a great moment to give the trap back, to be rid of it at last—right now, when I could hear the Beckers laughing. I only had to go to the window and I'd see the Beckers, all five of them, coming up the hill and waving at us over and over. Although they were still a good distance off, I spotted the huge sponge cake they were carrying, a gift for their hosts. I still remember wanting to compare their three kids, scampering ahead in their bright outfits, to butterflies in a flowery meadow. "Like butterflies, like butterflies," I wanted to call out to them.

I can still recall the kids, them and how the sound of their footsteps came closer and closer. Have you ever actually been to Calcutta?

II

Mr. Neitherkorn and Fate

"I needed a haircut," I began. "But either the hairdressers were busy giving manicures or were fully booked, or I ended up in a beauty salon." Mr. Neitherkorn looked up from his cup as if about to say something, but then just extracted a sugar cube from the bowl, dunked it in his coffee, and shoved it into his mouth to suck on. "Suddenly," I went on, "there was a shopwindow, and inside what looked like a swarm of barbers. Their customers, all people of color, were sitting in regal but well-worn barber chairs. The white men working around them didn't seem too happy, looked lost in smocks a couple sizes too large. They ran shavers across black and brown skulls and finished off by massaging the now bald heads with perfume. When a chair opened up for me, I demonstrated for a short lithe man, probably in his early forties, how much he should take off. He nodded, dampened my hair with squirts from a spray bottle, and picked up a comb. It wasn't very pleasant for either of us. I can't get a comb through my hair myself unless it's soaking wet. But I didn't complain. After a while my barber asked his neighbor something in Russian. But the man was so busy trimming a beard narrow as a helmet strap along the chin line of a shaved head that he failed to respond. I made some remark. The barber looked at me in the mirror as if enjoying watching me grimace under the tug of his comb. Where was I from? And him? From Bukhara. I said that I'd been to Bukhara once, and had enjoyed both the city and the desert. His comb halted midstroke, and we smiled at each other in the mirror. He described for me exactly where his apartment had been—across from the monument of a Hero of the People, did I remember it perhaps? Pumping cloud upon cloud of vapor from his spray bottle, he tried to prompt my memory with more details, but without success. He had trained as an engineer but had been living in the U.S. for a year now, along with his whole family. 'Better a barber in New York than an engineer in Bukhara?' I asked—purely rhetorically. And then he replied: *'Nu, chto delat? Eto sudba.'* "

"And what does that mean?" Mr. Neitherkorn asked, tracing his lips with the tip of his finger.

" 'Well, what's a man to do, it's fate'—fate, destiny, something like that. When I left the shop a half hour later—six dollars including a shave—three barbers offered a farewell handshake, and a fourth, who was having a cigarette outside, said: *'Shchastlivo,'* sort of 'Have a nice day.' "

"And that's why you want to write about it?" Mr. Neitherkorn was propping his forehead between his palms.

"It was pure chance. I could have chosen another word just as well," I replied. "But when somebody says that right to my face, and in Russian besides? Why should I come up with something on my own?"

"But if you're going to claim that there is no such thing as fate?" He looked up, and I could see the reddish rims of his eyes.

"I meant that I don't use the word myself. And besides," I added, happy that I could now put the sentence to good use, "besides, the only important issue is *why* we believe there is or isn't such a thing as fate."

Mr. Neitherkorn crunched down on the last bit of sugar and took a sip without lifting his elbows from the table.

"So the only important issue," I said, disappointed by Mr. Neitherkorn's reaction, "is why we use the term."

"If that's how you see it," he said. His tongue was playing with his dentures again.

Every day around one thirty in the afternoon, weekends included, Mr. Neitherkorn would arrive at the apartment. I always heard his key in the door, quickly followed by a key in the two locks to the adjoining room. Then it fell quiet, until he entered the kitchen around four o'clock, made coffee, and waited for me to join him. Usually the cotton plugs were still in his ears—he never went out on the street without them. He supplied the coffee, I bought the milk. If I didn't show up by five, he would knock on my door. If I was going out for the afternoon, Mr. Neitherkorn liked to be informed—he just wanted to know I was all right.

At first I had acquiesced. But then it became a habit and finally an effort, or simply a drawback of the apartment that justified the rent: $289 for 275 square feet on the seventeenth floor on the Upper West Side—there was nothing cheaper anywhere in Manhattan. And he was gone again by six.

I had found my way to Mr. Neitherkorn by a series of unusual accidents. His wife, also a German, had died early that year. He was now living in an old folks' home on West End

Avenue and dropped by just to organize "final matters"—or
that's how the friend who led me to Mr. Neitherkorn had put it.

I read the article on "Fate" in the *Brockhaus* lexicon in the
library of the Goethe Haus: "A term for the experience that
much of what happens to a human being or in the world at
large and in history is not the result of human will and action,
but is imposed 'from outside.' Fate can thus appear as the decree
of numinous powers, as 'law,' as the will of God, or in its secular
form as something determined for a person by biological,
social, or psychological factors." There in black and white was
everything you needed to know.

Grimms' Dictionary offers numerous examples of the use of
the word, for instance by Goethe: "Fate, before whose wisdom I
stand in great awe, may—given the accidentality by which it
works—wield a very clumsy apparatus." This sentence was the
answer to all questions, including those that had vexed me as a
schoolboy: Why is the historical mission of the working class
legitimate, and why must the working class be led by a new kind
of party? Because fate accidentally wields a clumsy apparatus.

There are two pages on fate in Hoffmeister's *Philosophical
Dictionary.* The first page uses as its point of reference the work
of a fellow named Gehl, who in 1939 published a book entitled
The Germanic Belief in Fate, in which he explains why among
Germans fate is necessarily imbued with a heroic character, and
concludes: "What lies concealed behind this is nothing less than
the proud belief in the utter freedom of man in the face of every
sort of coercion, a belief arising from the depths of the German
heart and finding its unflinchingly venerated culmination in a
death approached with a smile."

One should likewise consult Gehl as regards the merger of a personal belief in fate with a mystical, suprapersonal sense of "a common fate of all living creatures." This is followed by a few bibliographical references and the next article: "Fatuousness."

"Did you strike it rich?" Mr. Neitherkorn asked. "Have you discovered what fate is?" He rummaged in his shopping bag.

"In the Western world 'fate' is conceived of as either passive or active," I attempted to summarize. " 'Passive' means there is a point of origin, and after that events unroll more or less according to plan. If you regard it as more active, it functions generatively. You tough life out and hope you won't get sick. If your own life is more or less determined by outside factors, you assume fate is running the show. Fate is a secularized version of God. You don't want him to be in charge anymore. Left on your own, however, you feel overburdened. Even if I had found a dissertation on the correct usage of the word 'fate,' it wouldn't have got me much further."

"There's definitely a study of that sort," Mr. Neitherkorn said as he sat down.

"Sure," I said. "But aren't stories better than treatises?"

"You evidently don't have a very philosophical turn of mind, do you?" he asked, cutting the carrot cake in half, including the plastic wrap.

"Philosophy's never been my thing," I replied. "That level of abstraction always allows you to assert the exact opposite. Evil—that's what abstractions are; fate—that's other people."

Mr. Neitherkorn looked up. "Is that original with you?" He shoved me half the carrot cake and took a bite of his piece.

"It quickly becomes anything you want it to be," I said.

"Fate—that's Oedipus; fate—that's my language; fate—that's my comrades or my genes. Man's fate is man. I am fate. Fate—that's vodka or 7Up or our carrot cake here. It always works, if you don't apply it too clumsily, or maybe when you do. We should simply say, this and that happened. Why talk about fate?"

"People in fact use the concept of fate," Mr. Neitherkorn responded, "at the point when they don't understand what forces are playing games with us." He looked at the carrot cake he'd been nibbling and cleared his throat.

"Do you know what I don't understand? Why you're here." He ran a fingertip across his lips again and stared at his cup. That's an odd question to hear from your landlord.

"I've got a scholarship," I said.

"I know that," he said. "But why did you apply for it? Why do you write your stories here and not in Germany, when ultimately they're about Germany? Why have you left your wife alone for six months, with a monthly fax and telephone bill of six hundred dollars, spending your summer sitting in front of an air conditioner, in a city where a person can't even get a good night's sleep? I don't get it."

"Don't you like being here?" I asked.

"Not in the least," he said and suddenly sat up straight as a ramrod in his chair. "What would make you think that?"

Sunday. I've just received a fax.

"If a writer is going to meditate on fate, somebody should be reading *Job* softly in the background, the 'story of a simple man.' I had just run across a sentence for you while I was reading it this morning and wondering whether to get up and send it off to you, when the doorbell rang, around eight. Job was at the door, your Gypsy. His wife and child are in the hospital in Romania, he needs money. He'd already heard that you're not here but in America. I had 180 marks on me, so I gave him a towel to wash up with, made him breakfast, and then we headed for the bank. I took out four hundred. Why not more? He's learned that pleading beggar's look well, kisses my hand, thanks God. For what? For fifty more to bring the kids a little something. And for his father? I still had thirty left, and I held on to it. All the while I was thinking how it's no wonder bicycles disappear, and that it's not just contrary to convention but to nature itself to be alone. And this old house seemed a huge luxury to me. I turned taciturn and unfriendly, Job still running through my mind. I couldn't deal with very basic reality.

"Fate is simply life that you have to change. But that doesn't happen often. There's a passage in Roth—it comes when Mendel Singer's son Shemeriah is fleeing from the military, just before he's led across the border: 'Shemeriah drank some schnapps, he felt hot, but calm. He had never felt so safe before; he knew that he was living through one of those strange moments when a man has to shape his fate no less than the great forces that assigned it to him.' "

I've been trying to pay my telephone bill. For questions they give you a number to call. Beneath it the line: "We're here to help you 24 hours a day, 7 days a week." I've been unable to reach anybody—I mean no human being. After the first message you punch a number, after the next another one, and so on and so forth, from message to message. After I'd worked my way through the menu of five punched numbers, it looped back around to the start. I began all over again, pressed one number several times and finally ended up with a message that promised me "assistance" at last. "We're sorry," the voice said. "All our lines are busy." I should try later. But I had no idea how I had managed to get even that far along in the chain.

On Wednesday I went out to Fire Island with C. We stopped in Brooklyn to pick up his wife's car from the repair shop. C. wove through the streets of Hasidic Crown Heights, as far as the border with the Puerto Rican section. Repairs that would run fifteen hundred in Manhattan cost only five hundred dollars here, C. said, and laughed long and hard.

I stared at the men in their hats, sidelocks, dark glasses, and caftans. They move no more quickly or agilely than other people, but in that garb they seem to, since one unconsciously takes them to be much older than they are. But often what emerges from behind the glasses, under the hat brim, between the sidelocks is a child's face. Or is it the contrast to the black men leaning against the wall beside the garage? There must be ten different Hasidic groups. Menachem Mendel Schneerson was the chief rabbi of the Lubavitchers, whom many held, and still hold, to be the Messiah. Now that he is dead they say they were simply not worthy of him.

"If somebody believes, then he believes," C. exclaimed. "There's nothing you can do," and he laughed as if he had saved another thousand dollars.

He told me about his grandmother, who was the grand dame of Elberfeld back in the twenties. Before 1933 she contributed two million marks to Hitler. She was convinced that when Hitler said Jews, he didn't mean German Jews but the other ones, the Jews in Galicia. "It took a long time for her to abandon her belief." He laughed again.

"If we were to understand the Holocaust as fate," C. added, "that would also mean it could be repeated and we wouldn't have to ask who did it. There is a difference between saying, 'the fate of the Jews' or 'what the Germans did to the Jews,' you know?"

T. called. They're driving west in a rental from "Junk Body, A-1 Motor." Just outside New York, as they put it, they got into trouble. T. thought she was photographing a group of actors. They were Amish people. "They don't drive cars," she said, "don't have refrigerators, electric lights, no TV, no chemical fertilizers, no telephone. And you know what the craziest part is? They're completely right, from a practical point of view."

"I read in last week's *Newsweek*," I said, "that churchgoers are statistically much less likely to have heart trouble."

"There, you see," she said. "Another miracle."

As I came up out of the subway today a man thrust a piece of paper into my hand—nothing religious, not an ad, as the man proudly announced. Instead: "9 ways to find peace of mind." Under point one it reads: "Nursing a grudge depresses your level of happiness by 50% on average." This is followed by less concrete suggestions: You need to cooperate with life, avoid self-pity, but also not expect too much of yourself, etc. Point seven demands the reactivation of "old-fashioned virtues": love, faithfulness, thrift, church attendance. The culmination is point nine: "Find something bigger than you are that you can believe in." It claims that self-absorbed materialistic people are less happy on average than those who are religious and act out of altruism. In a study by Duke University the latter folks achieved "top happiness rates."

On the day after the NASA press conference announcing that traces of organic life had been found in the rocks of Mars, the Japanese guy at the sushi counter asked me a question. But I didn't understand because of his thick accent. Finally he wrote it down for me on a napkin: Did I believe in God? "No," I said, "I don't believe in God." He turned to a black man who was waiting for his take-out order. Of course he believed in God, he exclaimed. "Who made us if not the Lord?" He was angry at the Japanese guy because he didn't believe in God. The sushi chef asked me another question I couldn't understand. And wrote on the napkin again: "UFO." He believed in them. And me? I shook my head again. What did I believe in, he wanted to know. My mouth was full, and so I had time to think about it. "I believe," I said, "that the fish here is really fresh and tastes good." He beamed at me.

Along with my bill I got a fortune cookie whose baked-in message read: "A little patience is often better than a lot of good ideas." I stood in the elevator and wondered what that might mean in my case, for my time here was slowly running out. As always I stared at the round buttons with their illuminated floor numbers. Twelve was followed by fourteen. No thirteenth floor is listed. The owners' tribute to fate—to put it in a conciliatory mood?

"I really do understand," I said to Mr. Neitherkorn after telling him about my lunchtime conversation, "that it feels good to be able to turn to God at any time. But isn't it also a matter of self-dignity not to be talked into some consoling Band-Aid?"

"Consolation?" he asked. "For what?"

"That everything's pretty much an accident, our whole existence."

"Do you think so?" he asked.

"Yes," I said. "What's the alternative?"

This morning a woman called me. She spoke German, gave me her name, and asked how long I'd be renting the room. "Until the end of December," I replied. Then she could move in with Mr. Neitherkorn at the start of the New Year, she said. She'd have to arrange that with him, but I doubted that he'd be keeping the apartment himself much longer. "He's just organizing a few things yet."

"He's been doing that forever," she said with a laugh.

"What?" I asked. "Not just since his wife died?"

"Ah! She's been dead for more than fifty years. If he asks you for your address, you can go right ahead and give it to him. He won't come in any case."

"Come where?"

"Oh, it's all just talk. Whenever he's too cold or too warm, or the city's too loud or too dirty, he says he's moving back to Germany. I'll give you a call later on," she said. "Bye now!"

As I stepped off the elevator, I ran into Mr. Neitherkorn. He was earlier than usual today. "Where are you headed again now?"

"To the barber!" I shouted, because of the cotton in his ears. "I want to talk him out of fate."

Mr. Neitherkorn grumbled something, lowered his eyes. I stepped aside, and the door closed between us.

Already from the outside I could see that I didn't recognize any of the barbers. I no longer know why I went inside anyway. A black man dressed in a suit entered behind me, said hello, flung his gym bag on the mirrored green cabinet, and began to unpack combs, scissors, and various bottles. After donning a white smock, he was assigned a customer by the boss, and began to shave the man's head. Black fuzz fell to the floor, and I thought how that might be fun for me too. I was handed over to a white man with a crew cut. But he couldn't find a suitable comb.

The boss waved over an Indian woman. She had a larger comb and went right to work. A Japanese woman entered the shop and unpacked her bag in front of the mirror to our right. Her customer, whose Rastafarian locks were bound on top of his head like a sheaf of grain, wanted to have his head shaved up to ear level. I was enjoying the tickle at the back of my neck, the sense of being pampered, and lowered my head, turning it to the right, to the left—and saw my engineer from Bukhara enter. I made useless motions with my cape-covered hands and, I suppose, uttered some sort of sound. The Indian woman said, "Sorry," and pressed her thumbs to my temples. The construction engineer stepped up behind us and showed off his trick of rapping his hand and sending a cigarette flying up to be caught in his lips. The boss greeted him, both whispered something to the Indian woman, who undid the bow of my cape and left her station.

Before I could get up, the engineer had thrown another cape over me and announced that he would now give me a haircut— free of charge, he immediately added. I said that unfortunately someone had just cut my hair, and rocked my head back and forth as if to prove it. But I would be glad to chat with him. "Just a trim," he insisted. "It's free," and began tugging at my hair. All the while he had that same sad and serious look as the first time. I was careful about how I put my question. Why had he left Bukhara? He waved the question off. "That wasn't a life anymore," he said. And what had he hoped for from America? "America!" he said. Every question I put to him received only a curt answer. Finally I wanted to know why he had mentioned *sudba*. "*Sudba?*" He gazed at my reflection in the mirror. They had waited much too long—he only had to think about how far ahead they could have been by now. But next week his wife would be opening a beauty shop in Brighton Beach, and he had found a job as a mason and would show them what he could do. Even more important, his daughter had a good chance for a scholarship, and if she got it—he snapped his scissors triumphantly in the air and gave me a wink.

"Things are going great," I said.

"Of course things are going great," he replied, and snipped a big swatch of my hair. "If only we hadn't waited so long!"

Then we fell silent. He snipped and snipped, and I thought about what I ought to write now.

"My, my, my!" went Mr. Neitherkorn as he entered the kitchen. "Were you attacked by wild animals?"

"They gave me two haircuts for the price of one," I replied, giving my hair a tug.

"What do you mean?"

"I don't know how to explain it," I responded. "In any case it wasn't fate, if that's what you want to know."

"Will you finally get over that!" he exclaimed. "Don't you have eyes in your head? Haven't you had enough yet?"

I sat down in my chair. He shoved a cup of coffee my way, rummaged in his shopping bag, and pulled out some carrot cake. As always he cut it in two by slicing through the plastic wrap, laid my half next to my cup, and returning to his shopping bag, took out the milk and opened it.

"Thanks," I said. We drank coffee and ate carrot cake. I was afraid to go to my room and sit down in front of my computer. "I have no idea what I ought to write," I said after a while.

"Don't worry about it," he said. His tongue was playing with his upper plate again. "I'll tell you a story tomorrow. You can gussy it up a little."

"What sort of story?" I asked.

" 'What sort of story?' " he repeated without looking up. "About a 'Boy Who Left Home to Find Out About' . . . and so forth."

"Are you trying to play fate?" I asked.

"Oh no!" Mr. Neitherkorn cried, raising his arms with the palms turned heavenward, and held the position for a moment. "I'm just a barber," he then remarked, lowering his hands again. "But there's a lot to be learned there. . . ."

Writers and Transcendence

A few years ago, it was in February, I visited my mother in Dresden. We didn't see each other that often but did talk a lot on the phone.

We were sitting over a light supper in the kitchen when the front doorbell rang. My mother fell silent. I set my cup down without making a sound. We didn't even look at each other—whenever a disturbance threatens we play dead out of an instinctive reflex. We heard sobbing in the stairwell. "Christa dear," a woman's voice cried, "Christa dear." Then only more sobs.

"My Pushkin!" our neighbor Henrietta cried as she entered the kitchen. She embraced me—her eye shadow was smeared, tears had left black tracks on her cheeks.

Ever since Henrietta found a photograph of me in a local Dresden paper, in which she claimed I bore a resemblance to Pushkin, she has called me "my Pushkin." Henrietta came from Sverdlovsk in the Urals, which nowadays is once again called Yekaterinburg. She has been living in Dresden for thirty years.

Henrietta used to be a dentist, then she was unemployed, and now she's retired. Her husband has another wife, both daughters have long since left the nest.

In agitated tones Henrietta told us how our neighbor Frau X was demanding five hundred marks from her. The woman had been to see her just now, stomping about and screaming that she was owed the money for her table. Henrietta again broke into tears.

"What table is that?" my mother asked.

"Table from attic, from corner!" Henrietta cried.

It had always been the custom to store discarded furniture in Henrietta's corner of the large attic. If she couldn't use the items herself, she passed them on to Soviet officers and their families. A few weeks earlier, Henrietta had discovered what's called a kidney table from the fifties in her corner, taken it to her own apartment, and since it was too high for her, had sawed off about a hand's-breadth from each leg.

Setting out today in search of her vanished table, Frau X had rung Henrietta's bell as well. All unsuspecting, Henrietta had invited her in. At the sight of her maimed table Frau X had been beside herself and had called Henrietta some very nasty names. She was now demanding five hundred marks for her ruined property. And Henrietta had better not get any ideas about moving out before making good on the damage, either.

"Lady X!" I said, interrupting Henrietta. "Lady X should cut the grandstanding!" Even before 1989 it had been clear to us that Frau X and Herr Y worked for State Security and "looked after" our building. Both my mother and Henrietta had come across Frau X's reports in their files. That hadn't altered life in the building. Just as in the days of the GDR, curt greetings were exchanged and each went his or her way.

My mother nodded, but then made a suggestion that shocked me. Henrietta, however, stopped crying.

Two days later, on Saturday, Henrietta went to the beauty salon, put on her long dark blue dress, adorning it with a gold chain that had been her mother's, made coffee, and set the sawed-off table for two. Next to one setting she laid an envelope with five hundred marks and a folder with copies of documents. She lit a candle before an icon that had come into her possession a year before. From the record player came Russian choral music. Then Henrietta rang family X's doorbell and invited Frau X upstairs. When both women were seated across from each other, Henrietta apologized for the cropped table. Before she handed over the five hundred marks, however, she did have one more question. She would like to know why Frau X had written reports about her, Henrietta, and her family.

Frau X smiled and asked how Henrietta dared spread such slander. Henrietta shoved the folder across to her.

Frau X opened the folder, paged through it, paged and paged, her thumbing growing more and more hectic. "This can't be, this simply can't be," Frau X whispered. She had, she now exclaimed, written only a very few reports about Henrietta. Neighbor Y, Herr Y from the side entrance, he was responsible for this, and what she had passed on couldn't even be compared to what Herr Y or for that matter Frau Z had done. "It was Frau Z who wrote the most reports."

That was perfectly possible, Henrietta said, but her reports were the ones found in the file, after all, and nothing by Frau Z or Herr Y.

"A drink," Frau X whispered, jumping to her feet. "I need some schnapps." She tried to embrace Henrietta, begging her not to think too badly of her. She had been forced to write this stuff. "I didn't do it voluntarily," she cried. "I didn't do anyone any harm."

Frau X downed the vodka with a grimace, tears welling in her eyes. She heaved a sob and ran out. Henrietta poured herself a shot of vodka, picked up the envelope with the five hundred marks, and rang our doorbell.

Although my mother had not expected any other outcome, she found it remarkable that until now Frau X had evidently lived in the belief that we were still in the dark.

I admitted that I had already written off the five hundred marks my mother had provided. "I would've bet my life on it with someone like X."

"No!" my mother exclaimed. "I've always believed that justice prevails in the end."

A few weeks later I wrote up this story, intending to use it in place of a newspaper article I'd agreed to. Up till then, however, I'd never written a story based on real events. So that I found my plan a little eerie.

"I've written about you and Henrietta," I told my mother on the phone. Maybe, I said, the story would work better than rambling explanations to demonstrate how the defunct system's coordinates and behavioral patterns still shimmer through all our lives.

"Listen up," my mother interrupted. "There's more to it."

"Has X turned up again?"

"Oh, this is a totally different story."

Henrietta had moved out and been living in a high-rise in the center of Dresden for two weeks. For the move she treated herself to a new dressing table. In order to spare herself a delivery charge, she struggled her way home with the boxed item herself. Just short of her front door a young man offered her assistance, shouldered the heavy carton, maneuvered it onto the elevator, and up he went. Henrietta took the other elevator. When she got off on her floor she found neither her table nor the young man. She waited, returned to the ground floor, then back up again, and now ran up and down the stairs, calling out several times in the stairwell that her dressing table belonged on the eighth floor.

"What are you shouting about?" an astonished elderly lady inquired. Henrietta asked her if she'd seen a man with a big box, and told her tale of woe.

The woman gave Henrietta the once-over. Not to worry, she said at last, sent Henrietta back to her apartment, and took the elevator to the top floor, where she rang at a particular door and stepped inside. Two young men were busy assembling a dressing table. Go ahead and finish the job, the elderly lady said. Stealing from the mother-in-law of a mafioso, having his bodyguards show up, risking an ear or two—and all for a cheap piece of furniture. "Have fun!"

Ten minutes later Henrietta and her helpful neighbor unloaded the now assembled dressing table from the elevator. The glass tabletop had a few scratches, which Henrietta magnanimously overlooked.

I wrote the rest of my story just as my mother had told it to me. Of course neither Henrietta nor my mother knew what the neighbor lady had actually said, but the line of argument sounded credible.

I intended to end my story with the punch line that until 1990 a sign had stood atop the high-rise where Henrietta now lived, proclaiming: Socialism Triumphs!

"Are you going to show Henrietta the story?" my mother asked.

"Why should I?" Her name would be changed. And there was no chance Henrietta would ever read the newspaper for which the article was intended.

The next time I visited Dresden, I brought along the newspaper containing Henrietta's story. My mother collected such things.

To be honest, I wasn't exactly enthusiastic when my mother suggested I accompany her to see her former neighbor. Henrietta had just returned from Kiev; she'd been on a pilgrimage.

"Ultimately it's her you have to thank for your story," my mother said.

It wasn't until we were in the car that she confessed that Henrietta beheld the hand of God in our visit. Henrietta felt she had been charged to play missionary to Germany. A man named Misha, a former officer in Afghanistan who was later assigned to the GDR, had convinced her of this. He had announced to Henrietta that she would have to contribute four thousand dollars to the church he worked for. If she did not, within six months Henrietta would be standing in her kitchen, go "Oy!"—and fall over dead.

The building's entry and tiny elevator were filled with graffiti, top to bottom. Henrietta hugged and kissed me as well and gave us a tour of her two and a half rooms. We admired her dressing table—gilded frame, dark glass top—and gazed from her balcony to the slopes of Loschwitz above the Elbe.

The icon in her wall unit was flanked by a whole host of images of saints. In front of these lay, like a deck of cards, more gaudy portraits, each with an appropriate prayer on the back.

"If I do something right in life, then going to monastery," Henrietta cried. She was wearing a brown dress with a plunging neckline and low-cut back adorned with the fastener of her pink bra.

Henrietta had stayed in Kiev with Mother Maria, a miracle worker who could heal crushed hands and swollen legs by channeling heavenly energy. After hours-long sessions, people had departed from her free of pain and crutches. Had she not seen it with her own eyes—and at this point Henrietta fixed her gaze on us—she wouldn't have believed it herself.

With Maria, Misha, and other Kievites, she had traveled to Pochaev monastery in western Ukraine. Their small group had gathered at four in the morning to wait at the church door. This was followed by a kind of footrace, because each person wanted to touch the altar fence. I didn't know what Henrietta meant by "altar fence," but I didn't want to interrupt her story and forgot to ask later.

A monk, tall and with dark eyes, had admonished the believers: No matter what might be happening around them, they were not to worry, but to stay right where they were and trust in God.

Gazing now far beyond us as she spoke, Henrietta resembled a child singing its song. With every sentence she became more and more animated, while more and more Russian words found their way into her tale as she unfolded the scene before our eyes.

People become restive, they sigh, moan, groan, whimper. Henrietta holds tighter to the fence. In the same moment that the monk removes the Bible from the altar fence, a few people begin screaming. They throw themselves to the floor. "They make sound like horses, like horses and wolves. Hoohoohoooo!" Her Misha's hair is standing on end. "One makes sound like pig, makes like pig. Oink, oink, oink!"

When at last the monk begins touching the heads of the faithful with the Bible, the squeals and howls intensify to a deafening roar. A boy crows at the top of his voice, his mother pulls him back, a man thrashes about on the floor, oink, oink, oink!

"Fascinating," my mother whispered. "Truly fascinating."

All of a sudden everyone falls silent, no one stirs. A moment later, and they are brushing the dust from their clothes and looking furtively around. "They do not know what happen, devil driven from soul."

Here Henrietta segued to the topic of demons and black magic. Sometimes just a nasty look suffices, and the devil has entered one's body.

"And what happened to you?" my mother asked.

"No devil in me, but must cleanse myself anyway, everyone must do, you must do—you do too, when Maria comes, everyone invited to me."

I was ready to return to Dresden the moment the opportunity to make the acquaintance of Mother Maria should arise. Misconstruing my interest, Henrietta poured her heart out to me. She was telling everyone about the cleansing. Her great worry was, however, that she was not up to the task.

Four weeks later we were ringing Henrietta's doorbell again. Mother Maria was just finishing up the dishes. Before I report about the procedure she put me through, I should also mention that thanks to my mother's good auspices, I now possessed additional material—I was working on the sequel to my first story—and the only thing I was uncertain about was where to include it. Henrietta had seven sisters and one brother. Her father had fallen in the Great Patriotic War. At age fourteen her brother had stolen a loaf of bread, was arrested at home, and had never returned. She had learned from Maria, however, that he had survived imprisonment in a camp, married, and stayed on in Siberia, where he had died only a few years previously, mourned by his children and grandchildren.

Before proceeding with the treatment we had coffee. Mother Maria was in her midsixties, had a beautiful face and several gold teeth. I would, she announced out of the blue, marry a woman with red hair, presumably a Russian, by whom I would have children.

"We'll see," I said, and laughed.

In stocking feet, pants, and undershirt I took up my position opposite her, my face to the window. The sunlight was blinding me. Maria regarded me with a smile, almost mockingly. I grinned back. She didn't have to put on an act with me.

Maria stepped closer. Without so much as brushing against me, her miracle-working hands slid down from my shoulders and along my arms, then passed from neck to navel.

Translating Maria's findings, Henrietta announced I had heart and liver trouble. "Yes," I said. "That's correct."

"Fascinating," my mother whispered.

Maria's smile vanished. She fixed her eyes on me. It was not clear, however, whether she was inspecting my body or gazing right through me. She slowly lifted her arms. I was waiting to be scanned a third time when she ripped something out of me, ripped it out, wrapped it around her right hand, only in the next moment to shake it off like drops of water. I felt nothing. When she set to work the second time, evidently employing enormous strength in an attempt to tear out a tendon—rip!—I automatically flinched. But, as noted, I felt nothing. And on it went. Inch by inch Maria freed me of various evils and ailments, whereby, as per her diagnosis, there was an especial lot of work to do in the region around the heart and liver. At times it seemed as if the imaginary tendon or fish line from which my ailment hung would slip through her fingers. Then she grabbed hold again, sometimes with both hands. Her face contorted with effort, she squeezed her eyes tight. Meanwhile I was pondering whom Maria might have meant. But of the two red-headed Russian women I knew, I wouldn't have either as my wife. Finally—it had already grown dark—Maria turned to the treatment of my head.

"*Khorosho*," she said at last with a nod. We had not turned on any lights, and the only illumination in the room came from the streetlamps, but I could see how exhausted Maria was. She sank into the armchair my mother had just vacated, and closed her eyes.

I dressed and drank another cup of coffee. My mother gave Henrietta a hundred marks to pay for Maria's trip home. Maria was not allowed to accept money. Money would rob her of her powers.

I was feeling a bit queasy. I pressed my mother for us to depart. As if observing a minute of tribute, we then stood silent before Maria, now asleep in the armchair.

In the elevator at last, and before I could say a word, my mother pulled two of Henrietta's gaudy pictures of saints from her pocket and held them out to me. "Do you want this one or this one?"

In almost the same instant my mother's mouth wrenched, she stared at me. Her eyes seemed suddenly to grow larger as if she had just donned a pair of thick-lensed glasses. She backed up against the wall of the elevator, but then immediately bent forward again. I was about to ask what in the devil was wrong with her. But suddenly her face was far away, my knees buckled, I fell backward, slid to the floor, heard a shrill cry that made me want to laugh, and let out another squeal. A foul odor assaulted my nose, I felt as if I were being crushed.

As the elevator door opened, an elderly couple recoiled in fright. They eyed me warily and only slowly approached again. I didn't know how it could have happened or why I was still lying as if paralyzed at their feet. I had evidently stumbled, sending me sprawling. Mother helped me up. But because she was in far too great a hurry, I fell again. The couple didn't budge. "Did you hear that?" the man asked. His wife nodded. They whispered and gawked at us. I understood "writer" and something else that I won't repeat here.

"What a pig!" the woman suddenly cried—and loudly enough for the whole building to hear. "What a bunch of pigs!"

I wanted to reply that anyone could stumble and a little accident was no reason to insult me and be rude to my mother besides. They, both of them, needn't act so highfalutin. The way this place looked, walls all smeared over, and the stench—well, thank you very much, but I wouldn't want to spend a single night here. But instead I let out a disgusting belch.

"Pig!" the man shouted.

"Jackass!" I hissed.

"Pig!"

"Jackass!"

We stood toe to toe, sneered, and went on calling each other "Pig!"—"Jackass!"—"Pig!"—"Jackass!" until Mother dubbed my opponent a "limp pickle." She said it softly, more as if to herself. She didn't even say, "You limp pickle," but simply "Limp pickle."

"What, whaaat . . . ?" the man said, whirling around.

"Limp pickle!" she said, and pulled me along with her, out to the parking lot.

"What, whaaat . . . ?" he shouted, following us. But his voice now sounded so strangely drained that I looked back. He was in fact gasping for air, his eyes bugged out.

My mother quickly brushed the dirt from my pants and jacket, piloted me into the shotgun seat, and swung in behind the steering wheel. She made me spit on her handkerchief, which she used to scrub my right cheek. I hate handkerchiefy spits-and-scrubs, but this time I didn't fight back, in fact I did what I could to help my mother's efforts and pushed my hair out of my face. In the sun-visor mirror I watched the man brace himself against the car trunk. His blue-lipped fish mouth looked as if it were trying to continue to shout, "What? Whaaat . . . ?"

"Limp pickle," my mother said with satisfaction, started the engine, and drove off. The man vanished from the mirror. Exhausted by a surfeit of impressions and at a loss how to appropriately order or refine them, I closed my eyes.

Faith, Love, Hope Number 23

When Marek awoke he was alone in bed. There was a smell of coffee. If he opened his left eye, the sun burned a hole in the window casings. But with just his right eye, the room regained its clear contours: an old wardrobe, an unframed mirror, two chairs, and a clothes tree, with just one hanger, on which his jacket was draped. If he banished the posters and the big, smudged glass vase in the corner, the space looked like the hotel rooms in Osnabrück and Münster where as a ten- or eleven-year-old he had stayed with his father when the two of them had attended houseware trade fairs.

It had scarcely cooled off at all overnight. He heard music coming from a radio in the back courtyard. Marek heard the announcer, joined then by an incessantly clucking female voice. On the blue runner beside the bed lay Magda's panties, blouse, his shirt and underwear. It was shortly before seven by the alarm clock. His tie hung on a nail beside the bed, along with necklaces and other glitzy baubles. Marek rolled over on his side, pressed his face against the pillow, and breathed in the fragrance.

He had held Magda in his arms for hours, guarding her slumber, and then he had watched as she sat up and pulled off her nightshirt. He had never realized that there could be so much love inside one body.

Not twelve hours before Marek had still been sitting in Knesebeck Strasse working on a brief that he had to deliver at ten on the dot today to Herr Dr.—an honorary degree—Strobonski, owner of Assmann-Schibock GmbH in Hamburg, one of Continental's suppliers. He was supposed to evaluate the most elegant way—that had been the phrase—for Witold Strobonski to place the ownership of his firm in the hands of his three daughters.

Marek was accustomed to short nights. That's why he had a six figure salary. Just as the theme music for the eight o'clock news struck up, Strobonski's secretary had called and canceled the appointment. In the next instant Magda had appeared in the blue vest of a private courier service to hand him the piece of paper he'd been waiting for all his life—or so he had believed until yesterday at any rate. The order had been placed for new stationery, and after July 1 his name would appear on the letterhead of Baechler, Thompson & Partners.

In his cover letter Baechler had fudged by referring to "your name," since he could hardly have written "Herr Marek." In order to avoid his ostensibly unpronounceable last name, everyone called him Herr Marek. And now this Herr Marek would be a partner with Baechler, Thompson, and their twenty-two other partners.

To his dismay Marek heard the apartment door. He wanted to stay right here on his pillow and spare her the sight of a face strewed with red pimples. It was especially bad in the morning. Nobody at age thirty-four still had pimples like his.

"Well, sweet dreamer," Magda said, stepped up to the bed, bent down, and kissed him on the mouth, spreading both arms wide as if to keep the bag of pastries and the milk out of his reach.

To him it seemed as if she had gone out shopping wearing only her nightshirt and jeans jacket. He heard her bustling around in the kitchen.

Magda had asked whether she could use the office restroom, and laid her clipboard on a visitor's chair. Marek would have loved to sign his name again on the delivery form—larger, with a grand flourish, so that it didn't look as if it had slipped from under his hand. A signature, as one learned in the seminars Baechler recommended, betrays a great many things, practically everything. Bad luck, he suddenly realized, was not about to be changed, not even by a signature.

"Do you always have to work so late?" Marek had just wanted to hold the girl back for a moment, to get a good look at her. He had said there was cause for celebration, and she had replied that she wanted to do some celebrating of her own now too. A deft brush-off—or so he thought. And if she hadn't said, "Shall we go?" he would probably have stayed right there at his desk.

The coffee machine gurgled. Marek's feet had no sooner touched the floor than Magda stepped through the door, holding a tray at her tummy.

"Well," she said, sitting down on the edge of the bed. "Get enough sleep?"

Marek made room for her. He was afraid she would start talking, and like a chess player planning his next moves, he could see it coming—he would have to ask whether he could visit her again. Just as he had yesterday evening, he wanted to brush a strand of hair back behind her ear. But she was already cuddling her cheek in his hand, yes, clamping his hand like a telephone between her shoulder and head.

"It's so lovely here with you," she said.

"It's so lovely here with *you*," he said. It was almost unreal the way she had pulled all those needles and clips from her hair and shaken her head in that way he had only seen in the movies, sending her hair cascading down over her shoulders and back. Like a waterfall—but he hadn't said that, because that was a cliché.

"Are you coming back? Coming again this evening?"

"How can you ask?" Marek flared up, "how can you . . . ?" He knelt beside her on the bed and embraced her. He held her in his arms just as he had held her all night. The nakedness of his body felt awkward now. She shouldn't think that . . . And while he was thinking it and staring at the breakfast tray beside the bed, she whispered, "Lookie there, the curious young lawyer is back," and grabbed his penis as if shaking hands. "Good morning, Mr. Lawyer," she said.

The morning news at eight was coming from the courtyard when Magda carried the tray back to the kitchen, poured the cold coffee in the sink, and started to brew more.

"Why are you laughing?" she asked.

"I was going to ask you to give me your pillow."

"My pillow?"

"Yes," he said with a nod.

"But you'll have to bring it back every evening," she said in earnest.

"Yes," he said. "Definitely."

"But that's such a lot of trouble."

"But I don't want to be separated from your bed ever again."

Marek was afraid he'd said something wrong. Magda ran her hand through his hair. He closed his eyes. "Marek? Marek!" She waited until he laid his head to one side and opened his eyes. "It's never been so beautiful as with you, Marek."

He wanted to say that it had never been so beautiful as with *you*, but that would have sounded silly.

"Maybe I'm just dreaming," he finally said. "I'm dreaming that you came to the office yesterday and looked at me as if we had seen each other before."

"And you were sad," she said. "You got up, buttoned your jacket, walked around your desk, and said, 'Have a nice evening.' "

"And you smiled because I was so stiff, you were laughing at me."

"Not *at* you! I was imagining what it would be like to have children with you."

"Children?"

"You looked so respectable, respectable and sad."

"Because I thought you were going to vanish again in the next moment."

"That's why you were sad?"

"That's the only reason, only because of you."

"And what were you thinking?"

Marek shook his head.

"What's wrong?"

"I was just looking at you. I just wanted to go on looking at you, the way you were standing there, short, blond, and very tired . . ."

" 'Short and blond and very tired'?"

"I thought, She's so beautiful she has to be tired."

"Why's that?"

Marek lowered his head beneath her gaze. In front of him lay a half-eaten roll smeared with liverwurst. When the commercial for Höffner Furniture was over, Marek said, "If someone is beautiful, then she has a boyfriend, maybe a couple. And they're constantly wanting something from her. And so she doesn't get enough sleep. I mean—oh, you know what I mean."

"That in just one night I—?"

"No!"

"But you just said that I spend my nights with various men—"

"Boyfriends. I said 'boyfriends'—"

"With various boyfriends—"

"I'm sorry. Please, I didn't mean it that way. Please forgive me."

Magda took a deep breath and sat up straight. She didn't have to say another word, he knew he had ruined everything and that he should leave now.

"But if I hadn't asked about the restroom? If I'd just taken off before you opened the envelope?"

"I wouldn't have let you leave."

"I usually give the doorman stuff like that."

"I would have called the doorman to tell him to keep you there. I would have followed you, would have jumped out the window..."

Magda wrapped her hair around one hand and put it in some kind of knot. "So we're both dreaming the same dream?"

"Yes."

"Has this ever happened to you before?"

"No. Never."

"And does it go on and on?"

"Of course. Once it's happened, it's happened, it can't go on any other way."

"That would be lovely," she said.

Marek didn't understand why she was suddenly so sad. "Are you tired?" Nothing and no one would ever be able to separate him from her again—nothing and no one. He reached for her hand and said, "You know, nobody is going to believe this. Not this kind of good luck. They'll think I'm pulling their leg."

She smiled. "You don't have to tell them."

"I'm not going to."

"It's not allowed, not during the first week. The first week is sacred."

"Sacred," he said, and it sounded far more serious than he had intended.

"I'll be waiting for you from six o'clock on, and I'll wait and wait and—wait."

"I'll be waiting for you," he quickly said. "I'll be counting the minutes."

"I'm superstitious," she said. The sun was shining on her feet.

"Because it's the thirteenth? But it's Wednesday, nothing happens on Wednesdays. Besides, thirteen is a lucky number."

"Definitely not."

"But what about us . . . this morning . . . it was already the thirteenth."

"This morning?"

"And on the thirteenth they've made me a member of the firm, on June 13, 2001."

"Okay, fine, then it's a lucky number," she said. The alarm clock rang at that same moment.

When Marek stood up from the table, Magda followed him. He opened the shower stall and turned on the water. She was still standing beside him. He grabbed her nightshirt, and like an obedient child she raised her arms to let him pull it over her head. There was a mosquito bite on each shoulder. They entered the shower holding hands. He soaped her and rinsed her off, and then she laid her head on his chest, right next to the spot where the jet of water struck him. He couldn't understand what she said. But a moment later he heard it quite clearly: "The curious Mr. Lawyer."

Their hair still damp, they stepped out onto Nauny Strasse, and it felt like he was onstage, because everyone was looking at him—that is, first at Magda, then at him. But that wasn't the reason. It was the sun. It was already so high that except for a narrow strip along the right edge of the sidewalk it cast no shadows.

At Kottbusser Tor he waved good-bye to Magda, and although normally it would have embarrassed and upset him to turn around every few yards and raise his arm with total strangers looking on, he now even walked part of the way backward. Nothing, nothing should be different, he didn't want to miss a thing, not even the mosquito bites on her shoulders.

Marek walked up the stairs to the U1 el station. He looked about him like a tourist. Normally he took taxis. He didn't have a car, not even a driver's license. He had also never learned to swim, but nobody knew that.

Suddenly he had the feeling he had done everything right. Of course he regularly met with success, that was his job. But only through Magda had it all acquired meaning and significance.

Marek had been married once, as a student, but neither his marriage nor other relationships had lasted.

Marek found it depressing that he'd been unable to tell Magda anything other than that he loved her, that she was his lucky charm, and his darling, his one and only, and the most beautiful woman besides, and that he would love to have children with her—all statements he had used often before. He had wasted the words, abused them, worn them out, and now he could only repeat them for Magda, the only woman they were meant for.

As Marek came up out of the subway station at Uhland Strasse, a large Mercedes drove past. The guy on the passenger side was holding a Brazilian flag out the window.

He entered the building with its large-lettered rooftop sign: Baechler, Thompson & Partners. It was obvious that the letters had been braving wind and weather for three decades now.

"I thought you were in Hamburg?" cried Frau Ruth, the executive secretary, who looked at everyone as if she were gazing out over reading glasses. "Congratulations," she said and went on sorting files.

"Thanks," Marek said. The door to Baechler's office was ajar, he cast a glance inside. Baechler was on the phone.

Marek still thought Baechler looked like Sky Dumont, and it had bothered him to watch Sky Dumont dance with Nicole Kidman in Kubrick's *Eyes Wide Shut*—as if he had caught Baechler cheating on his wife. Old man Baechler was so handsome it was like a cliché, just as he, Marek, was likewise a cliché—the opposite one. Marek knew that people here too called him crumb cake, pizza man, or just pimple face. Why should it be any different at Baechler's, of all places, than it had been in school, in the army, in college, in law offices or restaurants? Strangely enough, after the first few iffy minutes, it proved an advantage with clients, as if someone who looked like him must be especially intelligent or talented to have been brought on board by the handsome Baechler.

Files clamped under her left elbow, Frau Ruth preceded him. She almost always wore a white blouse and something black to match her black or black-dyed hair. Marek's father would have called her a woman who took good care of herself. But after being hired by Baechler, Thompson & Partners, Marek had barely been able to hide his astonishment upon learning that Frau Ruth's daughter was only twelve. Marek considered Frau Ruth to be spiteful.

"Not in Hamburg?" Baechler exclaimed, leaning back in his chair but not offering him a seat. "Yes, my good man, hang together and get hanged together. Our heads are in the same noose now."

"I wanted to thank you, Herr Doktor Baechler. I—"

"No need for that, none whatever." Baechler waved his large liver-spotted hand adorned with a ring with a large black stone. "You know I've refused to do the same for my sons."

"If only for that reason, Herr Doktor Baechler," Marek said, who had been listening to him go on like this about his sons since day one. But even though—like everyone else—he joked about it, it never failed to impress him.

"What's with our friend Strobonski?"

"Canceled late yesterday evening. Ten minutes earlier, and I would have missed the courier."

"Even then, it would've arrived in time."

"And once again, my warmest thanks," Marek said and leaned across the desk to extend his hand to Baechler.

"Keep it in mind, Marek—our heads in the same noose."

"Happy to," Marek said. He was touched that Baechler had addressed him by his first name without the silly title "Herr."

"Thank you," Marek said turning to Frau Ruth, who gave him a startled look, as if noticing him only now.

In the elevator—his office was four floors down—Marek wondered if he should go directly to the subway at six or first go home and change. What he really wanted was to climb into a car right now and wave a Brazilian, or any other, flag. Ten minutes earlier, he reminded himself, and I would have missed her. The idea was so awful it seemed to protest his good luck. And if Strobonski hadn't canceled? Marek tried to think about other things. About the mosquito bites on Magda's shoulders or about how rattled he had been by the razor in the bathroom and how that had made her laugh. As if to make amends, to thank her for dyeing her hair for his sake, he had kissed the dark line of the part in Magda's blond hair. Marek was still smiling as he stepped off the elevator and walked down the hall, where he ran into Elke, the intern. "You're invited to join us, at one o'clock," Marek called out, and it pleased him that Elke stopped in her tracks and asked, "Me?" "Yes, you," he said. He would invite everyone who had the time, everyone—except Baechler, who was always served lunch by Frau Ruth in his office.

Around six he would first go home, pack his carry-on suitcase or gym bag and then—off to Magda's! For a moment he imagined Magda at his place on Bamberger Strasse, and the thought didn't sit well. He himself didn't want to go back to that apartment, to his crypt. Marek looked out the hall window. And for the first time, or so it seemed to him, the blue sky was meant for him as well.

Marek walked over to the coffee dispenser. He wouldn't get any work done today in any case, because a steady stream of people would be stopping by to congratulate him. He might just as well go on standing right here. Some would say they'd have to have a beer sometime, and others that they'd have to meet over coffee. And Karl-Heinz Södering, who was proud of having married a former Miss Nuremberg, would say that Marek definitely had to pay them a visit soon.

When Marek finally opened the top file to prepare for a Friday appointment, he was disappointed that everything was just as always. He loved his work. But today he wanted to celebrate, chew the fat, laugh. All he could think about anyway was Magda. There were moments when he actually believed he sensed her presence. And once he raised both hands to re-create the motion of his fingertips as they traced from her neck down to her breasts. Like a ski jumper, he had thought. But he had kept that to himself. Besides, both the gesture and the comparison belonged to another "body"—Silke, his ex-wife, had always used the English word "body."

Shortly after noon he called Joachim, who had started with Baechler at the same time he had, but had been taken on as an equity partner one year earlier. Joachim briefly congratulated him—he was speaking with a client at the moment, with whom he'd be having lunch. Marek ran into Christopher Heincken in the washroom. At first Marek had been quite proud to have an office on the same floor as Chris—everyone called him Chris. His UMTS contracts had earned Chris the title of best horse in the stable; he was assumed to be Baechler's crown prince. He clapped Marek on the back with a wet hand and, ripping away at one paper towel after another, said: "Now we both have our heads in the noose." That was meant ironically, right?

At five after one Marek appeared at the front entrance. Elke, the intern, seemed less peeved at his being late than at having to have lunch with just him alone. It had been embarrassing to have to admit to her the reason for his invitation, and she was as surprised by that as he had once been by the age of Ruth's daughter.

How had he ended up with Elke around his neck? Sven Schmidt, Frau Ruth's pet—they both came from Wetzlar—had shown him Elke's application, even though Marek no longer read applications, and he had underlined the phrase "career oriented" as if it were a stylistic gem, but Sven Schmidt had said that was a "must" nowadays. Elke's attempts to engage him in conversation bothered him. And at the same time his old self-consciousness returned, his old life. Marek kept a good half stride ahead of Elke. When she suddenly halted he expected to be scolded for not being more considerate. But Elke just slipped out of her sling pumps, brushed her forearm across her brow, smiled, and, one shoe in each hand, hurried after him.

"I have an idea," Marek said, offering Elke his arm. They crossed the street. Marek hailed a cab, passed ten euros up to the driver, and said, "KaDeWe."

The driver explained the various flags and T-shirts for Elke and said that Sweden wouldn't play for two days yet and that Germany, if everything went according to plan, would meet Sweden in the final eight—Sweden or England, but Sweden was better.

Marek rode with Elke up to the gourmet floor. While she was still inspecting displays of lobsters and oysters, he ordered a lobster tail for them to split and wine. "Marvelous, really marvelous," Elke exclaimed.

When she was finished, she leaned over on her bar stool, laid her head on his shoulder, and whispered, "Awesome, just plain awesome, Herr Marek." On the ride back they sat side by side not saying a word.

When after two more hours no one had stopped by to congratulate him, he was convinced people were avoiding him as a way of protesting Baechler's decision. Of course all the partners had had to consent, but Baechler's word was law.

Marek felt completely calm. He could handle clearly drawn front lines. Him against all the rest of them, that was nothing new. For a few minutes Marek managed to concentrate on his brief. Then he leaned back and closed his eyes. The universal snub had left him exhausted. He would open his own office, and Magda would work for him. Him and Magda, Magda and him. He would talk to her about it this evening. Suddenly he was afraid of seeing Magda again. A night like that, a morning like that—it could never be repeated. Maybe the bosses would rescind their decision, and then—Marek was certain of it—he and Magda would also come to a bad end.

When the phone rang it was accounting, a missing train ticket, and Marek promised to deal with it and to make a copy of his ticket in advance next time. He *had* turned that ticket in—he was certain of it. One pinprick of the thousands awaiting him.

It was five o'clock when Frau Ruth called. Would he be so kind as to come upstairs—yes, right away. She hung up without another word.

On his way in the elevator Marek decided the best thing would be for him to resign.

Baechler was standing with Heincken at the window of the reception room. They didn't return Marek's greeting. Frau Ruth stared at him with arched eyebrows, as if she had just asked him a question, and pointed to the conference-room door. It was ajar. "Dr. Baechler will be in soon," she whispered, and bent over her desk again.

As if hitting a wall, he recoiled from the darkness in the conference room. The blinds had been lowered to keep out the summer sun. He groped for the light switch. . . . Someone shouted, "Three, four!"

Marek was aghast. Lights, faces, laughter. To the melody of "For He's a Jolly Good Fellow" they sang: "For he's the twenty-third now, he is the twe-henty-third now, he's the twe-henty-thi-hird now, and so he's one of us."

His partners stepped aside—a cake decorated with a "23." And then they struck up their song again. He stared into Frau Ruth's mouth, he saw Chris and he saw Baechler, who was pretending to conduct. Yes, he was number twenty-three, in collusion with twenty-two others. Corks popped, and three waitresses passed trays of glasses. Someone shouted, "Speech!" And then others: "Speech! Speech! Speech!"

He wanted to ask why, of all of them, he was the one to receive such a posh reception. But it occurred to him just in time that he had in fact never been present when someone was made equity partner. They always celebrated among themselves.

His speech failed miserably. Nothing occurred to him, not one thing that could have made the others laugh for real. He was literally overwhelmed, speechless, and touched—which was what they had wanted.

The first ones left around seven. Everyone said their good-byes to Marek, invited him to join them for coffee or a beer or even to visit them at home, as soon as possible, while summer lasted, for a backyard barbecue. Wiener's Party Service started removing platters.

The loveliest part, however, had not been the surprise, but that while he spoke with the others he could think of Magda and that he would now walk out on the street, climb into a taxi, and ride to her place. And he thought, this is what pure luck feels like—pure good luck.

Baechler repeated his thing about heads in a noose, and as he extended his hand to Marek he placed the other hand on his shoulder. Marek resisted the impulse to give Baechler a hug. "Thank you," Marek said. "Thank you."

The last stragglers were gathering at the end of the conference table, from where you could look out on Savigny Platz. Now they could finally drink beer.

Sven Schmidt opened two windows, a pleasant breeze flowed in. And Joachim asked what they should do to follow up. "Tonight's my night out. I'm thinking a party at the very least, what with our heads in the same noose."

Chris had reserved a table at Dicke Wirtin for ten to eight, in time for the game with Brazil. "Marek has to treat," he shouted. "Marek needs to be fleeced. I forked out a couple thousand back in my day. An evening in front of the TV can't hold a candle."

"I can't," Marek said. And above the boos, he shouted, "Somebody's expecting me!"

They called him names—penny pincher, wet blanket—but it didn't sound like they meant it, and Marek was relieved.

"And it's set in stone?" Sven Schmidt asked.

Marek nodded.

"Call and tell them what's happened. A night like this comes once in a lifetime!"

"No", Marek said. "It really won't work. She's been waiting since six."

"She! Sex!" Sven Schmidt whistled through his teeth.

"How's that, Marek, a lady?" Chris asked.

"Yes," Marek said. And now that he had put it in words Magda no longer seemed to be a dream.

"Marek has a girlfriend!" Karl-Heinz Södering shouted. "Have her come along!"

"Congratulations," Joachim said. "And? Is she the one?"

"Yes," Marek said. "She's the one."

"Be careful," Chris said. "Don't go getting married tomorrow." They laughed.

"Day after," Marek said.

"A free night, and then look what happens," Sven Schmidt said. "But you're not going to slip away from us this easy, let me tell you. Not this easy."

Joachim hugged Marek. Marek said his good-byes, shaking hands with the others.

"Can you tell us the name of the lovely lady?" Joachim asked.

"Magda," Marek said in an almost toneless voice.

"Magda!" Sven Schmidt announced. "And she's very beautiful?"

Marek nodded.

"Blond, long hair, slender, and with a nice perky pair?" Sven Schmidt held his hands before his chest, rippling his fingers and looking at Marek.

"Believe it or not, yes!" Marek said.

"And she loves you," Joachim said. "And no night was ever so beautiful as with you?"

"Shut up," Chris hissed. "Let him go."

"She loves me and I love her, and no night was ever so beautiful," Marek said.

"Congratulations," Karl-Heinz Södering said. "Have a great evening, Mr. Lawyer."

"Shut your trap!" Chris shouted.

"What's with 'Mr. Lawyer'?"

" 'The curious Mr. Lawyer'? Is that her name for it?" Joachim asked.

Marek looked at Chris, then back at Joachim.

"Damn it, Marek," Joachim said. "It can't be. You didn't really fall for her?"

"I don't know what you guys mean," Marek said, looking from one to the other. "What do you mean by 'Mr. Lawyer'?"

"Your dick," Sven Schmidt said. "Svenya evidently hasn't come up with anything new."

"Her name's not Svenya."

"You're right there," Joachim said. "Her name's not Svenya, or Johanna—and not Magda either, Marek."

"Chris?" Marek asked. "Tell me what's going on here."

"Your new partners have said it all." Chris removed his jacket from the back of the chair.

"Now don't pass out on us," Sven Schmidt said. "Do you think the old man would send you the news by courier service, when Miss Ruth would only have to take the elevator down a couple of floors? Or that our majestic doorman would let her in?"

"Her name's not Svenya," Marek said.

"Only the old man himself knows her name," Joachim said. "So best leave her be."

"Baechler?"

"Oh, Marek! Of course Baechler, surprise, surprise! Welcome to the club."

"Baechler?"

"Do you suppose Miss Ruth does the job for him? A guy who loves it like he does?"

"Damn it, Marek. You Poles have got plenty of hot women, if anybody's got classy women, then it's you guys. You don't have to get mixed up with someone like . . ." Sven Schmidt said.

"He's really fallen for her," Karl-Heinz Södering said. "He still hasn't caught on."

"Shut up, will you finally just shut up," Chris said. "I'm sorry, Marek, but nobody here figured on this."

Three hours later—the match with Brazil was already over—Marek was still sitting in Dicke Wirtin with Joachim, Karl-Heinz Södering, and Sven Schmidt.

Marek was tired. He was close to letting his head sink to the table. But not to sleep, no, not that. There was simply no room for sleep, not at this table or any other. There would be no spot where he could get some rest, no matter how long he looked. Sleep was out of the question.

When Magda was suddenly standing before him, his first thought was that she was drunk too. Something about her wasn't right.

"Come," she said. "Come on." He was puzzled because she acted as if only he and she existed, as if they were all alone in the room. She knew Sven Schmidt and she knew Joachim, and she even knew Karl-Heinz Södering from Wetzlar, Frau Ruth's favorite. Why didn't she greet his colleagues too? They were all easy to recognize. Sitting here in suits—compared with everyone else they looked like a delegation. And then all the Swedes. The city was full of Swedes already. And of lawyers, four of them were sitting right here, four lawyers.

"Come on," Magda said. "Come with me."

Marek discovered you had to watch her lips to get what she was saying. Otherwise you could barely make it out. Something wasn't right about her. He first held one eye closed, then the other. But at this distance that didn't change anything. Marek saw what everyone saw. She was short, blond, and very, very tired. But maybe she knew some spot where you could sleep.

Estonia, Out in the Country

During that week of September 2000 that Tanya and I spent in Tallinn and Tartu, I was called upon several times to write something about Estonia. In every case I explained that while I was honored by such requests, writing a short story is not a matter of choosing a country and a topic and simply taking off from there. I knew nothing about Estonia, and our experiences of regime change were scarcely comparable. But I was talking to a brick wall. After all, I had written thirty-three stories about St. Petersburg, so surely I could come up with one about Estonia.

For a story set in a foreign country, I said, one needs to sense a certain affinity, a kinship of soul with how things developed there. But the more emphatic my arguments, the more I rubbed my hosts the wrong way. They were too polite to tell me straight-out that they regarded such arguments as mere evasion.

I was a guest of the Writers Union and had been invited to Käsmu, where the union has a guesthouse on the Baltic. Käsmu, as my hosts never wearied of assuring me, was a very special place. It was not only a spot for total relaxation, but it also inspired one to work as never before. What we needed was a trip to Käsmu.

I hope this introduction has not left the impression that we were treated inhospitably. On the contrary, ours was a royal reception. Never before had one of my readings been moderated by the chairman of a writers' union. He greeted us like old friends and invited us to a café where we could make plans for the reading. On our way there, every few steps someone would block our path to shake the chairman's hand, a steady stream of people rapped on the café window or stepped inside, until we could hardly exchange two connected sentences. When I inquired about the profession of a tall, handsome man who gave me a most cordial handshake and apologized for having to miss the reading that evening, the chairman said: That was the minister of culture. The minister's wife—beautiful, young, clever, amiable—interviewed me for television. It was just that they had all studied in Tartu, she said, and were now all working in Tallinn. They couldn't help knowing one another, right?

Tanya and I took our lunch and dinner in restaurants that were both upscale and empty, and despite a good number of beers we seldom paid more than twenty marks.

When we and a small group went looking for a restaurant after the reading, it was Tanya and I who could offer suggestions. My translator, on the other hand—who told us how she and the people of Tallinn, of the entire Baltic, had for so many years gathered to sing anthems in hope of independence—couldn't recall the last time she'd been in a restaurant. She couldn't imagine buying a book as expensive as mine—which converted at just short of seventeen marks.

Before I tell about our days in Käsmu I want to mention

another episode that has nothing to do with my story, really. Between a reading for students in the German Department of Tartu University and the public reading that same evening of the translated version of my book, some students invited Tanya and me for a walk through town. Toward the end of our little tour we passed a kiosk that offered the same beverages we have at home. There were two wooden benches out in front, and we invited the students to join us for a drink. Tanya said she was amazed at how everyone here roundly cursed the Russians but almost revered the Germans. Was that simply a matter of hospitality?

That had nothing to do with hospitality, it was simply how they felt, after all they were German majors. I was about to ask a question myself, when the youngest and loveliest of the female students, who until this point had only listened, exclaimed, "Why are you amazed? Germans have never harmed Estonians."

"Well maybe not Estonians—" Tanya said.

"I know what you're getting at," the student interrupted. "But surely you know that we Estonians had our own SS, and you only have to consider how many Estonians, how many people from the Baltic in general, the Russians killed and deported even after the war. Only bad things have come from Russia, and mostly good things from the Germans—people can't help noticing that."

Tanya said that one cannot limit memory to a particular span of years or to a single nationality, and that after all it had been the Hitler-Stalin pact that had robbed them of their sovereignty.

"That's true, of course it's true," the student said. "But why are you amazed?"

"Why aren't *you* amazed!" Tanya blurted out. After that we returned to the university and exchanged addresses.

On the drive to Käsmu in our rental car, Tanya asked me if she had come off as self-righteous. No, I said, just the opposite, but unfortunately I hadn't been able to come up with anything better to say. Tanya said she couldn't help being reminded of certain turns of phrase in those Estonian fairy tales we had been reading aloud to each other of an evening. Certain idioms kept popping up, like "She adorned herself in beautiful raiment, as if she were the proudest German child," or "as happy as a pampered German child."

We were looking forward to Käsmu. We had read in our guidebook that Lahemaa, Land of Bays, lies about twenty-five miles to the east of Tallinn, is bounded by the Gulf of Finland and the Tallinn-Narva highway, encompasses an area of 250 square miles, and was declared a national park in 1971. The guidebook also noted several endangered species to be found there: brown bears, lynx, mink, sea eagles, cranes, Arctic loons, mute swans, and even black storks.

We reported in to Arne, a gangly man with medium long hair and a beret, who runs a kind of marine museum. He greeted Tanya and me with a handshake: a signal, he said, to his two dogs—setters—that we now belonged to the village. Before handing over the keys, he gave a brief lecture about the especially favorable magnetic field of Käsmu. On the way to the guesthouse, however, Arne fell silent, as if to allow us to take in the view of tidy frame houses without any distraction and appreciate the peaceful setting to the full. The two setters bounded ahead of us, came back, circled us, and nudged against our knees.

When I think back on that week now, six years later, the first thing that comes to mind—quite apart from the incredible events I am about to recount—is the way the light turned every color brighter and paler at the same time.

The house had once belonged to Captain Christian Steen, who had been deported to Siberia in 1947 and has since been listed as missing. The entryway opened on a large, centrally located dining room, where, with one exception, we took all our meals alone at the huge table. At opposite ends of this space were the two guest rooms, and a third door led to the kitchen, which adjoined a winter garden. The dining room's high windows looked directly out onto the sauna cabin and a moss-covered erratic deposited by the last ice age.

The finest quarters, the Epos Room, had been reserved for Tanya and me. The smaller Novel Room was unoccupied at first, while the two Novella Chambers under the roof were home to a married couple, both lyric poets. We, however, caught sight only of the wife, who, no sooner had she announced in English, "Käsmu is good for work and good for holiday," scurried off again as if not to waste one second of her precious Käsmu sojourn.

Käsmu has a narrow beach. You walk through the woods, and suddenly there is the sea. Or you stroll out on the pier in the little harbor to watch children fishing and let your fantasy run free as you gaze at derelict cutters scraping garlands of car tires strung along on the sides of the pier. The town is nothing spectacular, but lovely for that very reason. Somewhere there must be a depot for wooden pallets, because pallets lie about everywhere, and once they have been chopped into firewood by the villagers, are stacked along the sides of their houses.

The one thing we had a knack for in Käsmu was sleeping.

Käsmu is worth a trip simply for its silence. As we sat in the winter garden in the evening—sipping tea, eating the wild-berry marmalade we'd bought from an old local woman, listening to the sea and the birds—time seemed to stand still.

Käsmu's peace and quiet were only disrupted of a morning, by two or three buses that came lumbering down the village street to deposit school classes at Arne's museum. The children stood staring in amazement at whalebones, shark teeth, ships in bottles, fishhooks, and postcards of lighthouses around the world. They would picnic on the lawn in front of the building, run out on the pier, and then be driven away again.

Tanya and I had tried to engage Arne in conversation and intended to invite him to dinner, but Arne resisted all contact with us. Even when we paid a second visit to his museum, he simply greeted us with a brief nod and then shuffled away.

On the third day—it had been drizzling since early morning—we watched from the window of our Epos Room as schoolchildren got off their buses, jiggled at Arne's front door, circled the building, peered in from the veranda, until finally their teachers, equally perplexed and upset, rounded them up and herded them back onto the buses, where we could see them eating their picnic lunch. That evening when we returned from our excursion to the high marshy moorland, the note we had left for Arne asking him to heat the sauna was still wedged in his door. The sky was clear and promised a beautiful sunset.

The fourth day was cold and so gusty we could hear the sea even with the windows shut, and we stayed indoors. Tanya made tea and crawled back into bed with Gustav Herling's *A World Apart*. Resolved at last to make use of Käsmu's favorable aura and do some work, I turned on my laptop and was staring at the file icons on my screen—when savage barking called us to the window.

A green Barkas van was standing beside the museum. Arne's setters were going crazy. I don't know where they had suddenly come from, but their baying didn't sound exactly welcoming. Although the day before yesterday these same dogs had obeyed Arne's every word, he now had to grab each by the nape of its neck and drag it into the house. But once inside they still didn't calm down and kept leaping up at the windows to the veranda, yelping their hearts out.

Arne on the other hand looked somehow younger—his beret cocked back on his head.

"If you can keep a secret," he called over, "I have something to show you." With a wide swing of his arm, he directed us to take our place behind him, inserted the key in the rear door of the Barkas, and opened it a crack. He peered into the van and then with a clownish pantomime urged us to do the same. I assumed Arne's daily encounters with schoolchildren were to blame for his exaggerated performance.

It was dark inside the van, and I recoiled from the foul odor. Tanya took more time. Then she glanced at me and said in a voice that sounded as if I had just asked her the time, "A bear, there's a dead bear lying in there."

Arne had dragged over one of those wooden pallets. Tanya opened the door till it caught in place, and Arne and I propped up the pallet to make a ramp. Arne took up his post beside it, Tanya and I retreated behind the opened door.

The bear didn't stir.

We watched as Arne pulled a can from his jacket pocket and, after opening it with his fingernails, plunged a stick into it. He handed me the stick, nodded as if to thank me or as if we had agreed on some signal, clapped his hands three times, and cried, "Seryosha! Seryosha!" He clapped three more times, took back the stick, and held it out in front of him like a fishing pole.

I'm really not all that much of a wimp, but when, at no more than an arm's length, the bear's head emerged from the darkness, I had a sense of the aptness of the idiom "so scared I almost shit my pants." "Let's get out of here," Tanya whispered. Arne, however, armed with just a honey-smeared stick, showed no sign of the jitters. He waited in front of the pallet with his legs astraddle, bending farther and farther forward—and given his height, it looked like some sort of gymnastics. The bear stretched its head out even farther but still refused to crawl down the pallet. Arne held the stick so close to Seryosha's mouth that he could take a lick and bite off a piece. He crunched the stick as he dined, and growled. From childhood on we learn that bears growl. But when you actually hear that ursine rumble, without the protection of a moat or a fence, it leaves a lasting impression.

Strangely enough my confidence was boosted less by Arne's honey-stick gambit than by the bear's behavior. When you know how this story ends, that seems a facile observation, but from the start I had the impression that this bear had himself under control, that he knew what he was allowed and not allowed to do. He stuck out a paw and pushed the pallet away from the van, measured the distance between the edge of the van's bed and the pallet lying below it, shifted his weight from one paw to the other, reached down farther with his right paw, and leaped out so quickly that Arne would have been knocked over if he hadn't performed a reverse buckjump. At the same moment the Barkas bounced with a metallic squeak.

Arne made a few quick jabs at the can. The crunching sound

resumed. And then it happened. At first I thought the bear was turning toward us. But then he kept going, spun around once in place, and then a second time, because Arne was applauding him. He turned and turned, swinging the rope around his neck with him. When we joined the applause, he suddenly stopped, lurched forward and backward as if dizzy, and ended with a somersault that was a little off kilter but still counted as a somersault. For his finale, the bear plopped down on his rear end and raised his paws, begging.

Whether Arne's stick was now too short or whether he was following instructions, at any rate he pulled out a handkerchief, dipped it in the can of honey, and tossed it to Seryosha, who simultaneously tore it to shreds and stuffed it in his mouth. Smacking his lips and grunting, he lowered himself onto all fours and set off on a stroll across the lawn. Arne had removed a basket of fruit from the passenger seat. He now tossed Seryosha a couple of apples and strewed the rest over the bed of the van. Seryosha actually turned around and jumped up into the Barkas, which settled onto its rear axle with a squeak.

It wasn't until weeks later, after we had told the story of Seryosha many times, that it struck me just how curious this little interlude outside Arne's house actually was. Why, after all, had Arne enticed the bear out of the van? Had he wanted to play wild-animal trainer for us? Had his vanity gotten the better of him? Was that the reason he had risked discovery?

Arne invited us to accompany him. And so, for the first time since our hitchhiking days, Tanya and I found ourselves squeezing into a Barkas—but unlike back then, Tanya climbed in first.

What I ask myself now is: Why didn't I jot down a single note while we were in Käsmu? Driving through the woods were an Estonian and a German writer, along with his one and only love, plus a bear in the back of their van—and it never once dawned on me that all I had to do to provide my hosts with the story they wanted was to write down what I was experiencing at that moment.

It would of course be an improvement if I could reproduce Arne's speech in the original. His German was tinged with the now-defunct East Prussian dialect, but I'm simply unable to replicate its odd syntax and broad vowels. Chugging out of the village in second gear, we at first said nothing. Arne was apparently enjoying keeping us in suspense and pretended that his slalom course to avoid potholes demanded his full attention.

"What kind of bear is it?" Tanya finally asked. In her attempt to look Arne in the eye, she bent so far forward that her forehead almost touched the windshield. "What are you doing with a bear?"

Arne smiled—a pothole sent us lurching forward. Arne cursed.

"Did you hear that?" Tanya exclaimed. "He growled, he's growling."

A couple of slalom maneuvers later, Arne began to speak, but what he had to say apparently had nothing to do with Tanya's question. He explained that the Writers Union was poor because its writers were poor. Except for one member, not a single writer in Estonia was able to live from his books, although of course the union also received a government subsidy. And for the quartermaster—that was in fact the term he used—for the quartermaster of a writers' retreat there was really not much left over, and he couldn't depend on the standard practice of tipping in their case either. Once in a while he let a few villagers use the sauna, but they paid, if at all, in produce. As far as his museum work went, all he got out of it was what he squeezed out of it himself. Even ten buses a day wouldn't do the job. "So, *chto delat*?" he asked in Russian. What was Arne to do?

But why was he taking a trained bear for a joyride through the woods?

Arne was looking for a turnoff. We drove at a snail's pace along the rutted path. Arne talked about the revolution, as he called it. They had achieved everything they had wanted: independence, democracy, a market economy, and soon the European Union. Except that by now all the islands and coastal properties had been sold to Finns and Swedes, some to Russians and Germans too, plus the finest houses in Tallinn. There was truly nothing left that hadn't been privatized and incorporated into the market economy. So what now?

Whenever we drove over a root or through a deep puddle, we could hear Seryosha's growls.

The only difference from the old days, Arne said, was that from time to time some Westerner might get lost and end up in Käsmu. And that there was nobody to tell him how to run his museum anymore.

Arne turned on his headlights because the fir trees had closed in over the path, so that it was like driving through a tunnel. After an eternity of two or three kilometers, a heather-covered clearing opened up before us. Arne stopped, turned off his lights, pulled the key out of the ignition, and leaned back with arms folded.

A friend of his in Lahti, who also ran a museum and to whom he had sold two old German telescopes at a friendly discount, had passed on an inquiry about whether he, Arne, could perhaps act as an agent to locate a house at a good price along the coast. Although he had not agreed to this arrangement, suddenly there stood Mika, along with his wife, a stunning Argentinean, and their three children. Nothing came of the house deal, but Mika had been wildly enthusiastic about the local forest—which Arne found surprising, since Finland had plenty of forests of its own. It turned out that Mika was a hunter, and he called this forest a Russian forest and suggested that surely there were bears in a Russian forest. He, Arne, had never seen a bear in Lahemaa, but, since the house deal had fallen through, he didn't want to dash Mika's hopes a second time, and so had promised to inquire about bears at the local game and forestry office. There were plenty of bears, so he learned, but it was forbidden to shoot animals in the national park. Unless—here Arne raised his right hand and began to rub his thumb against his first two fingers—unless the bear presented a serious threat to the life and limb of locals and tourists.

Arne had come to an agreement with the game warden as to how many Finnish markaa it would cost Mika to obtain the ruling. Mika agreed to the sum, half in advance, the rest on the hide of the bear. In March a family of bears actually turned up in Lahemaa. But to avoid additional difficulties, the game warden had requested the hunt be postponed until autumn.

But the family of bears vanished in May, and there had been no trace of them since. The game warden had telephoned him a week ago and confessed that unfortunately he was no longer in a position to pay back the advance. In lieu of the cash, the game warden gave him a hot tip: A once highly renowned circus from Soviet days was eking out a livelihood in a St. Petersburg suburb. They were trying to unload their animals because their upkeep was too expensive. And so yesterday, for a payment of three hundred marks, Arne had taken charge of Seryosha, whom his caretaker had smuggled across the border through the forest. And so now they had a bear.

In response to Tanya's question of whether he had informed Seryosha's caretaker what fate awaited her charge, Arne brusquely asked in return whether she would prefer that Seryosha starve. Thanks to his good work, the animal would at least die with a full tummy and the pleasure of having enjoyed a couple of hours in the wild.

The plan was to let Seryosha settle in at the edge of this clearing for a day or two. To ease the pain of separation, his caretaker had also given Arne a pair of her old shoes and a jacket. Arne pulled out a well-worn moccasin, like the ones I had worn as a child, and got out of the van.

I smiled, unable to suppress my suspicion that what Arne had told us was your basic cock-and-bear story. "You don't believe me?" he asked. I shrugged. "Tomorrow," Arne said, "Mika will be here. Maybe you'll want to apologize then." I apologized on the spot, and several times over, but to no avail. Arne had opened the van's rear door, and now clapped three times, called Seryosha's name, and with the shoes and jacket bundled under his arm and a sack of food thrown over his shoulder, set out across the heather.

Tanya and I stood beside the van. As he trotted alongside Arne, Seryosha was a beautiful sight to behold. It was not just his loping gait, which made it look as if he were dragging his paws behind him. Under that mass of fur moved a body no less supple than a tiger's, except that Seryosha's elegance was less obvious.

When we finally lost sight of them in the trees at the far side of the clearing, Tanya asked what I would do if Arne were to scream for help. "Certainly not run in his direction," I said.

On the drive back each of us was lost in our own thoughts.

Our good-byes were brief. Arne had enough to do calming down his setters—and a clutch of teachers and their students.

Tanya took it upon herself to walk over to Arne's that evening to ask him about the sauna, but either Arne wasn't there or he didn't want to be disturbed.

As we drank our tea in the winter garden, we tried without success to imagine the hunt. Would Arne clap his hands three times and call out "Seryosha"? Should we or shouldn't we hope that Seryosha had made his getaway? Did a circus bear have any chance at all in Lahemaa? Wouldn't he seek out the company of people, so that sooner or later he'd be shot as a dangerous animal? Seryosha's future didn't look rosy, and there was nothing we could do about that.

The next day was warm, the sky cloudless, and we made an excursion to Palmse, once the estate of a German baron. Afterward we visited a forest chapel, which was set in the middle of an old cemetery. (I've rechecked my notebook. In point of fact there is not a single entry about Estonia. Although Tanya did use two pages to record the names on the wooden crosses and gravestones. I now remember how ashamed I felt that it was she who jotted down those names and not me.)

On the drive home the weather turned gloomy, it began to rain. But once we arrived home our mood immediately turned more cheerful—smoke was rising from the sauna cabin. Arne had in fact heated it and filled the basins in the entryway with fresh birch branches.

As we entered the steam room, each of us dressed in no more than a towel over one arm, we found three men already huddled in the small room. They neither responded to our greeting nor moved closer together to make room for us.

Instead they ogled Tanya. From the corner of my eye I could see the one seated behind her trace a female silhouette in the air. We couldn't understand what they were saying, of course, but their stifled childish giggles didn't need an interpreter. Tanya left the sauna after a few minutes and returned to the house.

I was idiotic enough to believe I ought not yield the battleground to the Finns without a fight, so I was the first to go back inside and stretch out on the upper bench, leaving them to crowd together on the lower one. In the course of the next half hour I thought I could observe the other two brownnosing the guy with a blond mustache and a back sprinkled with moles. They held the door open for him and closed it behind him, let him be the first under the shower, the first to select a seat—and everything he said was met with a twofold echo.

Returning to the Epos Room, I immediately noticed something was up. I looked at Tanya—and she was already in mid-explosion. Our arguments always follow the same pattern. They begin with my failure to notice or notice too late what should be the appropriate response. In this case, since I had chosen not to take on those three louts directly, I ought to have at least followed Tanya out. But I was a man who could never forgo his pleasures, and by my behavior I had, whether intentionally or not, sided with them.

It is truly remarkable. Although I earn my daily bread by observing and describing situations and emotions, compared with Tanya I see myself as utterly tone deaf and dull witted.

The situation escalated when shortly thereafter the guy with the blond mustache sat down at the dining-room table to disassemble and clean two guns. While he worked he loudly whistled random melodies. I had to do something.

My suggestion that he could in fact tend to his weapons in

his room was ignored with a grin. When I insisted, he cried, "Arne! Arne!" as if Arne had assigned him to his task. But when I picked up the barrel of one of the guns, he shouted in English, "Don't touch it! Don't touch it!" and snatched it away from me. The upshot was that we spread our evening meal over one half of the table—the lyric poetess from the Novella Chamber was impervious to our request that she join us in defending the dining room. The other half was occupied by the Finn, who was still busy oiling his weapons. For a while he kept up his mindless whistling, but much to our gratification was the first to beat a retreat.

We were already in bed when there was a knock at our door.

After apologizing for the disturbance, Arne begged for our help. "You're from the East too, after all," he said. One of the group, we learned from his explanation, was Mika's boss, and Mika was in some kind of trouble. He didn't know anything more than that himself, Arne said. He would be truly grateful if, once back in Tallinn, we wouldn't mention the fact that the boss had been quartered in the union's guesthouse. If everything went well, they would all be gone the day after tomorrow anyway.

"Day after tomorrow?" Tanya said, "That's when we're leaving too."

"But you'll be here tomorrow?" Arne asked. He needed us because the Finns had come from Tallinn in a taxi. Could we drive two of them to the hunt?

"Only if they sit in the backseat," Tanya decreed.

Arne stepped closer and extended a hand to each of us. "Wake-up call at three thirty, breakfast at my place, departure at four thirty," he said, and hurried off.

It was a long time before we fell asleep. Around three o'clock our sleep was interrupted by what we first took to be a barking seal—a sound evidently emanating from the boss Finn under the shower.

It's a strange feeling to sit at a table with people you've first come to know in the buff. Their expensive outfits, which brought to mind an imminent polar expedition, looked to me like a crude attempt to conceal their true natures.

They politely offered us hard-boiled eggs and pickled herring—I bought something similar in Berlin a few days ago, where it's marketed as "Swedish Snax." Arne and the boss rode in the Barkas. Mika and the other fellow came with us. Both of them had small eyes and stringy hair—Mika's was dark blond, the other guy was a towhead. They both fell asleep immediately. The alcohol on their breath was tolerable only with a window down.

After the turnoff we rolled the windows down all the way and inhaled the forest air. It was moist and piney and somehow swallowed up the exhaust of the Barkas ahead of us. Any second I expected to see Seryosha pop up in the narrow beam of our headlights. "Let's hope, let's hope he's taken off!" Tanya whispered.

We halted just before the clearing and left it to the boss to shake his countrymen awake. Dawn was breaking by now, fog lay over the blanket of heather.

Arne assigned the hunters places every fifty meters. The boss was given a post on a low rise. Mika took a spot very close to us, the towhead stood farthest off. Arne passed out blankets. We could drive back home and get some sleep, he said, evidently worried about us, we didn't need to be back here for another four or five hours. But we didn't do Arne the favor.

How lovely it would be if I could describe what comes next

in the style of a Leskov or Turgenev. But I know neither the names of the birds striking up their songs, nor of the beetles crawling under our collars or up our sleeves, nor can I make a name for myself by offering some observation that testifies to my dendrological expertise.

Freezing, we jogged up and down under the firs and dreamed of the sauna, which surely ought to await us—at a minimum—in reward for our cooperation. But we never moved too far away from the car. Once fired upon, even Seryosha might turn cranky.

Between seven and eight—the sun had now risen above the treetops—I noticed some movement. Evidently the hunters had spotted something. Everyone except us had binoculars, which is why I'm dependent here on Arne's account. He would tell us later that it all began well enough, actually conditions were ideal, since Seryosha had been meandering along the opposite edge of the forest. For hunters who are good shots a distance of 200 to 250 meters is no problem, but Seryosha kept vanishing behind tree stumps and bushes. It makes sense that Arne advised against taking a shot, since he assumed that Seryosha could be lured closer.

In the real world, spectacular events always occur at great speed and usually almost coincidentally. And how can you be in the right place at the right time? To give truth its due, I ought to describe the finale with the brevity and speed with which in fact we experienced it.

Seryosha, then, had been spotted and was in the Finns' crosshairs. I'm certain the argument that broke out among the hunters at that point—in which Arne somehow managed to get involved as well—would have sent any other bear packing for good and all. According to Arne's subsequent report, the issue was who should fire first, the boss or the towhead, who was considered the better shot. The towhead had evidently lodged a protest, implying that his boss wouldn't have much luck at that distance. At any rate the ensuing rhubarb was worthy of a soccer field—then suddenly, a shot. Followed at once by another. Silence. Tanya pressed her fists together and whispered, "Beat it, Seryosha, beat it!"

The next sound we heard was a screeching female voice. Which is to say, at first I took it to be the wail of an animal so accustomed to the company of humans that it mimics them in its pain. So it was with real relief that we saw a woman rise up amid the heather, a woman in a black headscarf, throwing her arms into the air and spinning in place. She evidently didn't know what direction the shots had come from. We were standing next to Mika on the low rise, the towhead and the boss were a few steps to our right, with Arne behind them. Rooted to the spot, they stared through their binoculars. But even with the naked eye it was obvious the woman, whose screams now rose to savage yowls, was pointing to the far edge of the forest.

I have never used the following phrase, and will presumably never use it again, but in this case there is no avoiding it: I didn't believe my eyes. No, not even when I saw what was happening right before them. It was Seryosha. But he wasn't jumping or dancing or doing somersaults. Seryosha, if not with great skill, was riding a woman's bicycle. It looked as if his paws kept slipping off the pedals, and every few yards I expected him to upend, or go flying over the handlebars. But that was more a matter of the uneven forest floor. Seryosha was perched on the seat, pumping for all he was worth. Unfortunately, given the situation, I was paying no attention to the people around me. It wasn't until I heard a shot that I noticed an ashen-faced Arne, and saw the boss raise his gun and fire—followed by a second shot from the towhead, and finally one from Mika.

Now it was Arne who was screaming as he pushed the barrel of the boss's gun down. Any shot was irresponsible, even though the wailing woman was not in the direct line of fire and had in the meantime dived into the heather—at the sight of her commandeered bicycle, as we would soon learn, she had fainted. I took advantage of the brief skirmish that followed to borrow Mika's binoculars. Which is why I was presumably the last person to see Seryosha. He fled into the forest, soon breaking into an easy trot on all fours, and vanished among the fir trees.

I probably don't need to describe what was taking place among the hunters. Fortunately their shouting match was less about the bear's agility than about Arne's interference and their own failure to maintain an established hierarchy. They even forgot about the woman. Only after she reemerged from the heather, still nervously prepared to duck and cover, did someone come to her aid.

She was younger than I had guessed. At the sight of her bicycle—an old Wanderer model—she raised a howl to curdle your blood. The front wheel was a figure eight with extruding spokes. One shot had shattered the bearings in the rear wheel. But there were no traces of blood to be found anywhere.

The woman had come to gather blueberries, and while she held out her hand one bill of Finnish currency after the other was thumbed out until she fell silent. Arne carried the heavy bicycle to the Barkas and drove her home. Without sliding her own seat forward so much as an inch, Tanya watched in the mirror on her sun visor as the boss was forced to squeeze into the backseat between Mika and his chief rival, the towheaded sharpshooter.

By the time we handed over the keys to the Epos Room to Arne the next morning, thanking him and saying our good-byes, the Finns had already departed—in two taxis, Mika riding with his boss, whereas the towhead had to pay for his own taxi. Arne considered this a victory for Mika. Because, according to Arne, the open hostility that had erupted as a result of the hunting rivalry between the boss and his former right-hand man offered Mika a second chance, so that the bear hunt had paid off for him after all, if in unexpected ways. The woman gathering berries, Arne hoped, had received enough hush money. But if she still couldn't keep her mouth shut, which he feared would be the case, her punishment would be that no one would believe her story.

Arne promised to let us know as soon as he learned anything about Seryosha's fate. Sad to say, I've never heard another word from Arne.

Of course I ask myself why, after six years, I'm now writing about that memorable hunt. I've forgotten so many details in the meantime—from the names of the lyric poets at the writers' retreat to the make of our rental car, from exact prices to the route we took, and so on and so on. Besides which it's quite possible that things have changed drastically in Estonia over the last few years, so that my story has in some sense become past history. In any case, the fact is that not only my own life has changed. All our lives have taken a different course over the last few years. And that may perhaps—perhaps—be the reason I finally found myself in a position to venture a story about Estonia.

Incident in Cairo

"You picked up something while you where down there," the doctor on emergency house call offered as a diagnosis. While the air drained from the blood-pressure cuff, he added, "Or it was already budding inside you." I'm quite certain he used the word "budding," although that sounds so metaphorical. At any rate, since my return on March 1st I had been lying in bed for two weeks—totally sapped of my strength, gulping down antibiotics, and expecting my head to burst the moment I attempted so much as an e-mail. My recovery was so slow that even in April I still had to be sparing of my energies.

Once we had landed at Tegel, I told Sheila I didn't want to see her again. I said it even though between flights in Paris—where the drafty jet bridge had finished me off—she had bought a dark-skinned doll for my daughter, Anne, since I'd been unable to find a "brown" doll in either Cairo or Alexandria.

Sheila said that I shouldn't act so childish, she would take care of me, and after I was healthy again, we could discuss the whole thing. My jealousy at any rate was as foolish as it was unfounded.

We could talk about it again at some point, I said, handing the cabdriver my suitcase, but first I wanted to get well, and having her around would be simply toxic.

I hadn't intended to insult Sheila, but I wouldn't have gotten rid of her otherwise.

I mention my illness and separation from Sheila because if I don't, no one will understand why I didn't give a thought to the incident in Cairo for quite some time, let alone tell anyone about it.

From a psychological viewpoint it's easy to explain. My memory waited until I had recuperated and halfway overcome the separation from Sheila. At that point I began to talk about it, because I thought telling the story would help objectify it. By now I've told it often, quite often, blaming myself, admitting my guilt—all of which provides only short-term relief.

My story is about the next-to-last evening, when I joined Hoda and the other women to dine on squab or, far better, "pigeon"—for my sake we all had to speak English—and what a far more apt word "pigeon" is than the German *Taube,* because when you say "pigeon" you can literally feel the swollen, rubbery consistency of a stuffed squab as your lips touch it right before that first bite. I've never spent much time describing our little gathering, or the women, whom most locals took to be Christians since they were in European clothes, but who spoke Arabic. I've also never mentioned the vendors, the deaf-mute fortune-teller, the children, and a heavily made-up girl of thirteen or fourteen.

That evening, the whole absurd conference, the readings, my

illness, the virus slinking its way inside me—it all probably belongs in the story, as well as a restaurant called the Fish Market and the fishermen in the harbor basin of Alexandria. I've never described the cabdriver, who was at least as much to blame as I was. But what good does it do me to cast aspersions on the cabbie? Above all I've never told about Sheila, about Sheila and Samir and the previous days.

By that next-to-last evening I was sick, tired, wounded—I wanted to get back to the hotel, I didn't want to keep giving alms to beggars over and over, I wanted the cabdriver to finally pull away. But he took his time, chewing on his falafel. Luckily the cab doors were locked—a child to my left, a child to my right, children in a great swarm all around us, growing more and more brazen, spitting on the windshield—and then that loud bang as the taxi pulled away, as if they had all kicked it at once. The children were behind us now. The taxi zipped out onto the main road, I can't say if we were doing thirty miles an hour or fifty or more. As far as I was concerned it couldn't be too fast. And then, at some point, I see him, the boy, close to my shoulder, his eyes looking directly into mine, just a few inches away, wide-open eyes staring at me through the back windshield—with him hanging on my neck, so to speak. I don't want him there, I want him to finally leave me in peace, I turn around again, look straight ahead.

It began, if it ever had something like a beginning, with a call in September or October 2004. The country code in the telephone display meant nothing to me. A deep female voice whispered: "We want to send you a fax." At first I thought it was a call from

Kiev, the accent was a match for that of a Russian or Ukrainian, because in early March I was supposed to tour Ukraine for a week. When I saw the page that came out of the fax machine, I had to laugh, and I mean a real guffaw. It annoys me now that I laughed, but at the time I found it completely absurd for someone to send me a fax in Arabic. What was I supposed to make of that calligraphy? At the bottom, however, I discovered an address written in tiny roman type.

I showed Sheila the fax, Sheila can manage a little Arabic, and with the help of a dictionary she finally figured it out.

"The purpose of this correspondence," she said, "is to extend to you a very honorable invitation to an international writers' conference." Those were in fact her pathos-laden words. I was being invited to Cairo to deliver an address on "Literature and History," flight and accommodations paid for by the organizers.

It was clear to me that I ought not accept any more invitations. For a year and a half I had been living off an advance and debts. I needed finally to finish the new book, and there was that trip to Ukraine besides.

My guess was that Gamal al-Ghitani and Edwar al-Charrat were behind the invitation. I didn't want to disappoint them. But most of all I did it for Sheila. Sheila said it had always been a dream of hers to see Egypt.

Sheila's father is Algerian, her mother comes from Kamenz near Dresden, the same town where Lessing was born. Sheila's parents had both studied at the Technical University in Dresden. Sheila knows her father only from photographs. Sheila and I had met toward the end of 2003 at a reading in Koblenz. She had joined us afterward for dinner and, along with the bookstore owner, had accompanied me back to my hotel. Might she see my room and its view of the Rhine? she asked, as I was about to say good night. I had in fact enthusiastically recommended the view earlier.

I could get involved with Sheila with a clear conscience. But that was also the only advantage of having to live separated from the woman I loved, and my own daughter.

Sheila usually stands out because of her incredible hair and her vivacity, with its tinge of overexcitement. After flunking out of law school she worked in a notary's office. A couple of weeks after my reading in Koblenz she had moved in with a girlfriend in Berlin and, against the odds, immediately found a job here. From then on we saw each other almost every day, and soon we were being invited everywhere as a· couple. I did not, however, introduce Sheila to Anne, my daughter by Tanya.

Sheila was now reading nothing but Egyptian writers, and learning Arabic vocabulary every morning. I patched together a lecture from various texts, found the hook to hang it on in the relationship of the words "history/story" and *Geschichte/ Geschichten,* and finished with the conversation between Alice and Humpty Dumpty in Lewis Carroll's *Through the Looking Glass,* which implies that whoever has power also decides what words mean, which is why we storytellers, or so I planned to conclude, are so important. Because we . . .

I could see myself in a huge auditorium, with a horde of photographers thronging the space between the stage and the first row, heard myself say *shokran*—the word for "thank you" being the only word of Arabic I know—and felt myself being literally overwhelmed by the applause. I put my hand to my heart several times and bowed. Some people responded so enthusiastically they couldn't stay in their seats.

With the help of Elisabeth, the librarian for the Goethe-

Institut, who had smoothed the way for an Arabic translation of my *Simple Stories*, I arranged for readings at the university, the German high school, and the Goethe-Institut in both Cairo and Alexandria.

In early February—I hadn't learned until the end of January that the conference would be held the last week of February—it dawned on me that there wouldn't be much point in giving my speech in German. John Woods, who was sitting atop his packed possessions in San Diego, on the verge of a move to Berlin, translated the text in two days and wrote me a few encouraging words. Finally I spent an afternoon with Eleonore—nicknamed "Nörchen," a friend of my mother's who had grown up in South Africa—memorizing the correct pronunciation of the English words and a corresponding cadence for the sentences. The day before we were to depart I bought half a dozen German and Berlin calendars that I found on sale, as well as three smallish boxes of Mozart balls—prettily packaged chocolates are always well received. At KaDeWe I found three chunks of the Wall (the colorful ones) encased in Plexiglas for 6.90 euros apiece. People can laugh, or take this as a bit of self-irony on my part, but everyone who travels for business or an official tour knows how helpful such items are at that first encounter with one's hosts. Nor do I wish to hide the fact that I have the occasional weak moment when I consider myself a good representative of my country—yes, why not, of Europe and the West.

On February 22 we flew Air France via Paris to Cairo. The music played in the plane before takeoff in both Berlin and Paris was, remarkably enough, an instrumental piece by Michaela Melian, the title track from a CD that I had given Sheila for Christmas. Sheila likewise thought that was a good omen. This was our first trip abroad together. Closing our eyes, we held hands on takeoff.

In Cairo, before we even reached passport control, we were greeted by two young men. Thanks to their presence as ambassadors of the conference, they claimed with some self-assurance, we would be able to have our passports checked right away, no visa necessary—which turned out not to be true. We had to go back and purchase a thirty-five-dollar visa that looked like a postage stamp—the pragmatism of a country with lots of tourists, said Elisabeth, who was waiting for us on the other side of passport control.

The warmth, of course, was a gift from heaven. After our edgy drowsiness on the plane, the few yards from the arrival hall to the parking lot sufficed to instill euphoria. The driver of a shiny silver VW bus, an older gentleman in a suit, opened the car doors for us, stowed our luggage, and then we glided out into the early evening traffic. Soldiers in dark blue uniforms and armed with shields and billy clubs stood in cordons along both curbs—awaiting President Mubarak. But we were soon driving along elevated roads, gazing down at Cairo, and getting used to the ubiquitous honking of car horns.

As darkness fell we arrived at our hotel. Sheila called our room a "suite," since we had at our command both a living room and a bedroom, as well as a large bath. The view was blocked by the smoothly stuccoed wall of another high-rise, but far below we could see roofs with antennas. We left our bags unpacked and started off at once, made it hand in hand across a multilane road from which the hotel driveway diverged, and a minute later we were beside the Nile. We should walk along the Corniche, Elisabeth had suggested, to the Fish Market, a boat restaurant.

Not that I was unfamiliar with the term "corniche," but all the same to my ears it sounded as remote and exotic as the words "Tuscany" or "Broadway" once had. And now I was leaning beside an energized Sheila on the railing of Cairo's Corniche and watching the current as attentively as if a basket were floating there in the water. Neither the myriad boats draped with garlands of light, nor the hotel palaces on the far shore, and certainly not the streetlamps on the bridges and along the riverbanks were able to illuminate the Nile. It flowed along wide and heavy under a gentle cover of darkness. We walked upstream, past a disco and restaurants with just a few customers. The young people strolling side by side—there was a good distance between streetlamps—never touched one another. When they spoke it looked as if they were explaining very serious matters, at least it didn't look like chitchat. At one point Sheila stopped, hugged and kissed me, and said, "Thank you so much!"

We got the last available window table in the Fish Market. Silly of course, but it filled me with a certain pride to know that the river we were watching flow by beneath us was the Nile. And at the same time it seemed a kind of sacrilege, as if this were somehow presumptuous of us. Sheila pulled out her cell phone. "Mama," she exclaimed. "Guess where I am?"

The buffet was an elongated mountain of ice cubes, in which lay the rarest and finest fish. You saw only the mouths of most of them, and the waiter in charge of the buffet had to dig deep and extract them for presentation to his guests. Sometimes he displayed the fish like a precious necklace draped between his hands, sometimes he held one in each hand like a balance scale. Once we had made our decision, the buffet waiter passed the "Egyptian fish" on to a chef and turned to his next guests. Sheila returned to the table. I waited a while but finally followed her—

and was certain I had done something wrong. No one had given us a number or a chit. But no sooner had I taken my seat than our chosen fish were presented again for approval, our order was then repeated—"Yes, grilled, sir"—and served to us shortly thereafter, although we weren't even close to having sampled all the appetizers.

On the way back to the hotel we bought mineral water in a little shop. A young man sitting on the steps smiled and pretended to tug at his hair, pointed then to my long hair, and called out, "Very nice, very nice!" I felt not just flattered but right at home.

The next morning began with a misunderstanding. We arrived at the foot of the hotel stairway at the agreed hour and kept an eye out for our silver VW bus. I waved off the offers of a steady stream of snail-paced taxis, and Sheila had to repeatedly assure the bellhops that we didn't need one. When at twenty after ten still no VW bus had appeared, I called the Goethe-Institut. The driver, I learned, had also just phoned to ask where we were. Suddenly I heard my name being shouted from a battered old car, a Lada. We climbed in. The driver laid into us. He claimed he had been driving in circles for half an hour, that he wasn't allowed to stop here—a no-parking zone. Sheila said he was lying, that we had been standing there for a good twenty minutes.

Our outraged glances met in the rearview mirror. I was offended by their having sent us a gypsy cab instead of the nice gentleman in the silver VW bus.

Sheila and I now slid deeper into our seats, because in an attempt to make up for lost time, the driver pursued a slalom path through the lanes of the road, with every stoplight a kind of course marker. At major intersections, with traffic spinning in a vortex, he kept so far to the right that he was always in the first or at least second starting lane.

When we stopped at the courtyard in front of the Goethe-Institut our eyes met again in the rearview mirror. I had no choice but to thank him for the ride. He gave a gloomy nod, got out, and vanished into the building.

It's a great temptation to write about my readings at length. Given all the young women on the university campus, Sheila did not stand out. In the dean's office I was presented the university's shiny gold medal in a red-lined box. I returned the friendly gesture with Mozart balls and a colorful piece of the Wall in Plexiglas. The entire office was furnished like that of the director of a printing outfit in Leningrad in the eighties: bulky desks and cupboards, lacquered very dark and with numerous scrapes and scratches. A portrait of the president adorned one wall. The lecture hall was overflowing with women students, Sheila was seated somewhere in the middle, a few male students stood along the walls. All I could see of some women students was their glasses, the rest was swathed in black. Most of them, however, wore jeans and T-shirts or a long tunic and headscarf. I wasn't sure if they had even understood what I read. They were in their third and fourth years of German. Breathless silence, but otherwise no reaction, brief applause at the end. To my left and right sat the college staff, professors, who were to moderate the discussion.

The questions, asked in German, were much like those at home. Why do you write? How autobiographical are your books? Are the East Germans being oppressed by the West Germans? Why are your characters unhappy? That I made a living writing my books required some explanation. I intentionally said *my* books, to avoid having to say *two* books. The question about Israel, about which I had been forewarned, was not posed either here or later. When the moderators overlooked a raised arm and I pointed this out to them, a professor asked me, "Which of them would you like to have?" He later assured me that it was just a joke, he had merely been teasing.

We had to wait for Sheila, who had by now been subjected to more than a dozen of my readings, because she was still chatting with some students and a translator—to be on the safe side, my speech for the conference was to be made available in Arabic as well. Once in the VW bus, Sheila announced how happy she was to experience the university from the inside and not have to walk through the city as just a tourist.

It all looked as if this would indeed be a successful trip.

But then came lunch, and we met Samir over lunch. Elisabeth had hired Samir as our city guide. He was tall and trim, with a profile like an ancient Egyptian bas-relief. He wore a long white robe and handsome leather sandals. In addition to Arabic Samir was a master of English, French, and Spanish. His German and Russian weren't so good, he said—though his spoken German was close to fluent. He had beautiful hands with well-manicured nails, and wore a wide gold band with a black stone on his left hand. He walked with an easy grace. His voice on the other hand sounded high pitched to me. He seemed truly excited to meet a writer.

He had, Samir said, read two of my books, both of which were in the Goethe-Institut library and both of which—yes indeed, both of them—had been "a top-notch pleasure" to read. He planned to write novels someday, too, but the time for that had not yet come. (Samir looked to be in his mid- to late twenties.) He wished and hoped, however, that his book would then please me as much as mine had him. We toasted. When Sheila raised her glass—without the least hesitation Samir had ordered white wine—he looked at her for the first time.

Toward the end of the meal Elisabeth reminded me that we hadn't much time for a translation of my text, she needed it as soon as possible.

I've often thought: If she had said that earlier, if I had not foolishly left my shoulder bag in her office, if I had not had to walk back across to the institute with Elisabeth—and so on and so forth. I am well aware of how pointless such thinking is.

When I returned to Sheila and Samir twenty minutes later, the die had been cast. Both had propped their elbows on the table, Sheila's right barely a handbreadth from his left. Smiling dreamily to themselves, they both sat up startled as I approached the table.

Sheila began at once to tell me about Samir's passion for the Pyramids. He had had to promise his father never to leave the Pyramids for any length of time. Samir knew everything a person could know about the Pyramids. He demurred, and I said that it would be nice to take a stroll through the city.

We let Samir walk between us, although most of the time the throngs forced us to move single file.

What couldn't I write about the hours that followed, about the various markets or about how, after we had left the heart of town and were walking along a wide street, some young fellows blocked my path and indicated—or so I read their flurry of gestures—that I should check out a brush, a little plastic tub, and other housewares they were offering for sale. Their spiel grew more and more energetic, almost menacing, until Samir thrust them aside with a single motion of his arm and a few soft-spoken words. They fell silent, but as we moved on began shouting something that Sheila didn't understand and that

Samir refused to translate. Those weren't real vendors, just poor crazy kids, he said.

I understood Sheila's fascination, of course, and certainly ought to have reacted with greater discretion, but nothing could have saved me from the hurt I felt from the first moment on. It made no difference at all what I did. Every bit of attention Sheila gave me was purely diplomatic in nature, crumbs from the table. At first I thought it would be better for Sheila to take the lead. But watching her sashay ahead of Samir in her tight jeans, tossing her hair back, and once even coming to an abrupt halt for no good reason, so that Samir ran right into her . . . I knew very well just how resolute Sheila could be.

I first realized that I was in the way, that I was irritating Sheila, when we got to the Al-Azhar Mosque. I hesitated to follow Samir's example and shove my best pair of loafers (for which I'd paid just shy of two hundred euros) into one of the pigeonholes, where anybody could grab them instead of his own shabby slippers and scram. "You're nuts," Sheila hissed, hurrying off in her stocking feet behind Samir. Suddenly the men sitting at the entrance and watching me remove my shoes were my enemies.

When he was tired, simply worn out and in need of sleep, that's when he went to the mosque, Samir said. No place in the city was as pleasantly cool and quiet as this. I was entering a mosque for the first time and uncertain what was allowed and what wasn't. Anyone watching us would have thought it was Sheila who was our guide. The sight of several men asleep on a red carpet with a yellow design was simultaneously both unsettling and comforting. Upon discovering my shoes again, I turned downright cheerful and was prepared to accept Sheila's flirting with greater composure. That didn't last long. When we stopped at a booth of perfumes and scents—it had turned dark by then—Sheila and Samir started conversing in Arabic. Samir had the vendor open practically every little flask for Sheila, and at one point even asked him to mix two or three scents—which had to have made him a real expert in Sheila's eyes. She agreed with his opinion every time. Samir insisted on buying three flasks for her as a gift—they weren't expensive, in fact—and filled in the tiny labels himself, both in Arabic and in roman script. They moved on without ever turning around to look for me. Samir corrected Sheila's pronunciation and praised her extravagantly for the progress she was making.

I made several attempts to send Samir on his way. He had been so helpful the whole day now. . . . I wanted to go back to the hotel and then have dinner again at the Fish Market. Samir, however, had already reserved tickets for us, a performance of Sufi songs and dances—we didn't dare miss it.

This tourist spectacle took place in an old fortress. I barely remember the space itself, but I do recall working my way to a niche as far forward as possible, in the firm belief that Samir and Sheila were right behind me. At first I thought the two had vanished. But then I spotted them directly across from me. Sheila was standing in front of Samir, but so close that it looked to me as if she were leaning against him.

Later, in a tiny restaurant, we ate pizza from tin plates and drank almost frozen beer. Samir told a legend about taking the measurement of the Pyramids, which Sheila had already heard in the Arabic version. It was truly pleasant when Samir gave you his full attention. And along with jealousy I likewise felt regret at how much I was missing because Sheila was thrusting herself between us. I was just about to ask him if there would soon be a book where I could read about his story, when Sheila announced that the following morning she would be visiting the Egyptian National Museum instead of accompanying me to the German school for girls.

The worst part was that Sheila was right, of course. Since I always read the same stuff and couldn't always come up with new answers to the same old questions, Sheila's presence in the audience had become more of a hindrance by now, turning me into a man of few words, which isn't like me. Repetition leads to disenchantment, of course. All the same I regarded her decision as a betrayal.

The next morning, in the middle of breakfast, Sheila suddenly noticed Samir on the far side of the road, his gaze fixed on the hotel entrance. Although he had arrived an hour before the arranged time, Sheila ignored her hot pancakes, hastily downed her coffee, and moments later was bounding down the hotel stairway. It annoyed me that she kept pointing at me, until Samir spotted me too and offered the hint of a bow. I waved back.

I was angry at having to pack Sheila's things for Alexandria, too; I was scheduled to read there that same evening.

Later I vented my anger on the German teacher at the girls' school. It is really comical: Everyone makes fun of the question about what an author really means, and in the next moment someone asks that very question, and nobody notices.

At lunch—we had agreed upon the pizza place from the previous evening—I made the mistake of telling Sheila about one of the schoolgirls. She had worn a headscarf and had looked tired. Unlike her classmates she remained seated when she spoke. I left it to her to explain to the teacher what the relationship is between the written word and its meaning, and that whatever the writer himself may claim is irrelevant. Then she spoke about truth, and how truth is always an agreed-upon arrangement. What took place between the two of us wasn't flirtation, but rather—or so it seemed to me at least—our amazement at an intimacy attached to her every word, an intimacy that seemed to come out of nowhere. I can still see her smiling and nodding when I laid into her teacher yet again. I told Sheila that I would have loved to get to know the girl, but that we didn't even manage to say good-bye to each other because I hadn't wanted to risk speaking with a schoolgirl.

"Why was that?" Sheila barked at me. "Why didn't you try to meet her?"

"I was afraid it might arouse suspicion," I said. "I didn't want to embarrass her."

"Oh pooh, 'embarrass'!" Sheila exclaimed. "So what if it had aroused suspicion."

I assumed the matter was behind us, but Sheila wouldn't let it go. It was unsettling to watch her get worked up like that in front of Elisabeth and Samir.

I then had to leave for an interview at the Goethe-Institut library. Samir promised to get Sheila to the train station on time.

At two on the dot I said my good-byes to the journalist. Elisabeth came over and sat down beside me.

"The driver will let you know when he's here," she said with a smile. I nodded. We fell silent.

"I hope I didn't make a mistake," she said, "in introducing you two to Samir."

I found her insinuation tactless. "We'll see," I said.

"Did Sheila tell you?"

"Tell me what?"

"Sheila's not coming along," Elisabeth said. "We're trying to resell her train ticket. I thought . . ."

"That's news to me," I said as composed as possible and clicked my cell phone on. I had two messages in my mailbox, but I didn't know the code I needed to listen to them. I had never learned it.

"Alexandria is very beautiful," Elisabeth said. She sounded so sympathetic that I had to swallow hard.

Sheila let her cell phone ring. When she finally answered there was an infernal racket all around her. She had tried to tell me, she shouted, but my cell phone was off. She'd be spending the whole time sitting around anyway, on a train or at the reading. Besides, the most interesting part of Alexandria lay underwater. Since she was here, she wanted to see the Pyramids, too.

She could scramble up the Pyramids during the conference, I noted.

She definitely didn't want to miss the conference, she replied.

"You don't get to see Alexandria every day either," I said as if to myself, pressed the red button, and went down to the courtyard.

The driver of the Lada flung open a door, bellowed at me, and pointed to his watch. My cell phone was ringing. I took a seat in the car, slammed the door, and shouted: "Sorry, sorry, sorry!" although this wasn't my fault.

He threw me a hateful glance in the rearview mirror. My cell phone went on ringing.

Compared to this ride, our first one had been sheer dillydallying. Fine by me. I'd be exaggerating if I were to say I was hoping for an accident. But I was somehow strangely certain one would happen, and I waited for it as if it were a kind of liberation. I know how stupid that sounds, especially in light of what came later. But in those few minutes an accident seemed the easiest, the only possible way out of this screwed-up trip.

There were moments that left me cringing. At one point I actually did shut my eyes when a gaunt old man dressed all in white appeared before our hood as if dropped from heaven onto the multilane road. He wore a white cap, held a cane in one hand, and in the other—I no longer recall. To me he seemed like some mythical figure, an angel from beyond.

I could see him landing on the windshield, could hear the crash—and suddenly the car halted right before his knees, as if his conjuring outstretched arm had stopped us. The next miracle was that no one crashed into us from behind.

As it turned out, the driver of the Lada had been given the wrong time for the train's departure. And all of a sudden we were friends. He explained to me with something close to cordiality how and where I would catch my train—finding a parking space here at the station was out of the question. He promised to pick me up and zoomed off. Sheila called several times, but as far as I was concerned everything had been said.

Only now as I write these lines do I realize how the later incident has pushed everything preceding it into the background, and how difficult it is for me to recapture those days and hours.

In saying, "You don't get to see Alexandria every day either," I had, I believed, separated from Sheila. It had happened quickly. Just as Sheila had linked up with me at the first best opportunity, so she had ditched me at the first best opportunity. I rode toward Alexandria alone, and free. Good thing, I thought, I don't have to explain anything to Anne. I would write her a postcard from Alexandria and mention the train, which I hadn't exactly imagined would be the Orient Express, but not quite this dingy and ragtag. Even in first class the upholstery and curtains were beyond shabby.

I dozed away as if in a pleasant dream that relieves us of reality for minutes or hours. On my lap lay the marble gray bilingual Insel edition of Cavafy's poems, which I had carried around with me since army days. But I wasn't in the mood to read. Strangely enough I kept picturing the green triangle of the delta as I knew it from maps and had actually seen from the airplane. I was riding through the Nile Delta, and I thought how it was a sin to leave even a square foot of it uncultivated.

Entering Alexandria, you pass by buildings as intimidating as a scene in a Fritz Lang movie. That impression quickly fled when I was greeted on the platform by Mahmud, a truly handsome man in an olive-hued suit, gray shirt, and glowing red tie.

By the time we drove through the shopping district, with stores familiar from Europe, and suddenly turned onto the Corniche, where, beneath the gentle glow of lanterns lining the shore, the harbor basin and the sea now lay before me, I realized that I missed Sheila. Or maybe it wasn't Sheila I missed, it just seemed sad to experience this all alone.

In the three-quarters of an hour I had to spend in the lobby of the Windsor Hotel, because something wasn't right with my reservation, I reveled in a, if not painful at least melancholy, sort of pleasure—a somber mood to which I gave way entirely when I was served a cup of tea and a liqueurlike drink I had never encountered before.

When I finally moved into my huge room on the top floor and got the door unstuck to step out onto the balcony, I saw how the arc of lights along the Corniche turned the harbor walls into an almost perfect ellipse. As I breathed in the sea breeze blended with the odor of horse-drawn carriages, I resolved for good and all to begin an affair. I would meet a woman here with whom I felt the same sense of accord as with the schoolgirl that morning in Cairo. This curious euphoria kept me going—despite how tired I was, if not to say exhausted.

The Goethe-Institut is located in the old villa of some industrialist. As my text was being read in Arabic, I had time to check out the audience. Not a single one of the women present ignited my fantasy. The reading seemed endless, the discussion a marathon. Each word, as if it were a step up a mountain, sapped my energies. But all the same, I was in Alexandria. And so I trudged through the conversation, which lasted well past eleven. Then we set out and landed—in the Fish Market. There is also one of these restaurants overlooking the sea on the Corniche of Alexandria. Suddenly I wished I had Sheila there with me, picking up her cell phone and asking, "Mama, guess where I am?"

We were the last guests to be let into the almost empty restaurant. The buffet, however, was still full of fish. I arrived at my hotel between one and two o'clock, slept a few minutes, and then, kept awake by a strange agitation, tossed and turned in bed until dawn. Around seven I fetched Sheila's toiletry bag, spread her things out on the pillow beside me, sprayed some of her perfume, and dialed her number. As I waited for the ring tone, I pictured the room where Sheila was now sleeping. I was amazed she even had her cell phone on. I was sure I'd hear her mailbox intervene—where you heard her say a rather dejected, "Sheila Dietze"—when she answered. I asked if everything was okay.

"Yes, of course, everything's okay," she said. "And how about you?"

"I couldn't sleep. . . ."

"And I couldn't brush my teeth."

"Your own fault," I said.

"I'll meet you at the train, good night," Sheila said.

I would have loved to creep back into bed after breakfast, but the cleaning women were already in the adjoining room. While waiting in the lobby for more coffee and a cola with ice, I nodded off. But the fact was I had to be alert, had to explore the city, had to experience things Sheila would regret having missed.

Sitting in my easy chair at the Windsor and sipping at my cola as if it were medicine, I could watch a steady stream of children, couples, and a few dawdling loners stop along the parapet of the Corniche to observe something down on the jetty or in the water below. Soon they had formed quite a group of spectators, whom I then finally decided to join.

Before me I found a peculiar sight. At first I thought it was a rope that the five men were dragging. It was a fishnet. The man at the head of the towing line had thrown the end of the rope over his shoulder, the others held on to the net with both hands at their chests, hips, or—turning around backward—under one arm. At first I thought they were getting nowhere since they didn't appear to budge, but then they moved a few steps forward. The net must have been cast far out in the harbor. Following the great arc that it traced on the surface of the water by sweeping your eye to the right—that is, eastward, in the direction of the library—after about two hundred meters your gaze returned to the Corniche and a second group pulling on the other end of the net and likewise moving in our direction.

Dressed in a brimmed cap and a frayed sport coat, a short,

dainty old man with stubble on his chin glanced at me and whispered, "Hello." "Hello," I said. "Hello," he repeated softly and pointed to a horse-drawn carriage right behind us. I shook my head, put a finger to my eye, and then pointed at the fishermen. "After, after," he said, pointing at me and then the carriage. I rocked my head dubiously and went back to staring out to sea, when I felt a tug at my other sleeve. "Go! Go!" a man demanded and, presumably hoping I would follow him, took a couple of steps in the direction of his carriage—which riled the driver on my right. They began cursing each other, until the one who had first spotted me whispered, "After, after," and gave me a soothing nod.

I held my shoulder bag to my chest under crossed arms and kept my eyes fixed on the fishermen. They were, as nearly as I could tell, all older men, barefoot, some with chests bared, some with a jacket but no shirt. The barely perceptible movement with which the net drew closer, the effort exerted by the old men, the rags wrapped around their hands, their vacant stares, their gaping or tight-lipped mouths, the sweat on their swollen necks, their concentration, which demanded neither orders nor instructions, the short steps that brought them closer and closer to one another, until the two groups finally met and, without stopping or looking up for even a moment, marched past each other, crossing as if in slow motion—there was a staged unreality about it all that fascinated me. This fishing operation was something I could tell Sheila about.

Whenever the driver beside me raised his scratchy voice, I could be certain that competition was approaching. If he got louder still, in the next moment I would feel a hand touch me, only to be instantly shooed away by the short driver. At one point he even smoothed the wrinkles from my sport coat. The whole time he kept reminding me of his presence with low "hellos" and a hand raised in greeting.

The groups working the net had stopped about fifty meters apart and now, leaning back and treading in place, hauled the net in.

Two men sprang into the water from a small boat that had followed the net at the point of its widest expanse—only now did I recognize them as part of the operation—and where the ends of the net crossed began to stomp about and slap the water in hope of blocking the last escape route.

The groups working the net approached each other again, moving sideways until at last they merged into a single unit. The water in front of them began to stir; I thought it was the roiling of the fish, but it was only the stomping and splashing of the two swimmers. I joined everyone else and scrambled up onto the parapet. We were all staring at the net.

Because the driver was tugging at my pants leg, I missed the moment when the net was heaved onshore. What I now saw, however, as the men ran to deposit their catch in an assortment of basins, was devastating. Next to nothing—at best a dozen fish, none any larger than each of us had dined on the night before. The muddle of men and children swarming around the basins made it impossible to tell how the catch was divided up.

Tired and wanting to get out of the blazing sun, I gave in to the short driver and boarded his carriage. Sheila, of that I was certain, would never have ridden in a tourist carriage. And yet it really was better for the driver to earn ten euros rather than not to earn them—and after all, carriages are in fact made to transport people. Besides, in my present condition, Fort Qaitbey, which I believed I was duty bound to visit, was too far for me to have risked the long march along the Corniche. The fort, which crowns the western arm of the harbor basin, was erected atop the ruins of Pharos, there where the great lighthouse of antiquity once stood.

The relief I felt plumping down onto the leather seat removed my last doubt.

I sat leaning back in the carriage—the pedestrians we passed couldn't see me—staring at the driver's bent back, the horse's rear end, and, just above it, the knots of a whip swinging back and forth.

Now that all this is coming back to me hour by hour, I see the numerous details—which for anyone else would fit nicely into a normal travelogue—as a chain of clues, as evidence. All of it, or almost all, pointing toward the denouement.

I had him drop me off at the fort, followed all the paths like a good tourist, gazed out at the sea, surveyed the shore promenade and the library, and put up with schoolboys mocking my long hair—which evidently met with general disapproval here—even after their fourth or fifth barrage of *Luti, luti,* which I found merely disgusting.

My driver greeted me with a loud "Hello!" and suggested we take a detour past a long row of waiting carriages, past a real fish market in its own hall, outside which a couple of women were hawking small fish while repeatedly pouring water over them. We drove to a palace my driver thought I ought to see and, standing up in the carriage, I gawked at it through a massive grated gate. Three schoolgirls ran alongside us, giggling, calling out something, falling back, only to reappear beside me. I could come up with nothing better than a grin. They kept up their game until the old man jumped down from his box, shooed the girls off, and then resumed my dandified jaunt in the direction of the Library of Alexandria. I wanted to give the driver fifteen euros instead of the ten agreed upon, he had driven out of his way, after all. He, however, protested and demanded thirty. He began to bombard me with loud explanations. I gave him the thirty and took off, had a cup of coffee in the library, pictured Sheila swooning beneath Samir and whispering wondrous sweet nothings in his ear, and then dragged myself through the city streets. I had a headache, couldn't stop yawning, and cringed at the sudden blaring of a voice. Loudspeakers were hung on lampposts and facades. A moment later I was surrounded by kneeling men. Although it looked to me to be a normal business district, they were praying in the middle of the street and on the sidewalks. And I, the guy with the long hair, was the only one still standing. The voice from the loudspeakers sounded so menacing that it felt like it was directed solely at me. I fled in the direction of the Corniche.

Outside the famous Hotel Cecil I was greeted by a familiar "Hello!" My driver waved and patted his horse, which was feeding from its nose bag.

I had an appointment at one o'clock with Hosni Hassan, an Egyptian colleague, whom I had come to know through Edwar al-Charrat in Berlin six months before. Hosni has curly red hair, one of the reasons he's occasionally taken for a foreigner.

He led me to an eatery that had once been honored by the presence of the queen of England—documented by photographs on the wall—but that was now a favorite spot for families. Food is served on tin plates, and you sit at long tables. During the meal Hosni kept shoving new dishes my way, but I wasn't the least bit hungry, on the contrary, along with my headache I was feeling a little queasy. I dissolved two aspirin tablets in my glass, which was evidently considered impolite. At any rate people turned to look at me, and my host seemed somewhat perturbed.

Hosni asked why I hadn't brought Sheila along. It was probably due to my poor English that Hosni understood me to say she had fallen in love with the city of Cairo. I simply didn't have the energy, however, to clear up the misunderstanding. I preferred listening to him—he was quite optimistic. Within the next few months, he said, things would take a turn for the better in Egypt.

I was interested in what Hosni had to say, above all about his two years as cultural attaché in Khartoum. I also enjoyed his civility but was glad all the same to no longer have to carry on a conversation and instead spend the time until my train departed dozing in the lobby of the Windsor and drinking ice-cold cola. Mahmud, the amiable driver, who wore a snow white shirt to bid me farewell, brought me back to the train station and was so firm in his refusal of a tip that I actually pocketed it again.

On the trip back I practically froze because the entire first class was filled with military cadets who kept leaving the car to smoke, setting up a nasty draft each time. I huddled up but soon began to sneeze. I searched without success for a handkerchief. I was likewise depressed by the thought of having to confront Sheila and Samir again. I didn't want to fight, to argue, I just wanted a warm bed and peace and quiet.

A happy trio was waiting for me on the platform in Cairo. Sheila was standing between Samir and the driver of the Lada. She asked what had happened—I looked so ill. Nevertheless she pressed me to join her, Samir, and the driver for a meal at the Fish Market. It was her treat, we were her guests.

I said that except for a couple of aspirin I wanted nothing so much as sleep. I sneezed, and both Samir and the Lada driver pulled out tissues, which I accepted with a gratitude befitting a miracle.

Sheila commiserated but was dogged in her resolve to treat her companions to dinner. I encouraged her in fact. I wouldn't be fun company today in any case. She had, Sheila remarked once we were in the car, solved the riddle of the two dissimilar drivers. Our Lada driver had previously been engaged by the embassy of the GDR. Along with the building itself, he and his vehicle had been put to new use. The driver of the silver VW bus had always worked for the Goethe-Institut.

We stopped at a pharmacy, where Samir recommended a remedy that would vanquish my sniffles within a day. With the motor still running, the driver got out at the hotel and carried my bag all the way to the elevator. We bade each other a hearty farewell.

I spent a dreadful night, drifting back and forth between wakefulness and a sleep filled with disquieting dreams that exhausted me even more. Maybe I had just drunk too much cola. I had a voracious thirst for ice-cold cola. But once the cola had flowed down my esophagus, it seemed to gum up my works and ward off sleep. Even after I turned on the light and got up, I fell back into that state of dream-haunted wakefulness. Sheila arrived around two, fell asleep right off, and awoke at nine fully refreshed.

And right on time for the opening of the conference I was feeling really lousy. I had a craving for fruit, but otherwise wanted only ice-cold cola. At the breakfast buffet I piled half the melon slices on my plate and pillaged the grapes from the cheese platter.

Sheila went on and on about the Pyramids. The whole time they had done nothing but gaze at the Pyramids, watching the progress of their shadows. And Samir had told her everything that you could possibly want to know about the Pyramids. She was now addicted to viewing the Pyramids. There was nothing in the world to compare with them. For her, viewing the Pyramids was the best medicine—no, the best religion there was.

I didn't want to squander what little strength I had left on sarcastic remarks. I wasn't listening all that closely to Sheila anyway. But the longer she spoke, the more indisputable it seemed to me was the change she had undergone. I had encountered this same phenomenon only among the children of my friends, who at some point were no longer children and suddenly responded to me with either greater attention or detachment. Something of the sort had happened with Sheila. Despite her chattiness she seemed calmer, no longer so nervous and overexcited, more mature in fact. Suddenly I desired her again. Yes, it wouldn't have taken much, and I would have proposed to her.

While we were waiting for the bus, Samir appeared beside us unannounced. He would love to come along, he was very interested in the conference. I said I didn't know if it was all that easy to do. If I had no objection, he said, there wouldn't be any problem at all. I shrugged.

At that same moment a gray-haired man with a large nose and a mouth far too wide for his narrow face stepped up to us. As if by way of a greeting he ran his hand through his hair and addressed me in French. I don't speak French. As if by prearrangement, Samir soon interrupted our amiable colleague to provide a translation. The only thing I understood was *très bien, très bien,* which in Samir's version became "wonderful, simply fantastic." That pleased me, and I grinned like the Cheshire cat.

It turned out that a different Samir, that is Samir Grees, had sent his Arabic translation of *Simple Stories* to several authors, and this amiable gentleman standing here before me had evidently been one of the recipients.

Instead of thanking him directly, I requested our Samir to ask the man his name and then whether his own work had been translated into German or English. Samir hesitated briefly, supplied the name of my vis-à-vis, and then passed on my question about translations. After a firm *"Non, non, non,"* my Arabic colleague said, *"Au revoir,"* turned around, and strode off.

The conference opened in a large auditorium that I recall as being rather dark. I had asked Samir to inquire about earphones for me, but in vain, although meanwhile I kept an eye out for interpreter booths. Of the few writers whom I knew, I saw no one except Edwar al-Charrat, and he had more than enough to do greeting the many colleagues encircling him. A half hour later Dr. Bassalama, the signer of the invitations, entered in procession with his entourage. Had everyone risen from their seats and applauded, the staging would have been perfect.

I understood not a word of any of the speeches, of course, but did notice that Dr. Bassalama was mentioned repeatedly. The more frequently his name occurred, the more it sounded like an invocation. An earnest Samir sat ramrod straight beside Sheila and applauded enthusiastically after each speech.

An hour and a half later, as the participants of the conference streamed out into the lobby, I finally caught on: There were no interpreter booths and thus no earphones either. Samir confirmed my observation at once: "Only Arabic is spoken here." Then what, I asked Samir, was I doing here? He didn't know either. I grew even more upset when a few minutes later I tried and failed to find something to drink at a buffet table that was grazed clean within a few minutes. Only a few dirty glasses were left, and the container of orange juice had already been tipped forward so that a gentleman could dribble the last of it into his glass.

Sheila and Samir both declared their desire to stay. I rode back to the hotel, bought five cans of ice-cold cola, and dozed the afternoon away in my bed.

Sheila did not even appear for dinner, for which I was joined by Hoda Barakat. We had become acquainted in Yemen the year before and exchanged addresses. Hoda had fled with both her children to Paris from Beirut in 1989. I pumped her for details about Beirut, and she replied half in English, half in French. I needed the information for a character in my *New Lives,* the novel I was working on. While we spoke I spotted Sheila returning to the hotel. Around ten o'clock Hoda wrote down an address for me, the same one I later used for Vera Türmer: Beirut—Starco area—Wadi aboujmil, the building next to Alliance College—fourth floor.

When I returned to our room, Sheila had already departed again. She came back long past midnight. She asked where I had been and why I couldn't finally get into the habit of leaving my cell phone on.

The next afternoon—until then I had gone downstairs only for breakfast, and upon spotting Samir out on the street had retreated to my bed again—I was sitting with two colleagues whom I did not know on a podium in a space not much larger than an ordinary classroom, with very high-set windows revealing a white sky outside. After I was greeted and congratulated for something or other, I listened to my neighbor's lecture and finally to a very beautiful woman who read my speech in

Arabic. I had plenty of time to keep count of the audience, which was in constant flux. Although I could perfectly understand such a steady ebb and flow during the long, droning contributions of my colleagues, I was amazed nonetheless when the first listeners stood up to leave while my text was being read. There were never more than eighteen people in the room at any one time. Samir and Sheila sat stock-still side by side in the first row. Trying to keep from watching them the whole time was the greatest effort of all. At the end Samir once again applauded enthusiastically. There were two questions, neither related to my text.

"What am I going to do with you?" Sheila exclaimed when I announced I'd be returning to the hotel. I said that if Samir had time, she should have dinner with him, and climbed into a taxi.

On the hotel stairway I ran into Hassan Dawud. A few of his books have also been translated into German. He's the publisher of a newspaper in Beirut. We had likewise become acquainted in Yemen. Hassan asked me for my speech, he wanted to print it. I said he should first take a look at it. No, he laughed, that I was the author was enough for him. For a moment the pressure eased in my head, and I thought the worst might be over. Two minutes later I fell into bed.

The telephone rang. It was Hoda. She invited me to join her and a couple of her friends for dinner. No, she wouldn't hear of it, I was to come to along, it would do me good.

Just showering and dressing were Herculean labors, the walk down the hall to the elevator finished me off.

In the lobby Hassan Dawud waved me down, asked me to wait while he rummaged in his briefcase, held out a few pages to me—my lecture, it was incomprehensible, sorry to say. That might possibly be the translation, I said. Possibly, he said. I amazed myself with how calmly I took the news. But as I came down the hotel stairway I was on the verge of bursting into sobs.

How had I ended up in this farce? This conference could rot in hell. I felt deceived and humiliated. I hated Sheila, I hated Samir. I wanted out.

No one had come to the conference to hear lectures, Hoda said. The invitation was like a gift, you flew to Cairo, met some friends, enjoyed yourself—it was really a great time. It didn't matter in the least—she laughed—whether there were any interpreter booths or not. And I had the best deal of all. I didn't even need to have a twinge of conscience for playing hooky, I was a free man! Whereas since arriving in Cairo she herself had had to race from interview to interview—Hariri had been assassinated only a few days before.

Hoda introduced me to four women, including Leila, a writer from Kuwait, who gave me the once-over from behind dark glasses, as if suspecting me of being a spy. Finally she stomped her cigarette out and squeezed in beside me. Hoda shared the front passenger seat with a professor of French and Arabic literature from Cairo. The owner of the car had slid her seat so far forward that she was literally being pressed against the steering wheel.

Actually all I remember now is the women's laughter. And that I envied them, because I had probably never laughed so hard in my life as they did during our ride. None of the women, not even skeptical Leila, could bring a sentence to an end without being overwhelmed by her own laughter. To this day I don't know what they were laughing about. At one point Hoda slipped between the seats and fell against my knee, unleashing another salvo of laughter. She kept trying to explain something to me in English about the huge throngs at Nasser's funeral, but what was so terribly funny about that? There were brief pauses when they had to catch their breath, but the very next word was a spark that ignited a new explosion. Even the policeman standing beside a stoplight in a vast square grinned when he saw five people crammed together, holding their hands to their mouths and laughing to the point of tears.

A grated barricade in front of the Al-Azhar Mosque slid back and we were directed to a parking place. Passing begging women and children, we walked through an underpass and arrived at the square outside the entrance to the souk frequented by tourists. We were stormed by several waiters who tried to thrust menus at us and steer us to specific chairs at specific tables in a sea of tables and chairs. In the company of these women the waiters, as well as the beggars, vendors, and roving children, no longer seemed an annoyance.

Just the opposite—they were part of the scene and prompted new topics for a conversation that branched off now and then into English for my sake. Even a carpet vendor I was certain would be rebuffed—who would be buying a carpet at this hour?—had to fulfill his role. The price fell from 160 Egyptian pounds to 70, then to 60, to 55. At which point the vendor imitated strangling himself and, cursing and shaking his head, left our table, only to hail us cordially from a distance shortly thereafter—and was soon standing again before us. Because they were such wonderful ladies—for that was what they were—45 pounds. Hoda explained that 20 would have been plenty, and she could have had it for 20, but he had been unwilling to haggle. Leila waved over a heavily made-up girl who was screeching wildly as she fought off a waiter trying to ban her from his tables. Leila had the girl approach very close, gave her a talking-to, and when she tried to run off, swiftly grabbed her by the arm, held it tight, and went on talking until the girl gave several nods and said something in response. Only then did Leila let her go. Ten minutes later the girl returned, and Leila pressed a couple of bills into her hand. A beggar slinking up from behind suddenly bent down and gave Leila a loud smooch on the cheek. Leila screamed. But then, instead of being outraged, she laughed and rubbed the kiss from her cheek with a handkerchief.

Even now, after darkness had fallen, one tourist bus after another pulled up. One guide after the other hoisted a little flag, and one group after the other climbed out and vanished in the direction of the souk. A few of these mostly elderly ladies and gentlemen—whose flipped-up sunglasses made them look a little like insects—gazed wistfully our way, took a few snapshots, and straggled after their flags.

First the sense of exhaustion returned, then the pressure inside my head. I noticed our food being served, pigeons with their tiny drumsticks bound together. While we ate—pigeons don't offer much to gnaw at, the stuffing's the important thing—other pigeons searched for bread crumbs at our feet. One bite and I felt an aversion, something close to nausea. I couldn't take another, I wanted to but simply couldn't. I had to stop, my energies were exhausted. It's a miracle I was still able to sit upright in my chair.

After I had persuaded the women not to accompany me, they called the waiter, and the waiter called over a boy, and the boy went to fetch a cabbie. A price was settled on, and Hoda instructed me on no account to pay more than the fifteen pounds.

All I had to do was stand up and walk a few steps behind the driver—and they were all around me, a whole pack of boys. The youngest were maybe eight, the oldest maybe twelve or thirteen. But I've already told about that, probably far too often.

The worst part wasn't the kids. The moment I said good-bye to the women and began to walk away, memories flooded in. Or to put it another way, everything collapsed in on me. Sheila and Samir, the conference, my failed speech, my disappointed colleagues, the hotel room with its sweat-drenched pillow. The hour and a half I had spent with the women already seemed like some pleasant movie. Now I was leaving the theater and returning to reality.

I got into the taxi. Even now I can hear the boy leaping onto the car. I just thought—Well, there's another dent, as if this sort of damage was a normal risk in the business of transporting tourists. I didn't want to see anything else, hear anything else. I wanted the farce I had wandered into to come to an end.

I have no idea how he was able to hang on. With his fingernails in a crack somewhere? Or with the palms of his hands, his feet on the bumper? The driver of a car that passed us pointed to the boy on our trunk and shook his head.

I wasn't about to be blackmailed, I was determined to have my way in this.

Did it take me one minute, two minutes, before I shouted: "Stop, please, stop!"?

The taxi slowed down until we were moving at a walking pace, the boy jumped off, and the driver said, "Good idea," as he nodded to me in the mirror but filled the silence that had reigned until now with complaints that fifteen pounds wasn't enough.

I don't know if it was while I was still in the taxi that I tried to imagine what it would have sounded like if the boy had slipped off. With the windows rolled up, we probably wouldn't have heard a thing.

The cabbie wanted ten euros instead of fifteen pounds. I gave him thirty pounds, just to get away quickly.

Sheila and Samir were sitting in the hotel lobby. I think her hand was on his knee. But I didn't care about that now. Yes, I even found it annoying when she arrived in the room ten minutes later. I heard her use the bathroom, heard her lie down, turn on her nightstand light, turn it off again soon after, and fall asleep.

The next day she was never more than twenty feet from my side, about the distance from our breakfast table to the buffet, or from the lectern to the first row at the Goethe-Institut that evening. Over breakfast—Samir was nowhere to be seen—I told Hoda, whom I had no choice but to introduce to Sheila, about the boy at the rear windshield. Hoda scowled. It was a game, a way of testing their courage. If something went wrong it wasn't the taxi driver they went after, but the person with the wherewithal.

I scarcely remember that last day. I tried to cancel the interview before the reading because I simply couldn't utter another word—but for some strange reason it went okay in English. My head almost exploded during the reading.

It was still dark the next morning as we rode through empty streets to the airport. I had no idea how I would manage the long trek to check-in, then on to passport control, security, and finally the gate, with drafts blowing from all sides. And then came changing planes in Paris and standing for long minutes in the February wind of an open jet bridge, Sheila with the brown doll under her arm.

After landing in Berlin, as we waited for our luggage I listened to my mailbox. Maybe it was a mistake, maybe the Sheila beside me had nothing to do with the Sheila I heard on the mailbox. But I didn't have the strength to separate one from the other.

As I said, I've told the story often, very often, and have even written it all down now, but despite my expectations, it has lost none of its dreadfulness—on the contrary, sometimes I think it's worse. Nothing happened, I tell myself, nothing happened, I was lucky, everybody says so. But I live in the fear that I missed the one chance I had of breaking out of that moment, and that I am caught up in it now, for as long—oh, I don't know—for as long perhaps as it takes for a miracle to happen and, without a moment's hesitation, for me to shout "Stop, stop, stop!"

Not Literature, or, Epiphany on a Sunday Evening

Maybe I had had a little too much to drink. That would be the simplest explanation, of course, but any other explanation . . . well, what can I say. . . .

I can only provide you with bits and pieces of the context, but as for the heart of the matter—you're going to think I'm loony. Either you recognize it, or . . .

From the outside looking in things often seem so simple.

It's been several weeks now, anyway. It was on a Sunday. To escape the heat for one day at least, we had driven out to our dacha near Prieros. It's always three or four degrees cooler under the pines than in Berlin. Clara and Franziska can run around naked, we can wear shorts, everybody doing their own thing, and it's just a stone's throw to the lake.

Around noon my mother arrived, with a big bowl of potato salad in the trunk—I've known that ivory-colored bowl ever since I can remember. That bowl has, so to speak, always been there. And shortly after my mother's arrival, M. and E. showed up—two girlfriends who weren't supposed to arrive till later in the afternoon. It was a little embarrassing to have them catch me raking up pinecones and needles between the terrace and the shed. But believe me, it's very pleasant to walk over the moss barefoot. Besides, it would be pretty obvious if there were twigs, cones, and needles only at our place. Raking is just part of the routine for a rental property like this.

The heat meant that the electric grill was the only possible solution. The sausages and shashlik were from the supermarket, but they have very good meats. I seldom drink beer in the middle of the day, I'm a person who generally doesn't drink much at all. But what's grilling without beer? It was hot and I was thirsty, and the beer, left in the cellar from the time before, was cooled just right. I drank one or two bottles while I worked the grill and then one or two at the table. Everyone was drinking beer, except for the kids of course. The case was empty in no time. M. and E., agreeing as a couple, made fun of our diet potato salad, as well as the crumbly shortcake, the glaze was the only thing holding the strawberries together. But they polished off the potato salad all the same, and the sausages too. Natalia and I enjoyed the shortcake just as it was.

In the hope that the children would nap, Natalia and I set out on a tour with the double stroller, but the neighbors' dogs started barking, and Franziska kept going "Bowwow! Bowwow!" and Clara copied her. We gave up trying to get them to nap, packed up our swim things, and headed for the lake. Natalia and I swam to the far shore, while M. and E. sunbathed and my mother sat in a tied-up boat with Clara and Franziska and sailed off to America, back and forth, back and forth. In America, said E., whose son lives in California, we wouldn't be allowed to let the kids run around naked like this. Perfectly possible it would soon be like America here too, I thought. First the States, then here.

Before M. and E. took off we drank the prosecco they had brought—prosecco is their favorite drink—because it was finally chilled enough, and ate the rest of the shortcake along with what whipped cream was left. Then M. and E. drove off. We stood in the wooded lane and waved good-bye, and they waved from both sides of the car. The sun was shining through the pines and the dust they kicked up, and Natalia said we should stay the night—it would work if we drove back to Berlin early the next morning.

"We should have thought about that earlier," I said, as if we hadn't had a real Sunday. "Come on, kids," my mother said. "It's time for us to settle in nice and cozy now."

No one wanted to clear the table or do dishes. My mother just set the milk in the fridge. "Ah, there's still another bottle of prosecco," she called from inside.

"We'll drink it as our reward," I said. I have no idea what sort of reward I had in mind, but it was hot and it was really good prosecco.

I can well imagine how all this sounds to strangers' ears—pigging out and boozing.

Clara and Franziska strewed the old plastic containers they'd found in the shed across their sandbox. My mother was lying in the hammock and brooding over tricky solutions for the sudoku in the *Tagesspiegel* that, after a long discussion as a couple, M. and E. had left behind for her. Leaning back, legs crossed, Natalia was sitting at the table and attempting to read the rest of the paper in her lap. But Clara kept asking: "What does the Wicked Queen say when no kids will play with her? Is she sad because Sleeping Beauty is prettier than she is?" This can go on for hours.

Instead of getting into the car and turning on the radio, I called our friend S. to ask her how the game between England and Ecuador had turned out, and who would be playing that evening. She wanted me to tell her why so many writers think using the German genitive is pretentious and so no longer use it. I had no explanation for her but decided to make a note of her turn of phrase, "jeopardizing good taste."

With a still unread volume of stories by Ayala in one hand and a bottle with what was left of the now almost tepid prosecco in the other, I lay down on a blanket that had been hung out to air.

Suddenly I decided I wanted to be lying in a porch swing. I actually gave some thought as to where you could buy a porch swing and what one might go for, and figured that having it delivered out here would probably cost as much as the swing itself.

My sunglasses turned the sky as blue as in Italy, and our local pines had become stone pines. Now and then there was a sough of wind. To me it always sounds like a train moving through the forest, the way trains crossing the Dresden Heath used to. Then I tried picturing the sky as water and the pines as underwater plants. I must have nodded off for a few seconds— and woke up when Franziska came running by close to my head. She was laughing, almost hooting. She ran so fast I thought she'd go sprawling any moment, and since I hadn't swept the woods she was barreling toward, I was afraid she might hurt herself. I immediately thought of how last year a fox had risked getting as close as our garbage pit to watch us— a rabid fox.

Franziska pulled up short, bent her torso forward, held out one arm, and cried, " 'T's that, 'T's that?"

It was in fact very beautiful—a large perfectly unblemished piece of orange peel that someone had tossed over our fence. "An orange peel," I said. "What?" she asked. "An orange peel," I repeated. "What?" "An orange peel," I shouted. " 'T's that?" An orange peel, and one more time, an orange peel. And suddenly I got it. An orange peel! Franziska understood me at once. By the tone of my voice or whatever, she realized I had finally given her the right answer. We both gazed at the orange peel and, along with it, the miracle that there are orange peels and us and everyone and everything, the whole miracle of it. There's nothing more for me to say. We understood the miracle that we exist. Period. Should I say I saw us in the womb of the universe? But I saw not just us, but everyone and everything. Each man, each woman, each child, each thing, but not as some sort of panorama, but each man, each woman, each child, each thing up close. We were all at the mercy of horrors and of all things human, of every ugliness and every beauty. I wasn't standing apart from it, there was nothing in between—between me, us, and everything else.

I'm not loony, and I won't claim I saw electron clouds or Einsteinian space. But all the same, it was something like that.

As soon as I put it into words, however, it turns to nonsense. A bat of an eye, during which I understood everything. Nothing, nothing had ever been lost. I saw it and in the next breath knew that I saw it no more, that the curtain had fallen.

Ants were scrambling on the backside of the orange peel, setting Franziska laughing again, with renewed cries of " 'T's that?" and "What?" "Those are ants," I said, "ants," and turned away. After a few steps I looked around. "Ants," I said and walked back, intending to take the orange out of her hand. "No, no!" she screamed. And so I left her with the orange peel and the ants, and stretched out on my blanket again.

I can't say that I was agitated or happy or sad. I merely thought about how truly lovely it would be if in fact just before death we do see our life repeat at fast forward again, because this moment would be part of it, this moment and this afternoon.

But as I've said, maybe I simply had had too much to drink; it had been a really hot day. But when around ten o'clock I took a last look at the thermometer, the blue column of mercury was still showing twenty-nine degrees Celsius. Think of that— twenty-nine degrees Celsius at ten in the evening!

III

New Year's Eve Confusions

I used to be afraid of New Year's Eve. But then I was leading an impossible life. Only the professional side of things was functioning. Functioning even better than I actually liked.

When I try to cast about for the beginning of this story, I instantly find myself leaning back in my office chair, my right foot on the handle of the middle desk drawer, the tip of my shoe wedged in under the desktop. I'm holding the phone receiver in my left hand, while my right hand plays the spiral cord like a violin string pressed against my knee. The smoke above the ashtray assumes shapes—a rumpled handkerchief, an upturned ice-cream cone, a castle from a cartoon fairy tale.

Startled at first by the display showing a call from Berlin, I was as always disappointed to recognize Claudia's phone number. Claudia called me only when she couldn't get hold of Ute at our branch in the old city. This time, however, she was in a chatty mood. She wanted to talk about New Year's Eve, and I had no idea why she was telling me whom she would be inviting—the names meant nothing to me. But after a brief pause she added, emphasizing each word: "And your Julia too!"

This was on October 9, 1999, shortly before five o'clock.

Maybe you also have someone in your life who means the world to you, for whom you would sacrifice ten years of your life, for whom without hesitation you would leave your wife and child, give up your career. For me that was Julia, the Julia I first met at a carnival party thrown by the Arts Academy in Dresden in 1989. She was dressed as Hans in Luck, and could in fact have passed for a young lad, had it not been for the way she walked. She ordered a beer, I ordered a beer, we waited for them. I complimented her on her costume and went on to say that I had a thing for women who drink beer—a remark that leaves me blushing even now. We toasted. Julia assumed my general enthusiasm for theater—and in particular for a production of *Kate from Heilbronn* at the Leipziger Strasse rehearsal stage—came from my having recognized her. When the music struck up, we danced. Julia danced the whole evening just with me.

I was studying physics at the Technical University and working on my final-year paper. Julia was doing her year of practical training at the Staatsschauspiel.

The second time we met, as we sat across from each other in a milk bar near Goose Thief Fountain, Julia stretched her hands out to the middle of the table—and even a little farther—so that I couldn't help laying my hands on hers.

Despite a lot of big promises, she hadn't gotten hired in Dresden, and according to Julia the reason was her evaluation by the Berlin Acting School, which claimed she had problems "recognizing the leading role of the working class."

Julia was more than happy to land a spot with a theater in A., a district capital, although I found that almost more frustrating than she did. But since I was convinced that sooner or later someone would be captivated by her, I came around to believing that A. was better for her than Dresden. For an acting student to get involved with a guy from a technical university was unusual in those days, to say the least. The best her theater bunch could come up with was Dürrenmatt's *The Physicists*. They had no idea what it meant to plug away at five years of technical studies and—without becoming a party member— be granted a research slot, even if it was only at a technical school in B.

Even today I don't find it easy to describe Julia. It's like trying to supply reasons for why I loved her. It annoyed me when people called her a "standout," as if she were a precocious child. The most amazing thing about her was that, especially as an actor, she was scarcely aware of the effect she had. When I told her I knew of no other woman who walked in such an easy and yet decisive way, she said it was my infatuation. For Julia the most important thing each morning was to tell me about her dreams, as if she felt some need to confess. Julia never missed a party, even if it usually looked as if she was bored once she got there. She often learned her role on the train or would set her alarm for four in the morning. I loved everything about Julia—except the way she could encapsulate herself! From one moment to the next Julia could close up for apparently no reason whatever. She would then treat me as an object she needed to evade, even while she was flirting with a salesclerk or chatting for minutes on end with some stagehand we might run into on the street.

In June of '89 my left foot buckled under me while I was taking a run in the woods. I tore a tendon and ended up in a cast.

Julia dropped everything, including her graduation party in Berlin, to take care of me and cook for me—she even called the taxi that took me to the oral defense of my paper.

That cast marked the beginning of our loveliest time together. We were almost inseparable. When I could actually walk again, we took a trip to Budapest and Szeged, returning in the middle of August, which raised smiles on some faces at the time. But Julia and I had never so much as mentioned leaving for the West, just as we never spoke about having children or moving in together.

Later I asked myself many times whether I loved Julia because she was an actor. The mere thought that the same beautiful creature everyone was staring at would, once the applause ended, follow me back to my ghastly dorm and fall asleep cuddled up against me, that that voice would be whispering words in my ear, that those hands—ah, it can only sound banal to anybody else.

But believe me: As much as I loved Kate of Heilbronn, I loved Julia far more, who wanted nothing more than to be with me. With her everything felt easy and natural and effortless.

One time on the train—we were on my way to my parents', and Julia was sitting across from me reading—I was struck by the notion that we didn't know each other, a vision so terrible it actually left me with ice-cold hands. Without Julia everything was sad or at least incomplete. Even in the company of my friend C. or my brother, within an hour at the latest, I would be tormented by my longing for her.

Julia's first season in A. began that September and so did my assistantship in B. People in B. were far less uptight than at the Dresden Technical University. I could have ducked out on Thursdays. Julia said, however, that she needed more time now and more sleep, because she would have to concentrate completely on her work.

A week without her was endless, I barely lasted two. I didn't understand her change of heart. When she wrote me—neither of us had a telephone, and only emergency calls were allowed at both the theater and my lab—that she would be in rehearsal the next weekend as well and still had a script to learn, I took a train to A.

Julia had an evening rehearsal. I waited in the café across from the theater, missed her when she left, so that when I finally rang her doorbell she was already asleep—she was subletting a two-and-a-half-room apartment with no private bath. This was five days before her twenty-sixth birthday. I asked her where we should celebrate, in A. or B.? Julia said she wasn't up to celebrating this close to her premiere. Of course I grabbed a train for A. anyway.

The doorkeeper let me in solely out of the goodness of her heart. When I entered the canteen, there I stood—a bag of presents in one hand, a bouquet in the other—facing about two dozen people discussing whether they would be traveling to Leipzig for a demonstration the next Monday, October 2.

It was after midnight when we finally left. I hurriedly arranged a little birthday table. Julia, already in her pajamas, said, "You look like you're about to burst into tears."

I was in fact pretty desperate. But I hoped the spell Julia was under would be broken in that moment by one of our magic charms—and knew that I wasn't going to be able to go on like this.

On Wednesday, October 4, I participated in the meeting at the church in B., said something to the effect that in our country allegiance to the party meant more than doing good work—

a ridiculous platitude, but it was met with lots of applause. Afterward two men asked me if I didn't want to work with the New Forum in B. I should add that I was risking a great deal. My paper, "New Research on the Superductility of Aluminum–Zinc Alloys," had earned me some provisional laurels, preparations for the first series of experiments were proceeding without a hitch, and Professor Walther from Martin Luther University in Halle had held out the prospect of a position.

The premiere of Sophocles' *Antigone* was what is called a thundering success. I bore up under the endless premiere party without a peep, and was on my best behavior the whole time. It was not until the next morning when I told Julia about my statement at the church that she opened up.

To be admired by her was wonderful, but then she said that what I'd done would definitely please Ms. What's-her-face— I've forgotten the name of her director. I said I had no desire to please Ms. What's-her-face, to which Julia replied that I'd hardly have much of a chance in any case, since What's-her-face was a lesbian.

If you think that with that the definitive word was spoken, you're mistaken. I say this of course with no ultimate certainty, but precisely because the relationship between What's-her-face and Julia was so ambiguous, it left me in a quandary.

Things were proceeding in B. just as elsewhere in the country, except that the demonstrations in B. were never mentioned on the radio—which left us with a sense of disappointment and futility.

Before the New Forum in B. got a copy machine—smuggled in from our sister city K. in West Germany—we had to type up our initial proclamation over and over using four sheets of carbon paper. Ute, who worked in the lab at the polyclinic, and I were the only ones who could touch-type. The two of us would often sit typing until midnight in the "hobby cellar" of a dilapidated villa. This was almost perfect busywork for me—I wasn't alone and I didn't have to think about anything.

It was probably our work ethic that convinced the New Forum's "speakers council" that the copy machine would be in good hands with Ute and me. But beginning in early November when we had nothing more to fear and suddenly everybody had something they wanted to copy—we asked for twenty pfennigs a copy as a donation—we set up regular office hours, with Ute and me covering fifty-fifty.

Ute was in love with me from the start. On our trip to Coburg—we intended to spend our "welcome money" for copy machine cartridges—I told her about Julia and the fantastic summer we had had. But that made no difference whatever in her behavior.

When it becomes clear that you may touch the woman beside you whenever you want, yes, that she's waiting for you to touch her, you finally do it when the opportunity arises. I was surprised by how passionate and simple and beautiful sex with her was. We had sex almost every day, and afterward everything was always just as before. At some point I asked myself if it was possible for me to love Ute. Thought it just for a moment, one brief instant, and it seemed absurd of course—I couldn't leave Julia for Ute.

I made the trip to A. for Julia's Shakespeare premiere on November 26. The theater was practically empty. All the same I congratulated Ms. What's-her-face, who was quick to ask why my hands were so cold. "Are my hands really that cold?" I asked in amazement and held one hand up to my cheek, which sent What's-her-face into peals of laughter. Julia's expression took on a telling look.

In the middle of December what had to happen happened. Julia visited me in B. for the first time—someone had offered her a ride and she had grabbed the chance. The someone was What's-her-face. Later Julia said she sensed right off that something was wrong with me. She hadn't shown her face for three and a half months, and then there she was at my door with What's-her-face. Was I supposed to burst with happiness? I made coffee, put some cake on the table, and wished What's-her-face would go to hell.

What's-her-face enthused about the demonstrations in Leipzig and how they had turned everything upside down— "not just for us in the theater, but in the whole town of A." I asked who "us" was. "Well, all of us!" she cried, spreading her arms wide. "The whole theater!" Julia talked about solidarity among colleagues, about the incredible experience of being certain that they could depend on one another. "If they had dragged one of us from the stage, we all would have gone to jail."

What was I supposed to tell them about? Our copy service?

While What's-her-face talked, the thought of being left alone with Julia made me nervous. Julia was sitting on the sofa still wrapped in her coat, her hands in her pockets—I had opened the window because we were all smoking up a storm—and was presumably feeling much the same. The good-byes when What's-her-face left were extremely cordial. She apologized for having robbed us of an hour and a half of our time together, and even gave me a hug too at the end.

Actually everything could have turned out all right, but

when Julia remarked how happy she was that What's-her-face and I were finally connected, that working with What's-her-face meant a great deal to her, and that maybe I could understand now why she, Julia, hadn't been able to visit me—I saw red.

Was this how things were going to be with us from now on? I asked. And while Julia stared at me in utter dismay, I shouted, "I can't live like this!" I surprised myself with how angry and embittered I sounded. I wanted a decision. I wanted my Julia back. Either paradise or—all right—nothing. It all seems totally insane to me now, but at the time I thought I had suffered enough. Julia then made the remark that she had sensed something of the sort when she came through the door.

"I've been cheating on you," I replied, and tried to explain myself to her. Her pulling back like this had driven me crazy, but she was my whole life, without her I would simply freeze to death, I wanted nothing more than to be with her, just like it was before. But she said nothing, as if hesitating to summon the effort.

Tears were running down Julia's cheeks. We stood in the tiny entryway, listening to footsteps upstairs, to the click of a light switch, and to a very soft plop as one of her tears dripped on the floor.

She wasn't blaming me, Julia said, she'd noticed herself that she had never been able to satisfy me sexually.

No, I shot back, that was nonsense.

We didn't budge from the spot.

She wasn't holding it against me, she said, some silly little slip that probably had nothing to do with love.

And then something happened that I still don't understand even today. At that moment I thought of how I had wondered if I could live my life with Ute too. And instead of assuring Julia that the idea of my leaving her for someone else was absurd, I said that there'd been a smidgen of love involved.

Why did I lie? Because it was a lie—I swear, a lie!

Julia looked at me. "Well if that's the case . . . ," she said. Her voice sounded strange. For the first time it sounded like the voice of a total stranger. She went back to the living room to get her purse. "If that's the case . . ." were the last words I heard her speak.

On the way to the train station I showered her with declarations of love. I loved Julia, I loved only Julia and so never doubted that I could change her mind. I was certain that in the next instant we would embrace and kiss, that we would turn around and never be separated again. At the station, when Julia asked me for a cigarette, I thought the moment of saving grace, of awakening from the nightmare, had come.

Julia didn't answer my letters. I traveled to A. to see productions she was in. She wouldn't talk to me. She was sure I'd understand her someday, she said, thanked me for the flowers, and offered her hand. Her colleagues ignored me as if I were a stranger.

At first I thought Julia had put me on probation, but I didn't hear from her either on New Year's Eve or on January 13, my birthday. I started drinking, being alone was unbearable.

Almost everyone at the technical school had resigned their party membership. My senior adviser, Professor K., told everyone he could about the risk he had taken in preventing me from being discharged in early October. I spent most of my time in the office of the New Forum and until late into the night copied other people's theses, advertising flyers, and various calls to arms. We asked that 10 percent of every bill be paid in Western D-marks. That was Ute's idea, who headed up the business end of things. She was always there for me. I could also say she was at my beck and call, even though I was often mean to her. I couldn't stand it when she treated me as if we were a couple.

We passed on two thousand marks a month to the New Forum, and kept the rest. That rest grew from week to week, so that every Saturday evening Ute slipped me several times the amount of my stipend.

But telling it this way leaves the wrong impression. At the time I was no more interested in money than I was in anything else. Moreover it only slowly dawned on us what it was we were actually up to. It was clear to Ute—although I didn't give it a thought—that we were operating more or less illegally.

In the middle of March, the same week as parliamentary elections, she applied for a business license. We registered as a partnership under the civil code. As I said, I didn't have to worry about any of it. I signed whatever she gave me to sign, and did my work—I didn't want to have anything more than that to do with it. I lived in the expectation that at the first signal from Julia I would drop everything to follow her to wherever.

I gave up working on my dissertation. I was simply incapable of sitting there in my dorm and brooding. The reason I gave my parents was that all my advisers and mentors, including Professor Walther in Halle, had been given a leave of absence or fired.

Ute's days at the polyclinic were numbered as well. We ran "Copy 2000" as a kind of hobby. I learned how to roll coins, carried the bag to the bank for Ute, and watched the numbers on our statements climb and climb. I made two more trips to A., but then decided never again to set foot in the town.

Because most people we had started with in the New Forum

had wandered off into other political parties, no one except Ute and I knew who the machines—a second copier had been donated to us in December—actually belonged to. We moved them to a little shop at street level—Ute had arranged for an open-ended lease with People's Solidarity starting July 1, 1990. Compared with the three copy machines we bought on credit, our old ones were already museum pieces.

From the start we were the top dogs in B. We never turned down a job and worked late into the night if necessary, whereas our competition got bogged down trying to make a killing in computers and other office equipment. We invested in binding machines.

Ute and I slept together almost every day, sometimes even had sex in the office as we waited for the copiers to spit out the rest of a run. In that regard we were made for each other. With Julia—maybe she was right about that—I'd always felt a little inhibited.

"We sure do a lot of screwing," Ute once remarked. She said it the same way she might have said, "We sure do have a lot of business." But she might have claimed just the opposite without it having sounded any different. Do you understand? I mean, for her the only important thing was that we were together. Without batting an eye Ute would have dropped everything on the spot to follow me through thick and thin. I'm not saying this out of vanity. It was the same with me, except for me it was Julia.

At the end of August, it was just growing light, Ute's head lay on my chest and I was just about to doze off again, when she whispered: "I'm pregnant." She hadn't expected me to be happy about it. Fritz was born on February 28, 1991, he was named after Ute's grandfather Friedrich. His middle, and last, name came from me, Friedrich Frank Reichert.

All the same Fritz was Ute's child, hers alone. The boy didn't change my life in any fundamental way. He helped reconcile me with my parents, who had long been upset with me for having given up on my dissertation. And it meant more work, although within a few weeks Ute was at my side again in the shop.

I soon avoided being alone with Fritz. In his mother's presence, however, everything I said went in one ear and out the other. The older he grew, the more I irritated him—and at the same time the more devoted he was to his mother. Fritz turned on the charm for her in a way so unchildlike that it was almost worrisome.

Even before his birth we had hired employees. We used mainly students, who stood in line to get a job with us. But that's taking me down the wrong track. It works perhaps as a kind of backstory. The ups and downs of our business are not the issue here. I was a really good boss, at least a better one than I am today—and I know what I'm saying. Back then people actually considered me a cool guy, and I probably was, too, when it came to business. I didn't really want to be a success.

Do you understand? Nothing I did was done out of conviction. Nothing connected me with my work, it was just an accidental fit, with one thing leading to the other, as if in my worry and confusion I had landed in some parlor game.

Of course I could always have traveled to Berlin and rung Julia's doorbell—she'd had a couple of minor roles at the Gorki Theater in 1991, but after that only jobs on off-off stages. But a visit seemed an inappropriate, random act—a far too simple solution somehow. I was hoping, if you want to put it that way, for fate to beckon—ultimately for Copy 2000 to go bankrupt. It sounds ridiculous now, but at the time I regarded Ute and myself as two people running a company, business partners who also happened to live together.

Yes, I did hope that we would have to fold. All the same I couldn't bring myself to make mistakes on purpose. I wanted to lose out not to the competition but to circumstance. But evidently our responses were always the right ones.

In 1993—and by then there wasn't a soul who hadn't realized that there would be no economic miracle—we totally demoralized our rivals with our delivery service. But a year later, when we lost the bid for a copy shop at the Technical University, I figured that was the end. But then we started giving students and the unemployed a discount, kept our prices low—and what do you know, it wasn't us but Technical Copy that went belly up.

I wish nowadays I still had that same effortless flair for regarding difficulties as a mathematical problem, an equation to be solved. I knew that we had to grow, not because we had done any market research, but because B. consists of three zones, the old city, the new city, the Technical University. Besides which, three is a good number, the best, if you ask me. Once you have three copy shops in a city like B. you've sucked up the air for everyone else. Nevertheless I was surprised each time my calculations worked out.

After my separation from Julia, contacts with friends, in fact even my relationship with my brother—two years younger than I, an orthopedist—were almost totally broken off. Everyone suddenly had too much to do, or they moved away or simply faded into the woodwork, just as I had done. I didn't want to have to explain to anyone why I was living with Ute now instead of Julia.

Of course the pain subsided, I'd be lying if I were to claim anything different. But pain was still a constant companion, a shadow, sometimes a demon that could attack out of the blue. All it took was the fragrance of strawberries or for someone to speak Hungarian or just the sound of familiar music (I particularly had to beware of Brahms and Suzanne Vega). Often I had no idea what had lured the demon back. Summer months were the hardest, and strangely enough, autumn was my best time. But New Year's Eve was ghastly. Someone would say, "just two hours till midnight," and I would think: I've got two hours left to find Julia. And when it came down to counting minutes and finally seconds, I wanted to scream. What was I doing here in the middle of a meaningless life among strangers? Every year I was convinced that this would be my last New Year's Eve, I wouldn't be able to endure another. It took days, sometimes weeks, for me to calm down again. One year, it must have been in the midnineties, I lay wide awake on my back, beside Ute. Suddenly she asked me whether I still thought of Julia often. I barely had time to hide my face in my hands before I broke into sobs. It's a mystery to me how Ute put up with my theatrics.

Another woman? And how was that supposed to happen? It was difficult, impossible actually, for me to fall in love in B. An affair with one of the students who worked for us was not what I was after—which probably explains why there were never any sparks. And otherwise? I could hardly take out lonely hearts ads, although I constantly read them, looking for one that would be a match with Julia.

But then I did in fact hear about her.

Ute believed that when it came to her circle of friends I got along best with Claudia, whom she had known since kindergarten and grade school in Döbeln. Claudia worked as a bookkeeper for a theater in Berlin—it's not important which—and hung around, as Ute put it, with theater types. Ute must have said something to her about Julia. And so during a visit in Berlin in February 1997, I learned from Claudia that Julia had a child, a daughter. That upset me less than the fact that someone had spoken the name Julia in my presence and had called her (with a certain undertone—with Claudia there are almost always undertones) "your great love."

Until the call in October 1999 that I mentioned previously, it was never clear to me from the few things that Claudia told me about her if Julia was a kind of secret between Claudia and me or if Claudia likewise kept Ute up to date. What I'm trying to say is that hearing Claudia speak Julia's name had not been totally unexpected. But all the same it was like being awakened out of a profound stupor. "And your Julia too!"

So there I sat in my office chair, my right foot on the handle of the desk drawer, the tip of my shoe wedged in under the desktop, listening to Claudia chatter away while I gazed through the open Venetian blind out into the shop. Even when the place is bustling, at the beginning of the winter semester, for instance, our employees are still identifiable by their white T-shirts. To me the "Copy 2000" written across the breasts of female students always looked just a bit obscene. But it had been Ute's idea, and no one ever complained. The red lettering has faded on the shirts of those who have been with us for a while, but glows like a signal on new hires. I counted four of our T-shirts, recounted, but couldn't figure out who was missing. I tried to calm myself down. When Claudia mentioned Julia a second time, I couldn't take it any longer. "Julia?" I asked, reaching for the file of designs for our new logo, with the 2000 dropped from our name.

"Well finally!" Claudia groaned. "I thought maybe your ear had fallen asleep." This was followed by sentences that I could repeat here word for word, the last of which was: "She loves you more than ever, it's that simple."

And I—believed her.

Claudia asked how things were going with us. I told her about the problem of adjusting our software for the year 2000 and that we were considering changing the name of our company.

"Right," Claudia said. "You might just as well call yourselves 1900."

At the end she asked, "So you guys will be coming?"

"We'll be there," I said and felt myself reentering the present. All of a sudden there was a stab of pain in my toes, and I removed my foot from the desk drawer handle. I sat up straight and put the receiver back on its hook. I was glad—yes, I was proud—to have held out all those years, and limped out into the shop.

That evening I arrived home at almost the same time as Ute. She was in high spirits because just before closing an order had come in from the school district, and right afterward there was a call from the municipal office in Gotha, which wasn't even in our market area—meaning we had prospects of some substantial extra business.

I mentioned Claudia's invitation, and Ute said, "Why's she bothering you? She's got my number."

"Do you want to go?" Ute asked later.

"We're probably not going to come up with any better plan," I said. Ute had in fact tried to arrange something special, but Vienna was already fully booked, so was Prague.

"Then I'll follow through on it," Ute said, picking up the

phone and wandering into the living room with a half-peeled orange.

My mood over the next two and a half months could best be rendered as one of "Hail and Farewell." Unfortunately I can remember only the title of Goethe's poem and our German teacher's enthusiasm for it, but if called upon to describe how I felt, that was it exactly: hail and farewell.

I had just a little under a hundred thousand marks in my bank account, was driving a Mercedes SL that was almost paid for, and wasn't married.

I cleaned out my desk, dealt with the backed-up mail, worked through all outstanding accounts, including a few I turned over to a collection agency, and shredded piles of paper. Among letters from my father I found some contract bids that I had completely forgotten about.

I turned over all the odds and ends from the autumn of '89 to the city historical museum and tossed the receipt they gave me into a trash basket.

Two mornings I drove home to put things in order there too. Along with my passport and insurance policies I found a little red book published by Heyne: HOW TO SATISFY A WOMAN EVERY TIME . . . *and have her beg for more! "It Really Works!"* On the back was a picture of Naura Hayden—beautiful eyes, perfect teeth. "Vitamin C is ascorbic acid, and Nobel Prize winner Linus Pauling recommended a minimum daily dose of 3,000 mg. I take at least 15,000 mg per day, and have for many years," Naura Hayden writes on page 74. Ute would probably have been puzzled that I owned such a book, but in fact it had nothing whatever to do with her.

I shoved documents into transparent files, packed it all into a Lidl shopping bag, and headed for the door. Like someone who dared not leave any traces, I looked all around. What in this apartment belonged to me, actually? There was nothing I hung my heart on, nothing I'd miss, with the exception of a hand-made four-tiered Christmas pyramid from the town of Seiffen. It had been a present on my tenth birthday.

Ever since deciding on the Berlin option, as Ute called it, she had been eating nothing but veggies and fruit for supper—because Claudia had invited her to come along for a swim and the sauna. I reduced my supper to small sandwiches, gave up pastries, and when I ate out ordered steamed or boiled dishes with lots of rice. If the meal was fried herring, I removed the skin. Ute even went to a fitness studio for courses like "Fat Burners" and "Power Yoga" and took an adult education seminar in makeup—and ended up being talked into spending oodles of money for a mountain of cosmetics.

We gave away two big bags of pants, jackets, skirts, and sweaters to charity, and I finally tossed out all the old socks and underwear I had been in the habit of saving for polishing shoes. The weather was as fickle as in April. There was an early snow and a couple of gusty storms, and then it was back to springlike weather.

Those were crazy weeks. And meanwhile business was hopping as never before. It felt like life were casting off its waste products, losing fat, and building muscle instead.

The whole time Ute talked about Claudia and her new boy-friend Marco. Marco was in the film business and got along well with Dennis, Claudia's son. Ute likewise knew that Claudia couldn't sleep without earplugs, that she stuck big clumps of Ohropax in her ears every evening. And that Marco was a very jealous type but a good lover, and that he had a short, fat cock.

I asked Ute whether she gave out information of that sort

about me. "No," she said, but it sounded pretty flimsy. And not until I asked her a second time did she erupt with: "What do you take me for?"

Claudia thought of Marco as robust. Ute said she hoped I would never get that fat. Marco must have been making very good money at the time, otherwise they couldn't have afforded their two-story penthouse plus terrace with a view across to Friedrichshain Park.

On TV they were constantly talking about the countdown. And at one point I almost gave myself away. Someone mentioned a cute numerical landmark, it was 666, I think. "Just 666 hours left here," I said. But Ute didn't pick up on it.

It wasn't until Christmas that it dawned on me what sort of betrayal Claudia was planning. Or was she just toying with me? You're sure to object that someone like me shouldn't be pointing fingers. But I never made any false promises to Ute. She knew that she was not my great love. Whenever she tried to force me to express myself more clearly—sometimes it was about marriage, sometimes about another child—I would answer no every time.

Except for Julia there was nothing about Claudia that might have interested me. Yes, I found it difficult to put up with Claudia, who I assumed was anorexic. Not a word passed her lips that wasn't too loud or accompanied by a gesture that would somehow set her black shoulder-length hair swaying. Her gestures seemed in fact to demand words be put to them. Above all, when she laughed you sensed something vulgar about her—not to mention the way she ran through men.

"That's just how she is," Ute said, adding how she actually admired Claudia even though that wouldn't be a life for her.

" 'With candles five, a flame we've kept, now Father Christmas has overslept,'" Claudia recited the last time she called. And Christmas that year did in fact seem like a fifth Advent Sunday. I gave Ute a suitcase, and had bought one for myself as well. Our contribution to the festivities was to be the champagne, and I'd had the Aldi market reserve four cases for me.

On the morning of December 30 we both got on the scales. I had lost eleven pounds, and Ute a little under nine. It wasn't even light yet when we drove off. That made my farewell easier.

No, I hadn't given a thought to where and how I would find another job, and of course I realized what I was giving up. But that's exactly what it was supposed to be: a sacrifice! A huge sacrifice, do you understand? I wanted to just say yes to Julia, no matter what might happen.

On the way we ate slices of apple and bell pepper, and only just before Berlin did we stop for a lavish breakfast at a Mövenpick. We drove up the Avus autobahn, then exited at Kaiserdamm and headed eastward—the best route to make you feel like you've arrived in Berlin.

Claudia welcomed us in a loud yellow sleeveless dress—as if it were the height of summer. After the greetings she shot me a look that seemed to say: We're partners in crime. When she bent down to pull on her boots I saw that evidently the dress was the only thing touching her skin. Marco helped me load the Aldi champagne onto the elevator and stow it upstairs in an empty man-size refrigerator.

The rear courtyard apartment on Käthe-Niederkirchner Strasse where we were to spend the night was not even two hundred meters away. There was a break in the facades opposite, so that from the living room you could see across the vacant lot, where a bulldozer was at work, to Hufeland Strasse and a flower shop, above which Claudia and Dennis had once lived. While

Claudia—after first sort of shaking off her coat rather than slipping out of it—strode from room to room turning up the radiators, I watched as the bulldozer below our window suddenly lowered its jaws and set to work.

The apartment belonged to one of Marco's friends, who had fled to the Maldives. "Spotless," Ute said when Claudia showed her the kitchen and bath. The bedclothes—which I first thought were silk—turned the bedroom into an Oriental chamber.

Fritz had stayed behind with Dennis. Ute and Claudia wanted to head off right away for a spa near Zoo Station. I escorted them to the bus stop in front of a movie house, where, when Ute stopped to look at posters, Claudia took advantage of the opportunity to whisper to me: "Take a little walk in the park. You just might hit it lucky."

Then the bus pulled up, and Ute called out as if by way of farewell: "Those posters don't tell you one damn thing!"

Instead of crossing to the park I walked back up the street we'd just come down, and stopped at a drugstore where an effusively friendly man talked me into a powder for my sweaty feet, a product that dated back to GDR days. On the next corner was a Vietnamese grocery, where I bought coffee, milk, bananas, and rolls, and in the Italian delicatessen next door I found some pastry, red wine, and mortadella. Finally I purchased some roses that were so sinfully expensive that they earned me the admiration of the salesclerk. While she was wrapping up the bouquet, I watched through the store window as the bulldozer piled its small mountain higher still. As I walked along the street with my shopping bags and roses, I experienced a kind of happiness when it struck me that I might be taken for a local—just as if Julia were waiting for me in the apartment on Käthe-Niederkirchner Strasse.

No sooner was I in the apartment than I ran back downstairs. A minute later and I was in Friedrichshain Park. It looked deserted, the café was closed. A few dogs were being walked, a jogger passed by now and then. I walked up and down along the path beside the pond, then climbed the somewhat higher hill on the right, from where I could see Karl Marx Allee and Strausberger Platz, switched to the lower hill, which was hardly higher than the illumined row of windows in Marco's penthouse across the street. I suddenly realized I admired Marco and Claudia, felt a need to tell them that they were right to live such an extravagant life, that a person has to take risks. In that moment I wanted nothing so much as to drive a car with Berlin plates.

I descended the long flight of steps and walked back to our apartment, ate all the mortadella, and watched for a long while as the bulldozer built its own ramp to dig its way deeper, piece by piece.

That evening we invited Claudia and Marco to join us at a large Italian restaurant on a corner exactly halfway between our two apartments. The owner, Marco whispered, had had to flee Italy—he had once been a lefty activist. It annoyed me that Ute nodded as if she knew all about it. Claudia had pulled on a heavy sweater over her yellow dress and now divvied up the baguette of white bread with her long fingers. Without looking up, she gave her order, then started talking to us again, holding the menu over her shoulder until the waiter took it from her. We ate fish and drank carafe after carafe of wine. The owner strolled from table to table, kissed both of Claudia's hands, and, laying an arm around Marco's shoulder, smiled a frozen smile, as if posing for a photograph.

Ute suffered the whole evening from an almost pathological need to show her approval, used words like the "industry" and "normals," and wanted to know where Marco got his inspiration from and if he didn't need a creative pause now and then. Marco's favorite word was "leverage." Ufa had "leveraged" the series, he couldn't "leverage" the movie all by himself, they'd all have to "leverage" together. The restaurant, our apartment, the park were "class locations" and only yesterday he had "greenlighted" another contract or—as he explained to me with a little bow to emphasize how antiquated the phrases had become—given it his okay, had cleared the way for the film. Marco of course knew all about the bulldozer. "Construction begins in 1999, for credit purposes."

It was far too late when we picked up Fritz. Ute wanted to know what was the matter with me. I said her devotional pose, her stupid questions, had got on my nerves. Lying stretched out in bed, I was certain this would be our last night together.

When I got up to go to the toilet—several cherry bombs in the stairwell had wrenched me from a deep sleep—I could see the bulldozer, brightly illuminated as if onstage, its jaws raised and open wide. Although it was close to one o'clock, maybe a dozen people were scrambling around it, with several vehicles in the street flashing their blue lights.

It's with considerable reluctance that I report what happened next. I was watching the goings-on with the bulldozer and, recalling Marco's explanation, presumed it was some sort of police raid, when I noticed something moving in the only window with lights still on, kitty-corner across the street—a head was bobbing up and down in a regular motion. I didn't want to believe it, but I knew right away what was going on. I fetched my glasses from our bedroom, where Ute was snoring lightly and the odor of fiber carpeting hung in the air. All I could see now was the man, half lying, half propped on an elbow, not that unlike the position of Michelangelo's Adam. In the window adjacent, the silhouette of a naked woman appeared, but then took a few steps and vanished from my view. The man followed her, they met in the middle of the room, they embraced. Then they walked side by side toward the hallway, so that against the backlighting I could now see what slender legs—just in general what a beautiful body—the woman had. I missed the moment when they returned to the lit room, because I decided to likewise make my move to be closer to them. My hand was already on the door handle when I remembered that Fritz was asleep in there.

Back at my window, I saw the woman sitting on top of the man now; with one hand she brushed her long hair from her face and, leaning back slightly, braced herself with the other on his thigh. I followed her motion as he held her by the waist with both hands.

Her breasts appeared exaggeratedly large, like a *Playboy* caricature. I had to kneel down to see her face, which otherwise was hidden behind the window's sash bars.

You may find it odd, but it was not until I realized this was not some video I was watching, that I felt a twinge of the heart. This was not a staged scene. What was happening over there was reality! Plus there was my own sense of humiliation at not being able to tear myself away from it.

After I had pleasured myself, I washed, returned to bed—but a few minutes later was standing at the window again. Now I could see her back, her long hair falling down it. She was bending back and forth, and those hands were still clasped around her waist. Deciding not to put myself through this, I began to inspect the video cassettes, row upon row. The titles, almost all in German, meant nothing to me. When I looked across again for the first time to check if they were still "doing it"—a phrase I couldn't get out of my mind now—she was facing him again, but leaning forward with his hands on her breasts. I drank a glass of water in the kitchen and forced myself to go on sitting there at the table.

You can't imagine how relieved I was when there was only one small light left on across the way. Although I couldn't make anything out, I went on staring at the light until it was finally turned off.

The to-do around the bulldozer had quieted down, although the number of people had not noticeably diminished. Strangely drained of energy, I lay down in bed. But sleep was out of the question.

The whole circus began a little before seven—a half hour earlier and I would have welcomed it—just as I was finally dozing off. The doorbell rang several times, then came a knock at our apartment door and somebody shouting. Marco had said not to pay any attention to the telephone, but if the doorbell rang it might be a package.

When Ute returned to the bedroom, she asked me to please come with her—and it sounded as if she had found traces of my nocturnal adventures.

We were to vacate the place by 8:30—the bulldozer had uncovered a bomb in the courtyard, a five-hundred-pounder, as we would soon learn. Although I was hardly of a mind to get up, this news filled me with a childlike glee. While I drank my coffee, Fritz and I tried to persuade Ute to stay in the apartment, the worst that could happen here would be a couple of broken windowpanes. "You guys talk big," she said, but we had trouble persuading her not to pack our bags.

One window was tipped open in the apartment from the

night before. Either those two were already on their way or weren't about to leave their bed. Out on the street lots of people were milling around with suitcases and blankets, as if a film about refugees was being shot. A radio reporter asked Ute how she'd be celebrating New Year's Eve. A woman emerged from the building directly across the street with a tray, a thermos, and cups and served coffee to the reporter and two firefighters. In early May, she said, this street was a sea of pink blossoms. We'd have to come back in May sometime.

The front door to Marco's building was ajar. We took the elevator up, rang the bell, and I thought I could hear footsteps in the apartment.

The neighbor's door opened. An older man with a bag of garbage in each hand stepped out. Could he be of any help? Ute told him about the bomb, and that we were here much too early. At first I didn't even notice the woman who appeared behind him in the dark entryway. She was standing at the threshold now. While her husband repeated Ute's story, she observed us from deep-set eyes. Her mouth and nose were almost abnormally delicate, a good match for the gesture with which she now invited us in. No need to be bashful, the man said, and then asked if we lived in B. proper—he'd seen our license plates. He had studied in B. for a year, shortly after the war. They and their apartment gave off the odor of underclothes that have lain in the drawer too long, of a cleanliness that does without deodorant or perfume.

The man winced at the sound of creaking floorboards behind Marco's door, but then went thumping down the stairs with the élan of a good skier plunging down a steep slope. His wife had already vanished into the darkness of their entryway as the locks on Marco's door began clicking.

Marco looked dreadful, bloated, with reddened eyes and a grubby bathrobe gaping enough to reveal a strip of belly. He asked us in. We apologized and, under the pretext of fetching breakfast rolls, set out again at once. A stroll in the park might have been fairly pleasant had the place not seemed so bleak somehow. Ute and Fritz trotted reluctantly behind me up the big hill. We were the only strollers among the joggers and dog walkers. Ute remarked that our encounter with Claudia and Marco's neighbors had made her realize that there were hardly any older people in the neighborhood.

We bought our rolls at the Vietnamese grocery. I was instinctively keeping an eye out for the woman from last night. I wanted to see her up close and hear her voice.

Over breakfast Marco said there were considerably more bombs in the sand around here than hagstones on a beach. He explained for us the system behind the bombing of Berlin. It was probably purely accidental that early on bombs landed in neighborhoods that had been the first to declare themselves "free of Jews." Unfortunately accidental, he added. Here in Prenzlauerberg there had been hardly any bombing. I knew nothing about all that, had never heard his theory either, and hoped that Ute wouldn't start in again with the story about her grandparents and Dresden.

Claudia tried hard to keep Fritz entertained while he waited for Dennis to finally get up. Ute said that for some reason she found the bomb depressing, which was followed by much too long a silence around the breakfast table.

I sensed that we were both just in the way at this point, and even assumed I knew what Claudia would most likely call us— "wet blankets."

Marco asked about my work. I told him about our discounts

and the kinds of binders we provided and how important service contracts were for us, which was another way of adding to our coffers. "That's always a good thing," Marco said. Claudia said that if our shop was in Berlin we'd definitely be making a small fortune. "Marco always has so much paper to push, right?" Marco nodded with a full mouth. Then Claudia told about how upscale things had become at Ufa, and that in the passageways linking sets there was enough free fruit and coffee to keep a modest eater like herself well nourished. She followed this with: "They fight tooth and nail to get Marco onboard."

I asked who all they had invited. Claudia managed to insert Julia's name so offhandedly among the others that I felt no need to react.

Ute said we had nothing planned and could lend a hand anytime today. There was the constant racket of fireworks outside, and at one point a boom so loud that Ute exclaimed: "The bomb!"

By the time we took off without Fritz around one o'clock, the whole bomb hoopla was over. No one barred us from returning to our apartment. I felt privileged to have a key to a Berlin apartment.

"We're keeping the roses," Ute said, put on some music, and wriggled out of her sweater and pants. She moved through these strange rooms with a sense of belonging that suddenly made me feel like her guest, as if in fact I were visiting a strange woman. Did I like her new bra, her new lingerie, Ute asked—it was really very comfortable.

She left the bathroom door open. I followed her. She smiled at me in the mirror and closed her eyes at the first touch. As I've said, when it comes to sex we were made for each other.

Ute held on to the windowsill, so that looking over her head

I could see into the apartment from last night and, just by shifting a little to the left, the construction site. The bulldozer was now at the edge of the lot. The red-and-white barrier ribbon ran, oddly enough, right through the cab.

Later as we lay under the Oriental blanket, Ute kept running her fingers through my hair. I had already seen sleep's first images when she said, "I've slept with Claudia."

"You and Claudia have . . ."

"Yes," Ute said. "Once and never again." I could feel her warm breath on my neck, the tip of her nose was cold.

"When?" I asked.

"Before you came along."

I sat up in bed.

"The really stupid part," she said, "is that I never told you before."

For a moment I hoped that her disclosure might change things between us. I wondered if I ought to take advantage of the opportunity, to jump up and shout: "Why did you do that? It's over!"

"And why," I asked, "are you confessing now?"

"Let's leave it behind in this century. It's over and done with, we won't mention it ever again, okay?"

I'd have loved to ask lots of questions—how it came about, what Claudia had done, what her touch had felt like and so on.

I asked her whether Claudia really had nipples as big as I thought I'd seen yesterday in that low-cut dress.

"All you had to do was join us in the sauna," Ute said. That settled that, as far as she was concerned.

We slept way too long, and it wasn't until almost eight o'clock that we set out again. At first I thought the haze was smoke from fireworks, but it was genuine fog—you could barely see anything of Friedrichshain Park—weighing down on the city with a real sense of doomsday.

Claudia looked as if she had had no time to change. She was wearing a thin, very delicately knitted, almost fuzzy sweater that was not exactly opaque, plus an everyday knee-length skirt. In contrast Ute had put her hair up and looked downright sophisticated in her long skirt and plunging neckline. She'd find another man quick enough.

When she held a cup of coffee under my nose, I realized that Claudia had been keeping an eye on me the whole time. "So you'll have stopped yawning by the time Julia arrives," she whispered.

Everybody was waiting for the arrival of an actor whose name meant nothing to me—but I'd recognize him, Marco remarked, the moment I saw him, from television.

Claudia kept introducing me as the fellow who had been driven out of his apartment by a bomb that morning. In response to which I then had to tell the story in detail, and Marco, dressed in a ruffled white shirt and black suit, would then usually repeat his comparison with hagstones on the beach. Claudia gave a loud laugh, kissed Marco, and said, there was a whole "treatment" in that one image.

Was it the coffee or the alcohol or simply the fact that at any moment Julia would be standing at the apartment door with its three locks—at any rate, my palms were sweatier than they had been in ages.

I washed my face and hands, and as I was looking for a guest towel I heard the doorbell. I saw myself smiling in the mirror and stepped out into the hallway. There in front of me was the woman from last night. No doubt of it. Her hair was now in a braid that hung down to her breast on one side.

My greeting was perhaps a little too cheery. "Do we know each other?" she asked.

"Frank Reichert," Claudia said, "let me introduce Sabine, my dearest colleague, and her husband, Matthias." I almost burst into laughter. Handsome as her husband was with his shaved head, he was not the fellow from last night. Sabine actually blushed when I asked if they didn't live in this neighborhood too. "No, in Hellersdorf." It was a pleasant voice. Her neck sported a red spot just below her right ear, only half hidden by her turtleneck sweater.

"Be careful where your eyes wander," Claudia hissed, and followed the two into the living room. I found a spot to stand where, in the course of the choreography of greetings, Sabine would have to pass by me again. Ute had been leaning in a bay window the whole time, talking with Renate, a matronly friend of Claudia's whom we had met previously.

When Sabine was right in front of me again, I would have loved to whisper some double entendre in her ear. I didn't recognize myself now. I was even itching to pick a fight with her husband, although he was clearly bigger and in better shape than I.

"Can it be," I heard myself saying, "that I saw you around here yesterday?"

"Ah, so that's why you're acting this way!" I could have sworn that Sabine sounded disappointed. "We were in the Ore Mountains yesterday," she said softly. "And where was it that you saw me?"

At that same moment Claudia thrust her arm under mine—sorry, but she had to kidnap me. Once in the hallway she closed the door behind us, and pointed in the direction of the kitchen.

"There," she said and, crossing her arms, waited for me to follow instructions.

I was very calm as I walked toward the kitchen door and pushed it open.

"There you are," Julia said with a smile, and got to her feet.

I had never pictured to myself how those ten years might have changed her, but I was truly startled. Nothing, nothing had changed at all. There before me stood the very same Julia who had deserted me ten years before.

We hugged, at first tentatively, then more tightly. She pressed against me, I could sense her flushed body.

"Did you run all the way here?" I asked.

"Well, I did hurry," Julia said. We kissed, she wove her arms around my neck. "Here, of all places," she whispered.

"Better here than not all," I said. Everything was exactly the way I had dreamed it for ten long years.

I no longer know how we managed to sit down at the table. I held her hands in mine, and Julia explained that she had arrived so late because she had had to take her daughter, Alina, to Mecklenburg.

"And so what are you up to?" she asked, then laughed and gazed off to one side as if embarrassed by her own question.

"Run a copy service," I said. "And you?"

"Another kind of copy service, but it doesn't pay as well."

Whenever our eyes met, we had to smile. I kissed her hands.

The curious thing was that although I had thought of Julia every day, I had never pictured the shape of her fingertips, the slightly reddened skin at the base of her nails, or the tiny scar on her left thumb.

"You can't go on kissing and cuddling here like this!" Claudia called from the doorway. "So come on, let's go. People are going to notice."

We obediently stood up, I followed Julia and was almost over the threshold when Claudia's arm blocked my path. "Always keep a proper distance," she said, "and your head on your shoulders."

"I need to be excused," I said like a third-grader, pointing in the direction of the bathroom.

"Oh, really?" Claudia didn't budge. She looked at the floor. When she raised her head again I expected to be chastised or given some new instructions. Claudia, however, let her arm fall.

"Thanks," I said and moved past her.

Once in the bathroom I held my hands under lukewarm water and gazed in the mirror. There was a knock, and Claudia slipped through the door. She locked it, raised her skirt, and sat down on the toilet. I was just about to ask which was the guest towel as her stream hit the water.

"Everything okay?" she asked, plucking paper from the roll, dabbing herself dry, and letting her skirt fall as she stood up.

"Everything's fine," I said, and dried my hands on a long white towel.

At first I thought Claudia wanted to leave, and stepped aside. But now she laid her arms around my neck.

"Thank you," I said. I was truly grateful to Claudia, and so I hugged her too—and could feel how her back, her shoulders, her whole body trembled under my touch. I felt like a bear. I've never embraced a woman that delicate. Did she nestle against me, or did I pull her closer? I felt her lips at my neck, I could hear her breathing, I heard my name. In my numbed state I heard sounds so intimate, so plaintive and lustful, that I lost control—or maybe I should say my bearings. My hands hitched her skirt up, groped at her butt, I thrust them between her legs. We kissed. Claudia was so light, so incredibly light.

Before I could even get my trouser button open, it had happened—Claudia bit into my shoulder, grabbed my hand, went rigid. It may sound a little eerie, but I could swear she stopped breathing. I didn't dare make the slightest motion until Claudia awoke again and, as if wary of some injury, pushed my hand down and stepped back.

"Your turn will come later," Claudia whispered, kissed me on the mouth, tugged at her sweater, adjusted her skirt, cast a glance with raised eyebrows at her reflection in the mirror, and unlocked the door.

I sat down on the toilet or, better, sank onto the lid and stared at the diamond pattern in the tiles at my feet. Claudia's intrusion—or attack—hadn't lasted five minutes. I could still feel her body against my chest, fuzz balls from her sweater were stuck to my left hand. I could probably have gone on sitting there like that if a man hadn't burst in, but then beat such a hasty retreat that all I saw of him was a gray suit and a burgundy tie.

I washed my hands and face again, inspected the damp spot Claudia's lips had left on my jacket, and then also discovered the little pile of folded towels in a wall inset and the basket for used ones below it. Determined to step firmly with head held high, I left the bathroom.

Ute was still carrying on a conversation with Renate. Claudia was sitting on the couch next to Julia and waved me over. "She looks totally different now," Julia said, while I examined a photograph of Alina. "Where," I asked, "did she get that hair from?"

"Obviously not from me!" Julia plucked the picture from my

fingers and stored it in her wallet. I had to be careful, I no longer had myself under control. Claudia said that now that train service had been discontinued, it took almost a whole day to get to the village where Julia's mother lived. I asked Julia if she had a car and if her parents had gotten divorced.

"My father died a year and a half ago," Julia said, and smiled at me.

When Marco came around pouring red wine, I held an orphaned glass out to him and then drank it down at once.

Suddenly there was Fritz. He wedged himself in between me and the arm of the sofa.

"He's older than Alina," Julia said.

"By two years at the most," I said. Julia laid a hand on my knee but then immediately took it away again.

Marco sat down across from us and talked and talked. Since he told it several times, the only story I remember is the one about the whiskey: It was in the garden of the villa that belonged to the same actor we all were waiting for. They were lying in lounge chairs drinking whiskey. "The carton it came in was beside my chaise," Marco explained. "When I tried to put the bottle back, it didn't fit, it stuck up a little. I tried three or four times, so I forced it down in, hard." Marco made a motion as if screwing something into the floor. "When I take the whiskey out again the next evening, there's something sticking to the bottle." Marco pretended he had a bottle in his hands. He felt the bottom of the bottle with his fingertips and cried in triumph, "A squashed toad!" Claudia, who had listened the whole time on the edge of her seat, burst into a snort of laughter.

People were still laughing as a man in a gray suit sat down on the coffee table, raised his glass, and called out to Marco: "Here's to your not being let go!" I took it for a joke, but Marco turned to stone and Claudia set her glass down. This did not prevent the tall guy from finishing off his wine in several quick swallows. His shirt collar stuck out from under his jacket, which drew your eyes to his pointy, bobbing Adam's apple. Then, as if making a crucial move in a game of chess, he put his glass down among ours. With a smack of his lips he stood up and left the room.

Claudia's friend Sabine, who probably wasn't the woman from the night before after all, said she hadn't been able to arrange for a taxi before three o'clock. She said that on a night like this money was no issue, but that she herself wouldn't work tonight, not for all the world, because nothing could compare to a change of millennia. Julia asked what she would be paying the cabbie tonight, twice or three times the usual?

Somehow everything seemed to go off track. Later on Julia started making one weird remark after the other. It used to be, she declared, that we at least got something of an education in comparison with schools nowadays. At one point she mentioned her father, too, and it sounded as if financial difficulties had put him in his grave. Marco said that she should be glad that she could finally live in freedom, and Claudia's colleague Sabine added that she wouldn't give up her freedom for anything now.

"Which freedom do you mean?" Julia asked, which brought Marco to his feet. Shaking his head, he made for the buffet.

It wasn't till Ute was standing in front of me that I realized Fritz had fallen asleep under my arm. Ute extended a hand to Julia. Since this required a slight bend of the knees, it looked as if she were curtsying to greet her. Claudia introduced her two good friends to each other.

There wasn't time now to take Fritz back to our place. So I

left him on the couch and helped Marco open the champagne. One after another the guests found their way up the narrow spiral staircase to the penthouse, where the door to the terrace stood open.

At midnight I toasted with Ute, I toasted with Julia. I toasted with Claudia, I toasted with last night's doppelgänger and her husband, I even wished the tall guy in the gray suit a "Happy New Year!" Ute and I went back downstairs to wake up Fritz so he could watch the fireworks, or at least what could be seen of them in the haze.

After that I had to assist Marco and Dennis. Although we kept firing off several rockets at once, it soon got too cold or too boring for our audience out on the terrace. I wanted to go downstairs as well, where people were dancing now. Ute took Fritz back to our place.

Julia was dancing alone. Again and again our eyes met. When she left the room—Julia still had that same unique walk she'd always had—I took it as an invitation. She was waiting just outside the kitchen for me. I took her by the hand and opened a door at the end of the hallway—the master bedroom. It was cold and smelled, to put it politely, unaired. We embraced, we kissed, I stroked the back of her neck.

My life was suddenly like an equation that's easily solved. What I was doing now seemed to be automatically derived from what I had always dreamed, as if I no longer had any need of my will, or my courage. I was caught up in the feeling of having come to the end, having achieved finality—and all was well.

"I didn't know," Julia whispered, "that you were married."

"I'm not married," I said and noticed the narrow band of light coming from the door and falling across the unmade bed and nightstand with two lumps of Ohropax on it.

"It's the same thing, you live together."

We held each other tight, two actors at a rehearsal, waiting for the director's instructions. I even attempted to slide my hand inside Julia's blouse, but quickly gave up.

"I'm leaving now," Julia said. We kissed one more time and returned to the living room together.

It took a while for Julia to say her good-byes. Claudia saw her to the door.

When after a good while Ute had not yet returned, I was pretty sure she had decided to stay with Fritz.

Claudia asked me to dance. It didn't take me long to get into the swing of things.

I couldn't remember the last time I had danced.

Sabine, Claudia's favorite colleague, didn't budge from my side. Surprisingly, she danced in a lumbering sort of way, just kept repeating the same moves, no matter what the music. Claudia on the other hand was a wonderful dancer, she must have taken lessons. Marco was fairly drunk. He bad-mouthed the actor who had never showed, and soon vanished into the bedroom.

Once she started to dance Claudia evidently no longer saw herself as a hostess. She stopped seeing people to the door and helping them find their coats.

Each time a guest left, we nodded to each other as if counting the ones that remained.

By about four thirty the tall guy with the gray suit and pointy Adam's apple was the only one left. He had moved in close to us as we danced, swinging his burgundy tie above his head like a lasso. Now he was watching us from an armchair— the tie was dangling from his pocket. It wasn't hard to see what Claudia and I had on our minds.

Claudia then said the party was over, and turned off the music. I helped her gather up glasses. The tall man was holding his empty glass with both hands and grinning to himself. Suddenly he said, "I still get a peek." We could barely make it out, he was slurring so heavily.

"You've had your peeks," Claudia said.

He checked her over from head to toe, rocking his head and thrusting out his lower lip in approval.

"Clear out!" she said.

"Still wanna peek," he muttered.

We laid into him—which is to say, by now Claudia was so angry that I hardly got a word in edgewise.

"I wanna fuck," he blurted out. "And it's you I wanna—"

The tip of Claudia's shoe met his shin. He fell silent, bent forward, rubbed his leg, raised his head, and grinned. "Ouch, ouch," he said. "Bad girl."

Claudia gave another kick, but as if expecting it, he grabbed her foot. Claudia stumbled, he took hold of her other ankle, jumped up, and yanked her upside down as if trying to hang her by her feet.

I'll never forget the look of that mug, the ogling, the grin. It was the most disgusting thing I've ever seen.

I punched him in the face, then landed one to his belly—all of it stuff I've only seen in the movies. We fell onto the sofa, Claudia's legs between us. He wouldn't let go of her. We slid to the floor. Was it panic, was it rage—I didn't know how to go at his neck and head. I couldn't start strangling him or knocking his teeth out or smashing his nose. So that it was actually a relief when he finally let go of Claudia's ankles and we began to wrestle. Normally, if he hadn't be so sloshed, I would have been no match for him. Claudia jumped around behind us and kicked him in the ribs, again and again, and with each kick he bellowed like an ox. Then Marco showed up.

The three of us expedited the tall guy out, stuffed him into the elevator, tossing his coat in with him, and pressed the button for the ground floor. Marco never even struck him, all he had to do was just haul back with his massive balled fist. Curses boomed from the descending elevator car. The neighbor's door closed with a click.

Marco thanked me repeatedly. He looked more bloated than he had early that morning. He kept reaching under his pajama top to scratch himself.

We each drank half a glass of whiskey, and Marco did his routine again of how he had pressed the bottle into its carton.

Then the three of us waited for the elevator. Claudia gave me a good-bye peck on the cheek. Marco rode down with me and never stopped scratching for even a moment. He walked outside and then waved me out, as if I were in a hiding place some distance away. "The coast is clear," he said. "Take care!"

I didn't have a key and had to ring the doorbell. The front door immediately buzzed open. Ute came down the stairs to meet me. She was wearing a dress I'd never seen before. She looked as if she were going out somewhere. Candles had been lit in the living room, on the table were my roses, and two champagne glasses.

"I love you," I said, and at that moment it felt like a greeting, the greeting of a man returning home. Ute made a face. She probably thought I was drunk. She had tried, she said, to call Claudia, but we had all apparently been too busy. Fritz had thrown up a couple of times, which was why she had stayed with him.

It wasn't until I picked up the champagne glass that I realized my right hand hurt. It was swollen. Out of solidarity, Ute toasted with her left hand as well. She found some ice cubes in the fridge, and while I told her about the tall guy, she folded them into a dish towel that she wrapped around my hand.

In bed Ute said, "My hero." She really meant it.

I was awakened by her caresses. She begged me not to be angry, she just ached for me so much. Still half asleep I raised my head. All the buildings outside the window were still there and still looked as they had in the previous millennium, a state of affairs I found all the more satisfactory because I believed I had played a certain role in that miracle.

"I love you," I said, caressing her with the fingertips of my injured hand. Ute beamed like a child. By late afternoon we were on our way back to B.

In early March, Claudia made good on her promise in Erfurt, where she was attending a training course. We met in her hotel room during the noon break. Whenever an opportunity presents itself, we make good use of it. One time I traveled all the way to Warnemünde, only to turn around an hour later and race back home. Why do I do it? Why not? It's beautiful, and it has nothing to do with Ute. It's a game. I don't mean the role-play scenes that Claudia comes up with, I mean the other life I live in those hours when I'm with her. Why should I forgo that happiness, the moments in which a moody, snippy, anorexic, and slightly vulgar female is transformed into a woman full of such intense tenderness and passion that I can imagine I'm the only man who knows her?

And at the same time, I'm happy with Ute. January 1, 2000, was the beginning of my love for her. We got married in 2001, and if things had turned out as we'd hoped, we would have had a second child.

New Year's Eve Confusions

Although Fritz will be turning sixteen in a few days, I don't get the feeling he wants to move out or that he's even rebelling. Just the opposite, we get along better and better with each passing year. And who knows, maybe someday he'll take over the business. He already pitches in when we're short on help, and doesn't even mention money. My love for him and Ute hasn't just reconciled me with my life, it has in fact made life as a whole precious and sweet for the first time.

But that indeed is my problem. I no longer have to worry about New Year's Eve. I have other things to worry about.

In my euphoria of early 2000, I bought one hundred thousand D-marks' worth of stocks. You know what happened then. All the same, every few days some flunky calls trying to soft-sell me into investing money with him. Normally I say: Sure, happy to, I've got three hundred euros in loose change that I can risk. But sometimes I simply lose it. I can show you the spot where my cell phone crashed against the wall like Luther's inkwell up on the Wartburg.

I'd be quite content if I could recover just half of my old effortless flair, that knack for good luck that you need in business. Fear is not a good consultant. Given all my problems it's a miracle I've been able to keep the same weight I had on that remarkable New Year's Eve.

There's nothing more to say. That's my story. We've celebrated the New Year in Berlin three times now. Because Marco wanted it that way, Julia wasn't invited back, or the tall troublemaker, of course. Ufa fired both him and Marco on the same day. Ever since Claudia separated from Marco and Dennis went off to study law at a Dutch university in Leiden—he's interested in outer-space jurisprudence, or so he says—she visits us often. Because we're the ones who throw the big parties now. I need them to get my mind on other things, to forget the business for at least a weekend. By now we really know how to have a good time. We don't wait around for guests to leave, and we certainly don't send anyone packing. But when it's all over and it's just us three, we dance into the dawn.

A Night at Boris's

I need to preface my account of that evening, that night, by saying that Boris, who always spoke of himself as my oldest friend, is no longer alive. I don't mention this here because Boris is dead. I would think of him no differently were he still alive, nor do I have to reproach myself for not having told him how much that evening, that night, means to me—quite apart from our confusion and embarrassment when we all finally went home.

It was truly the most extraordinary party I've ever been to, even if I did play only a marginal role.

"You can always get new stuff, except for an old friend," Boris often said. And Susanne said: "Better no friends than one like him." In her opinion Boris and I were friends purely out of habit.

What's more, Boris never used to be my friend at all. He was one year ahead of me in school, and our morning route led us there from opposite directions. Our paths crossed during our army stint, we even spent a couple of leaves together—and immediately lost sight of each other upon discharge. It wasn't until 1994, when Susanne and I moved in together in Berlin, that I saw Boris again. He was living on the fourth floor of the run-down building directly opposite ours on Esmarch Strasse. We had morning sun, his balcony—its balustrade, both summer and winter, topped by a tall, folded-up laundry rack—would catch a bit of evening sun from March or April on.

We ran into each other shortly after Christmas as we stood in line at the Extra supermarket waiting to use what turned out to be a defective bottle-return machine. Boris's response was, or so I thought, a bit over-the-top, but he invited me to dinner—he'd cook. It was an odd situation when afterward we kept bumping into each other among the rows of shelving, not quite knowing what to say and mutely mustering each other's shopping carts. At the time I thought that the bottle-return machine might well have contributed to his reaction too, since it smells just like our old neighborhood junk shop used to.

Once I had disclosed to Boris that we could see directly into his window, I sometimes saw him peering from his balcony over at us. If he spotted us, or thought he had—in winter the blinds move in the warm air coming from the radiators—he would start waving and calling across until I opened the window. Boris even claimed he and I had gone to the same kindergarten, Käthe Kollwitz kindergarten in Dresden-Klotzsche.

In flight before a plethora of construction sites and baseball caps, Susanne and I moved to the west side of the city in 1997. We made regular appearances, however, at Boris's birthday parties. He would call months ahead and ask us to leave that special evening open for him.

There were, of course, a few things that didn't speak in Boris's favor. Injunctions such as: "Look me in the eye when we toast, or you'll have seven years of bad sex!" or stupid clichés

("What I don't know can't hurt me") earned Boris failing grades with Susanne. But above all it was her mistrust of a man who always has a new woman on his arm. I said that was a reason to be grateful to Boris, otherwise we'd never know that sort of life doesn't make you any happier. But Susanne doesn't see anything funny in things like that.

In the middle of May last year, three weeks before his forty-fourth birthday, Boris died of a stroke while swimming in Schwielow Lake. In the early nineties he had become a badminton instructor ("Shuttlecock coach," Susanne called it) and "business was good." He had leased an old glider hangar in Pankow, formerly East Berlin, which he later bought, and he knew all sorts of people. You seldom met the same person twice at his place. This was also true of his girlfriends, all of them terribly young and thin. He visited us only once or twice. The thing was, he loved to cook.

The last time we visited Boris was not for a birthday party but for what he called his "housewarming."

Sacrificing two evenings for him inside of three months—it was now early September—was way too much for Susanne. Even though it was she who accepted the invitation on the phone—according to her, she'd had no choice. Boris had sounded so proud of his apartment that she couldn't bring herself to do it. . . . The sole topic at his birthday party had been his new condo. He sent me an e-mail asking for my expert opinion of the girl who would be at his side—the judgments of an old friend counted a lot for him. He had often asked me for my "expert opinion," so often that I read right past the word "girl," instead of taking it as a warning or, at the least, an attempt to set the tone.

Boris had requested wine from the Saale-Unstrut region as a

housewarming gift, and so Susanne and I carried one case each of Müller-Thurgau and Sylvaner up four flights of stairs. The elevator goes directly to the penthouse, which is now home to the people who used to own the entire building.

As Boris came down a few steps to greet us, his legs looked longer than usual and his silly pointy shoes much too big for the stairs.

Two other couples had already arrived. They were still holding packages and bouquets, plus wadded-up wrapping paper. Needless to say, we didn't know them.

Boris told us to put the stuff on the coffee table and strode on ahead through the room, his heels rapping against the hardwood floor.

Except for a few new pieces of furniture—we made a point of admiring a long dining table and two large sand-colored "four-seaters"—the rooms were empty, in some even the baseboards were missing. Boris showed us what were to be his office and a guest room, and emphasized the southern exposure. The bath, kitchen, and bedroom—with boxes from the move still piled high—looked out onto the rear courtyard.

Boris railed at the ambulances that for no earthly reason, but with sirens howling just that much louder, raced up and down Greifswalder Strasse, but Marienburger Strasse was relatively quiet. Susanne had especially liked the big bathroom with its black-and-white tile floor. She said in her next life she'd play shuttlecock too—that way at least she'd make a go of things.

"It's called badminton, bad-min-ton!" Boris barked and led the way back. Suddenly there she stood right before us, on the broad threshold between the entryway and the living room, her shoulders hunched forward, a stack of large white plates in her hands.

"This is Elvira," Boris said, laying an arm around the girl's shoulders. Elvira cast us all a fleeting glance, the corners of her mouth twitched. Susanne came to her assistance and carried almost the entire stack of plates to the table. Of all the women that Boris had introduced us to over the years, Elvira was the most diaphanous and the youngest.

As if trying to explain the dark rings under her eyes—he evidently noticed our uneasiness—he said that Elvira had spent the night on the train. Her mother had in fact recently moved south, to the Allgäu region. Elvira shook hands all around and vanished again into the kitchen without our having heard her utter one word.

As Boris filled our glasses, I was afraid Susanne would make some remark within his earshot about the age difference. But she just accepted her glass with a smile and nodded graciously when Boris excused himself to follow Elvira into the kitchen.

As always at the beginning of evenings at Boris's we were now left to ourselves, which I found rather strenuous. With each successive year I had less and less interest in getting to know total strangers I would never see again.

The black-haired couple were Lore and Fred—she was a carpenter, he a structural design engineer with the plodding gait of a farmer. Pavel made his living giving piano lessons at the music school in Spandau and played keyboard with a band called the Wonderers, or something like that. The only reason Pavel played badminton was to please his redheaded girlfriend Ines, whom Boris had introduced to us as a colleague of mine—her latest plan being to actually write a book.

Lore and Fred had done work for Boris. Lore had built the black shelving for his CDs, five rows high and running the full length of the room. Fred had done the calculations for the extra steel beams needed to bear the weight of his library—Boris collected lexica of every sort, most of them foreign-language editions. In fact he read almost nothing but lexica and allegedly even took a few volumes with him on vacation.

Fred said he had never met such an interesting and multifaceted person as Boris. And Lore found his collection of CDs overwhelming—she hoped to borrow the whole lot over time. It made her very happy to think how at some point she could have much the same collection at her disposal—even though the CDs she burned wouldn't look as fancy as Boris's originals.

Shortly before dinner an ex-colleague of Boris's named Charlotte—we'd met her at the birthday party in June—appeared. She was now teaching courses at Jopp, a women's fitness studio. She was wearing the same lilac dress as before, and she'd also done her hair the same way—a ponytail that emphasized the high vault of her forehead.

Pavel, to whom Susanne took a liking—she later said his face was so striking it was as if he had pondered every note he ever played—busied himself inspecting CDs, but finished the task fairly quickly. He asked us how we knew Boris and Elvira. Instead of answering his question Susanne divulged that a few weeks earlier Boris had introduced us to a different woman—a remark to which no one had a follow-up. Although Charlotte, who was standing at the window smoking, did set her bracelets clinking softly and gave a telling nod. A moment later Boris entered and pretended not to notice our silence. Balancing a large tray at his belly, he followed Elvira, who filled plates with food and deposited one at each setting. Once they had circled the table, she started to head back with him to the kitchen. "Stay put," Boris said somewhat angrily. "I can manage."

I had sensed something wasn't right between the two of

them. But it wasn't easy to watch Elvira wince before turning around with head held high and crying, "Dinner is served!" Most of the time I'm far too busy imagining what Susanne is thinking and how she will react. This time, however, I likewise found the situation beyond the pale. What was this child doing here with us? What was she doing at his side?

Oddly enough there were place cards—he got the idea, Boris claimed, after discovering Elvira's calligraphic skills. Even Boris could barely conceal his own discomfort. For him, the perfect host, it was a major glitch to have opened only one bottle of red wine. As he set to work on the second, the cork broke, and he cursed much too loudly. Pavel took over the job, and Lore remarked that two months ago no one would have believed we'd ever be sitting here together like this so soon. In early July, Fred added, they had still been balancing their way on his beams. Pavel inserted a CD—tango music, but barely audible.

I sat directly across from Elvira, the perfect spot for observation, so to speak. She was wearing lipstick plus a little eye shadow. A narrow stripe of untanned skin was noticeable at the top of each arm.

In Boris's presence you quickly get the sense that you're witty and articulate, because he takes almost every remark as his cue for a story or at least replies with a burst of laughter that encourages you to continue.

That evening he evidently needed some encouragement himself, otherwise he would not have thanked Pavel so profusely for the music and uncorking the bottle of wine. Several times he asked, "Well, enjoying your food?" although everyone had already praised his cooking.

It was mainly Pavel's questions that gradually helped Boris hit his stride. "There's a story," he suggested, "behind every square meter here." By which, to be brief, he meant the hassles he'd had with drywallers, electricians, tile layers, painters. I had already been informed about a good half of these squabbles.

During the main course of fish—the supermarket kitty-corner had a fantastic fish counter—Boris described how over the last three weeks, because he had to be out of his old apartment, he had tried spurring the workers on with fifty-euro bills, but nothing helped. They hadn't been paid by the general contractor, and so they simply stopped showing up for work. Boris, as I knew him, was a born storyteller—according to Susanne, a windbag. When he got to the part about the stolen window handles he'd had to replace, he gave a wide-sweeping gesture with one arm that signaled he was winding down again. He paid no more attention to Elvira than to Susanne and me, since we were not providing him any cues to pick up on.

Unlike Susanne I'm not uncomfortable in such surroundings. Susanne always claims I'm a harmony freak, and that what I see as arguments are really quite normal discussions. And I admit it—lately I like it better if people don't argue. We, by which I mean our circle of friends, of acquaintances, used to strike a different tone with one another. Not that we were always of the same mind. Of course we each found various things to be good or important, but there was never anything fundamental, let alone personal, about it—even if someone believed in God or in the party and someone else didn't. But that's in the past, at the very latest since the Kosovo war or since Afghanistan. I thought there might be some improvement once everybody could see where the Iraq war has gotten us. Except for Susanne no one knows how I vote. And she just thinks I've got a screw loose. I don't mean to say that friendships have been

ruined over it, but they're not like they once were. You first stop
and think about what you will or won't say.

Until we got up from the table and distributed ourselves
over the four-seaters, nothing much happened worth telling
about. I might say that over the course of the meal I got used to
Elvira, yes, even found her pretty in some way, and that my eyes
returned again and again to those narrow pale stripes at the top
of her arms. Thus far I hadn't heard her say a word, except for
"Thanks a lot" and "More fish?"—phrases that betrayed her
uncertainty as to whether to use formal or informal pronouns.
Elvira had helped Boris serve and clear the table, something forbidden his guests. We were to amuse ourselves, which we managed only with difficulty without him.

Once we had transplanted ourselves to new seating arrange-
ments, our general self-consciousness returned. It was as if we
had taken seats to hear a lecture or see a movie. Pavel had
selected the music—early Pink Floyd stuff that everybody
knows, but that can leave you drowsy and down.

Susanne, however, had made a beeline to secure herself a
spot near the window in the middle of the four-seater, but then
slid over a little to let Pavel and Ines join her, and had sent me
away again, so that when Elvira finally appeared with pretzel
sticks, hazelnuts, and raisins, she had to end up beside her—
unless Elvira went to the trouble of pushing another chair
closer. And like a trap snapping shut, Susanne began to draw
Elvira into conversation. I admire the way Susanne handles
such situations, especially because she can make it all look quite
coincidental.

At first Elvira sat up ramrod straight, holding a bundle of
pretzel sticks in one hand and fixing her eyes on Susanne like a
deaf-mute. Her face slowly took on life, and when she smiled

she would close her light brown eyes as if reveling in a lovely dream. Soon they were facing each other, their knees almost touching.

It seemed to me that the rest of us were talking just so these two women could converse without interruption. Boris obliged us with another tile-laying story. He had come home about ten in the evening, only to discover what a mess had been made of the job, climbed into his car, and roused the tile layer from his bed, "to save what could be saved, while you could still pry the tiles loose!" And he flung his arm wide again. "It sounds crazy, but you're better off doing it yourself."

"Or don't let them out of your sight for a minute," Lore said. She and Fred smiled at each other—you might have taken them for brother and sister. Lore's black hair was shorter than his and sprinkled with tiny icicles. His wiglike ponytail and his gap teeth gave him an antiquated look. (One of Susanne's coworkers at her agency has actually hired Fred to play a role in a medieval pageant in Frankfurt on the Oder.)

As she spoke Susanne gazed straight ahead, balancing her wineglass on her knee with just two fingers. Elvira went on holding her bundle of stick pretzels clamped in her hand, without eating a one.

"It can happen," Pavel said.

"Sure can," Boris said. He wiped the sweat from his brow with his forearm, leaving the little hairs at his wrist pasted against the skin.

Once Elvira noticed that everyone else had fallen silent, she spoke even more softly. No one except Boris, who was sitting closest to her, knew why Susanne suddenly threw her head back and put her hand to her mouth.

"Can we laugh along with you?" Pavel asked.

"Of course, go ahead," Boris said, and walked to the balcony door. He opened the Venetian blinds and pulled them up, but so out of whack that they drooped on the right like a fan. Elvira went on speaking softly.

"May I?" Pavel asked and held the bottle up. Elvira nodded. But she didn't have a glass. There were several volunteers, including myself, who offered to fetch one from the kitchen. Lore won the contest. Pavel stood smiling in front of Elvira and Susanne.

"He wants to laugh along," Boris said as he tried to adjust the blinds to horizontal. "You've finally managed it. Now everybody wants to lend an ear."

"Oh leave her be!" Susanne exclaimed.

When Lore appeared with the wineglass, Pavel carefully lowered the neck of the bottle to the edge of the glass and poured. "I don't drink red wine," Elvira said, never budging. Pavel apologized, took the glass from her hand, and went back to the kitchen.

"So now you'll all be treated to a fine story," Boris said. "Something very special."

"She did tell it so well," Susanne said, as if that was the end of it.

Elvira seemed to be reconsidering her vanished glass. I was sure she would refuse to tell her story again on command. But then she said, "Well, okay," laid her bundle of pretzel sticks on the table, and rubbed her hands together. "I'll start over again."

"Once more from the top," Boris scoffed as he tipped the window open and then returned to his seat. "Everybody's just wild to hear you tell it."

"I thought," Elvira said, "that if I'm going to live here I ought to do my part—"

"Hear, hear!" Boris shouted. "A very wise approach."

Pavel offered another glass to Elvira, this time filled with our white wine, and when she didn't react, set it down in front of her.

"So I made coffee, five or six times a day, because Boris just has one of those glass gizmos that you press the coffee down into—"

"An Alessi."

"But no coffee machine, and the gizmo makes at most four cups. I used a good pound of Prodomo every two days. Their favorites were meatballs with onions and ham and eggs—"

"She means the workers," Boris said.

"And cola, coffee and cola, always 1.5 liter bottles of cola. Most of them drank their coffee black. At first I thought East Berliners drank theirs with milk and sugar and West Berliners black, but suddenly the Easterners wanted black and Westerners blond and sweet. They were all friendly and polite, even the painters, who kept having to come back. Boris had them paint the hardwood doors—"

"I didn't want to come home to a forest," Boris said with a nod my way. "Am I right?"

"They did the job without a grumble."

"There was nothing for them to grumble about; it's in the contract."

"When I asked if it bothered them, they all nodded. But they were always friendly."

"No sooner do you look the other way," Boris said, "than they disappear, and you have to make a hundred thousand calls to get them back again—hours on the phone."

"They were always polite, and they carried those tin lunchboxes, blue ones, red ones, just like I had as a kid in school."

"So what are you trying to say?" Boris asked.

"I just wanted to say that everything here was always in an uproar, for one reason or another, and—"

"Just what do you mean by that?"

"Would you please cut it out!" Susanne cried. "Don't pay any attention to him." She selected a pretzel as carefully as if she were playing pick-up-sticks.

"Life here inside was pretty normal," Elvira said, "until those guys showed up on the balcony." There was a roughness to her voice, as if she ought to swallow or clear her throat every few moments. "It was the sound of the welding torch—all of a sudden I wanted to know what that noise outside was. At first I thought they'd gotten up here by climbing the trees, that they'd swung through the trees on ropes."

Susanne burst into laughter.

"If any of you see any trees around here, let me know," Boris said, turning toward the window. "That's utterly absurd."

"They weren't just on the balcony, they were moving around on the scaffolding, like a crew busy reefing sails."

"I thought," Boris said, "that you were going to tell them—why don't you go ahead and tell them?"

"I was busy with the guys here inside, making coffee and sandwiches, the whole nine yards—"

"The whole nine yards! The whole monkey business!" Boris said, stood up, and left.

Elvira watched him go in shock. Nobody said a word. Everyone's attention was riveted on her, as if we were all waiting just to hear her speak.

"He really did remind me of a monkey," she said, half defiant, half intimidated.

"Who?" Charlotte asked.

"The guy I let in—who was doing the metalwork. I couldn't pretend I didn't see him. If I'm making coffee and sandwiches, then the guys outside should get some too. I rapped on the window. There he squatted beside his welding torch as if it were a campfire. He didn't even hear me open the door. It was a smell like a sardine can, only stronger. I had to shout for him to understand me. His mouth was hanging open—absolutely perfect complexion, hair like ropes, shiny ropes, just a few strands of gray, and pale blue eyes. And not an ounce of fat on his body. He was glistening with sweat. He held up both hands, he didn't want to come inside. So I set his coffee down on the tiles, the milk and sugar beside it, and watched through the window as he picked up the spoon between his huge fingers and shoveled sugar into his cup, like he was playing with dollhouse china— but he did it so deftly, like a watchmaker. The cup vanished in his hand, and I thought, That's not nearly enough for him."

"Was he King Kong?" Fred asked, but no one laughed.

"He never started before three o'clock. The whole day other workers would be out on the scaffolding or in the apartment. They were there by six or six thirty in the morning. But he never showed up before three. Late afternoon and early evening I was always alone with him out on the balconies, this one here or the one in the guest room."

"What sort of metalwork was he doing?" Susanne asked.

"The joints along the railings and the ones between the tiles and the wall."

"And then he came inside."

"Yes, the third day he came inside. I wasn't prepared for it, I didn't know what to do. He knocked on the balcony door and stepped in. Raising his shoulders high, he walked around inspecting the room as if it were a museum. Suddenly he stopped in his tracks and noticed the footprints he'd left behind. "Sorry," he said. That was the first word I'd ever heard him speak. All I'd ever seen were gestures or him shaking his head. 'Real nice,' he then said. 'Real nice, but if all you do is work and sleep you never get to see it.' "

Now Elvira picked up a pretzel stick too, but didn't eat it, just held it like a pen between her fingers. Except for Boris's puttering around in the kitchen, total silence reigned.

"The man was a giant. At first I thought maybe he stuttered, but he wasn't a stutterer at all. But he kept blinking the whole time. And he didn't budge from the spot. Then he asked to take a pee. The guest toilet wasn't finished, so it had to be the bathroom. It felt strange to let him in there. As he came out he was drying his hands on his pants legs. He said: 'I call it mange, it's deep under the skin, y'know, mange is what I call it.' " His hands were an anthracite color, like the lead in a pencil. 'Pipe in, water out, that's all it takes,' he said. I didn't quite get what he meant. He went on leaving footprints behind and looking straight at me, as if I'd said something, but I couldn't think of anything to say. I sat down with him at the kitchen table. He didn't want a sandwich, just coffee and a cigarette. 'Junos'—he meant the brand of cigarettes—'I settled on them.' And then he just kept looking around and saying things like: 'Gotta cost a pretty penny too, but if all you do is work and sleep, don't matter much.' He talked about 'Mercedes wages' and 'a whole day for a working stiff' and 'three weeks just for the rent? Don't need to watch that pot boil.' "

"But he didn't harm you, did he?" Pavel asked.

"I was afraid of that too," Susanne said, giving Pavel a nod of approval.

"He told how he'd 'headed for foreign parts right off,' in '90.

223

Hadn't done anything wrong, no arrests, but when he came back a few years later, his building had been sold and the account where he'd sent his rent was closed, and that was the only reason for his record, he said 'record.' But he'd taken time to do good work for us. 'Corners,' he said, 'my corners get an A, customers care about corners.' Passing the television, stereo, and VCR on his way out, he said: 'VCR, gotta keep the economy hummin', I bought me just five tapes and got the knack of it, but then gave it away, not my thing.' "

"Knows her master's voice!" Boris shouted as he came in with a tray. "And now she wants to swing from vine to vine with him, living with him like Jane of the jungle. She's thinking about getting a pad of her own, not some palace like this. End of story. Next topic!"

Boris did not set the tray with the teapot down easy. Susanne later said he slammed it on the table. I figured I was the only one who could calm him down, so I said there'd been no mention of that whatever, and that we wanted to hear Elvira finish her story.

But that just sent Boris over the edge. I'd never seen him like that before. We had probably all underestimated how much his new place meant to him, how he'd been working the whole time with no other goal in mind, and how hurt he was by Elvira's turning down his offer. "It's all for her, too," he shouted. "For her, for nobody else! She doesn't have to bad-mouth it like this!"

We sat there frozen in place, like schoolkids when the principal flies into a rage. I thought Elvira might get up to leave now, or that Boris would throw her out. The worst part was that our silence seemed likely to provoke something of the sort. I was about to say that I could understand what Elvira was getting at, but then Charlotte bent forward, stubbed out her cigarette, setting her bracelets clanking, and said, "I know what you mean. Something of the sort happened to me, too, back when Paul and I were still together. He always knew how to use the system, or so he claimed, and—without saying a word to me, of course— gave our address to an agency, in case they might need a location for commercials or stuff like that."

I was so relieved somebody had said something that at first I wasn't even really listening. Taken off guard by this turn of events, Boris stood there for a while, but then poured himself some tea, added plenty of rock sugar, stirred his cup noisily, and finally retreated to his seat. Charlotte held her ashtray in both hands like a precious antique and never looked up at us, as if her story demanded her full attention.

"So some guy called and asked if he could stop by, because they had something that might work. He was teed off that he first had to explain it all to me. But the next day he called again, he was just outside our building. So I had no choice but to let him in. The way he marched right in, the way he strode over the threshold, it was clear I'd made a mistake, I shouldn't have done it. That actually did cross my mind then and there. But you never listen to your own inner voice. With a head stuffed full of doubts and scruples, you listen to your own voice least of all. We're taught to be too polite. And so the guy shuffles his way through our eat-in kitchen, from the hall door to the window, from the window to the hall door, squats down as if trying to see if the table has been dusted, rounds the sofa, and is so intent on his own job he doesn't answer a single one of my questions. And suddenly he says, 'Okay, you win.' I ask him what we've won. And he goes, 'The film! They'll be filming at your place here. This Monday, eight a.m.' He tells me we need to find a hotel for three days—four stars would be okay, not exactly the

Intercontinental, but a good hotel. And only then do I begin to catch on: We have to leave, we're going to have to move out of our own apartment, for three days. What's so bad about that? he asks. We'll be living in a hotel and raking in three thousand marks besides. If he had a place like this he'd do it every week. Martha thought it was awesome, she couldn't wait for the hotel, and Paul kept asking me if I knew of any other job where you could earn three thousand marks in three days. One did cross my mind, but I didn't want to risk it—he'd have gone ballistic."

Charlotte leaned back, the ashtray in her lap now. And we gazed at her as if our weal and woe depended on her going on. Boris, however, had stretched out his legs and was staring absentmindedly at the tips of his shoes while he stirred away at his cup.

"Not even Paul realized," Charlotte continued, "what we'd gotten ourselves into. Not in our wildest dream did we think those no-parking signs on both sides of the street had anything to do with us. On Monday there they were, one van after another, twenty or thirty of them, some of them big jobs. The doorbell hadn't even rung yet, and they were already outside our window, on a platform lift, spotlights and more spotlights. I knew it meant trouble. We had no idea they'd be wrapping the whole building. They spread cloths up and down the stairwell—walls, steps, railing, the whole shebang! Claimed they had to do it for insurance purposes. And so everything got draped, inside our place too. Or wait—no, first they photographed everything, even Martha's room—I wondered why they were doing that, all they wanted was our eat-in kitchen."

Charlotte bent forward, set down the ashtray, picked up her glass and drank. Her bracelets rattled. "Nice vintage," she said, toasting Boris, who didn't look up.

226

"It was enough of a bother," she went on, "to have to go to a hotel after work. There's no way you can have one rational thought in a room like that. Martha and I started squabbling because of her homework—she thought we were on vacation. And as we sat waiting for menus in the restaurant, and they didn't come and didn't come, I started sobbing. I've never had such an attack of homesickness. I really did feel like a hooker, and then we had to laugh at how absurd that was. And Paul said that I should show him a family that earns its money by sleeping. We could have gone home after two nights, but the guy who called us—the same one who'd marched in the door—said if we wanted to stay put, he'd have the apartment repainted for us, it was in the contract, even though it wasn't necessary and they hadn't made a mess—in their own advertising they mention a possible mess—but they'd do a total renovation, that way we'd arrive home with no stress involved and everything in its place. And, since he didn't want to make the same mistake twice, Paul asked me if that's what I wanted. And I said, yes. I did think about Martha, but Paul suggested we make a big surprise out of it for her, or whatever. We hadn't even set down our bags at our building door and they swept down on us, our lovely neighbors, for not having told them anything about it. Well okay, I don't even want to go into that. I just thought, Home at last—enough anticipation and excitement—all I wanted was to step inside at last. And then there we stand in our own four walls, and everything is exactly like before, just freshly painted. But it's weird somehow. Paul notices it, I notice it, but we don't mention it. We say, 'Not bad,' stuff like that, and walk around, and I'm thinking: Just like the guy checking out our apartment. And then suddenly Martha starts bawling, she's standing at the door of her own room, and wails louder and louder. I look inside, no reason to be upset, I think, the photographs and posters are all hanging pretty much where they were before—except one poster has been torn down, and I ask who did that. But it was Martha herself. She had ripped it down, and the next one now too, one after the other, even though they were all hanging in the right place. I don't know how to describe it."

"Like burglars," Susanne said.

"Not that anything was missing," Charlotte said, pulling the ashtray closer and picking up her pack of cigarettes. "Just the other way around—everything hunky-dory, but that was just it, absolutely eerie, really. . . ."

"They touched everything, they picked up everything," Pavel said.

"Something has happened," Ines said, "but you can't put your finger on it, nothing you can grab hold of, you can't even see it, but it's there."

"Don't remind me," Pavel said as he leaned back, shaking his head and clasping his hands behind his neck.

"I know what you mean, Charlotte, I've been through it," Ines said. "Our last vacation trip was a horror, just this past June, in Croatia—"

"Dalmatia," Pavel said. "An utter horror. You tell it better."

"There's not much to tell. That's the thing—you can't get at it." Ines stared straight ahead.

Elvira bent forward, trying to get a look at Ines at the far end of the four-seater.

"Well, give it a go," Susanne said.

"The Kornati Islands," Ines said, shaking her head. "We had heard about them in Zagreb. When we said we wanted to drive to Zadar, the first thing you heard was the Kornati Islands, from all sides, the Kornatis. And Roman, who booked our stay for us, even talked about how Oscar Wilde called the Kornati Islands a paradise. From our balcony we could see the sea, and to the left, a little hidden by trees and a sliver of land, you could sort of make out Zadar, two-thousand-year-old Zadar. We had read in our travel guide that Hitchcock had seen the most beautiful sunrise of his life in Zadar, or something like that, at any rate Hitchcock had been there, and after '45, once the rubble had been cleared away—the Allies had bombarded, because of the Germans or the Italians—they discovered a Roman forum under all the debris. Zadar isn't as spectacular as Split, no Palace of Diocletian, but the churches are lovelier, and on Saturdays there are several weddings in each of them, with musicians standing out in front and men swinging Croatian flags. I liked Zadar right off, if only because of Anja, our landlady. She had waited two hours for us in the supermarket parking lot. Anja rode ahead on her red Vespa, her white helmet leading the way. Pavel fell in love with her on the spot, with her big breasts and long black hair."

"She was incredibly likable," Pavel said.

"She must have had her three sons while she was still very young, the oldest is fourteen. I could tell right off that Anja had kids. She just radiates something."

"She spoke German, really first-rate German."

"She kept asking Pavel whether that's how you put it—even though they understood each other anyway, Polish and Croatian are practically the same thing—"

"She said her husband could take us out to the Kornati Islands. And we thought, Why not? From the shore the islands look like a chain of mountains, a marvelous view."

"The first thing you asked was whether she was coming along—"

"I did not," Pavel said.

"But Anja didn't want to come along. Whenever we met she would start in about the Kornati Islands, how her husband could take us out in his own boat. All her guests made the trip— and that put me off right away, I didn't like the sound of it. And then here it came: Three hundred euros, that was the price for friends. Pavel immediately agreed. Three hundred! I said no. No is always my job. But that was including food and drink, and whatever else we might want. Besides which we'd be starting from here, practically at our front door, and we could pick the time. Then she described the steamers we'd otherwise have to take to the Kornatis, as if it was our duty to visit these stupid islands. I said no, half that, a hundred fifty, one hundred fifty was tops, that was all that was in our travel budget. Okay, Anja said, one hundred fifty euros. Haggling is so ugly."

"But the apartment didn't cost us a thing," Pavel said. "We had it for ten days for free, all paid for by Roman's outfit in Zagreb."

"It costs thirty-five euros a head on a tourist steamer," Ines said.

"Must be a living hell, though, we'd had a look at one. But as for her husband, and that's the point, we'd never seen him, although he lived in the house next door. Anja came every day on her Vespa and cooked for us, and then took off again, never stayed on, never spent the night."

"And how do you know that?" Ines laughed.

"Because her scooter was never there, she wouldn't arrive till around eleven on her scooter—"

"Always at eleven? I never noticed it was always at eleven, but it doesn't matter. At any rate we didn't see Peter until we got to the dock. He stood there like a mast on his cutter, at least six foot eight, with rimless sunglasses, wraparounds . . . ," Ines brushed both temples. "A guy with a deadpan face, frozen like a reptile's. You never knew if he was even looking at you. Plus his weird English."

" 'Guuuhd morrnink,' " went Pavel. " 'Uoun hanntert feeffti, uoun hanntert feeffti yuurro, guuuhd morrnink, madd damm.' "

"I thought how even a hundred fifty was too much for this guy. But we were seated comfortably and were alone, and when he asked if we wanted music and we said no, that was fine too. The racket from his *Kalypso*—that was the boat's name, *Kalypso III*—was pretty loud as it was. There was something mythical about it, chug-chugging along among islands with a man tall as a tree and silent as a grave. It always startled us when Peter would turn around to bellow his bits of tour-guide wisdom. We passed a church where there's a pilgrimage every August, because it was supposed to have snowed there one August—that's the only thing that registered. I envied people on these islands, spectacular homes, all with a view of the water, and I envied people in their sailboats, and even those on the excursion steamers. But the farther out we got the less there was to see, the islands got bleaker and bleaker, bleached crags, uninhabited rocks, with just property lines visible, separating somebody's lot from somebody else's, and here and there a kind of pattern, as if someone had passed over it with a trowel in a semicircle, a petrified arch, except you can't see what's below the opening. So we chugged along, farther and farther, and I asked—had to shout, of course—when we would finally get to the Kornati Islands, because to our right and left now was open sea, not a single island. I'd pictured the islands as a kind of jungle, Anja had talked about rare animals. 'This is Kornati, all this are Kornati Islands!' he yelled, and shook his head. He was

laughing at us, making fun of us. A hundred fifty euros for that!
We then entered a bay and tied up at dock with other boats like
ours and a few steamers. We were supposed to visit a salt lake.
Then we'd have lunch. Everybody was romping around at the
salt lake—what a horror. The lake gets water only from rain or if
storms flood it with high surf, though it's a riddle to me how
that could happen. We sat around with nothing to do, saw
schoolgirls do their changing-into-swimsuits ritual, taking
their time until all the boys were gawking at them, and watched
tiny crabs and mussels with long spiral shells like baroque wigs.
My good mood slowly returned—I knew we'd be heading back,
that the worst was over. And the meal that Peter served up was
really good, huge steaks, salad, bread, then fish he claimed had
just been caught. To prove it he threw bread in the water—and
just like that, a huge school of fish. Peter pointed to a net, as if all
he had to do was scoop them up. It was really first-class, with
linen napkins, starched and ironed linen napkins, and white
wine, a whole canister. They were eating on the excursion
steamers, too. The smell of fried fish drifted clear over to us. We
watched the day-trippers hold the fish heads with backbones
attached over the railing. Gulls dived in and ripped them right
from their hands, people were screeching and gulls were
screeching. What a madhouse! We were glad now we hadn't
ended up on one of those steamers. I asked Peter what he did
professionally. 'Scientist,' he replied. 'But not here, not here.' He
pointed off in some direction—"

" 'Far away,' Peter said, 'far away in the past,' " Pavel added.

"I didn't want to risk asking any details, you never know
what can of worms you're opening up. But that one question
alone was too much, or maybe it was the madness with the gulls

or simply the alcohol. He'd been hitting the white wine hard. And grappa, there was also home-brewed grappa. Then suddenly we took off, a sharp turn around the bow of the steamer, gulls scattering every which way. Peter was now driving a lot faster than before, and not back home but toward the south. At first it was actually fun racing through the water and being tossed around by the waves. We pulled on our jackets and held on tight. The sinful part was how close he shot by past other boats. All we saw were shocked faces, and in the next moment enraged faces. He sped right for other boats like a kamikaze pilot, and only turned away at the last second—"

"I tried," Pavel said, "to work my way forward to him—"

"I didn't think that was such a good idea," Ines interrupted. "And Peter, maybe because he saw Pavel coming in his rearview mirror, went into such a tight curve that I was sure Pavel would be thrown overboard."

"I just bumped my head."

" 'Just' is good," Susanne said.

"Yes, 'just' *is* good, because it could have turned out a lot worse," Ines said. "So we hunkered down, with the Croatian flag behind us—and then suddenly it was over. At first I thought the motor had quit or we were out of gas, but Peter had just pulled the throttle back and was chugging along now in wide curves. I yelled at him, and Pavel yelled at him. I couldn't think of anything better to say than 'We want to live! We want to live!' I don't know how many times I shouted it. Peter just waved me off in disdain, real disdain, and snapped his thumb and middle finger and roared, 'It's like nothing, like nothing!' "

"No, 'Life is nothing,' is what he said. 'Life is nothing!' " Pavel corrected her.

"He said, 'It's like nothing,' and said it with a snap of his fingers."

"Yes, he snapped them, but he said, 'Life is nothing,' because otherwise it might have meant his speeding was like nothing at all."

"Who the hell cares?" Boris said. "At any rate he was a nut case. You should have demanded your money back, whether it was 'like' or 'life.' "

"It was so unreal," Ines said. "First the kamikaze bit, and then nothing, as if it was all in our heads. We putt-putted home, it took an eternity. From the water there's nothing special about Zadar, not like Greifswald or Stralsund. At first I thought it was Anja waiting at the dock, at least there was someone there with a white helmet and a red motor scooter. But once she saw us, she was off in a cloud of dust. Well okay, and then came the moment that had me scared shitless—saying good-bye to Peter. I wanted to give him a piece of my mind. By now I was embarrassed at screaming, 'We want to live!' I wanted to tell him how outrageous it was to put people in that situation. Except I didn't know how to say it in English. Pavel can never get his mouth pried open for stuff like that, it's always up to me. We tied up, Peter jumped ashore, we groped our way forward. Peter was standing with one foot in the boat, the other on the dock, he held out his hand to me. I grabbed it, and I looked at him, directly into his bad eye—a ghastly dead eye, not even a glass eye, just a socket. I could smell the alcohol on him. Bracing me under my elbow, Peter pulled me up, and I jumped ashore."

"That eye shocked me too—" Pavel said.

"We stood there like pillars of salt, watching as Peter cast off the line, jumped back in the boat, and started the engine. He waved at us and called out, 'Ciao, ciao.' He had put his sun-glasses on again. But the most remarkable thing about the whole story is that somehow it came as a relief, I mean his eye—"

Boris burst into laughter.

"Not the way you think—sure, when I consider how he had no depth perception and was speeding like a bat out of hell, but I mean it was good that we at least had that eye, that there was something visibly wrong, some hint. Maybe it sounds perverse, but when I saw that sewn-up eye socket, I calmed down—it was a kind of explanation even if I haven't a clue what was up with that eye—it could have been an accident, didn't have to have anything to do with the war."

"Wait a sec," Pavel said. "The way you tell it, nobody's going to understand it. Zadar was under siege for two years, bombarded, for two years. The Yugoslav army left its barracks and headed for the mountains, and then fired down at the town from up there—at everything, houses, churches, libraries, everything. And the people in town, they had nothing, at least to begin with, but nobody talks about that, or almost nobody. Roman told about running with his little brother on his back and not knowing if they would make it or not. And when he got home, his mother was washing windows. She had forbidden him to fight, even though she'd been on the front herself, as a doctor. And when he said that he didn't want to have anything to do with this war, that he knew of no earthly reason why he should fight, she threw him out of the house. Even though she'd forbidden him to fight, understand?"

"And Anja?" Lore asked. "Was she still together with this Peter guy?"

"In some way, yes. At least she spoke of him as her husband. But she never spent the night with him. She came at eleven and then headed off somewhere."

"How could you live with someone like that?" Susanne said.

"And what if someone said that about you?" Fred asked. Susanne leaned back and pretended that Fred had addressed his question to everybody.

"Sometimes you can't help it," Fred said. "Just as maybe your Peter couldn't help it. Something happened to me once, nothing to do with war, of course, but it can happen so quickly—you tell a stupid joke, lose self-control, do something raunchy, that's all it takes." Fred paused as if he wasn't sure whether to go on or not.

"We'd met at dance classes, in Dresden," he then began. "I was seventeen, she was sixteen. Her parents liked me and even invited me to come along on outings with them; they had a car. In the late sixties that was still something special. But for her sake—her name was Ines too—I found excuses not to. I really loved Ines, and I think she loved me too. We hadn't slept together yet. I always thought that was the last step, the one thing still lacking for us to be truly intimate with each other."

Fred sat bent forward, letting his head hang and kneading his hands.

"It was the end of August, just before the school year started up again, and she was back from the Baltic with her parents. She had a great tan, and her hair was almost blond. She had written me several postcards, but brought them all back with her. Next year, she said, we would take off together, just her and me. I was happy, but I needed a little while to get used to Ines again, although I'd thought about her the entire time. When I told Ines that my parents would be gone for the weekend, she said she wanted to stay with me. And so Ines came over, and I suggested we ride our bikes out toward Moritzburg, past the harvested fields to the woodland ponds. Directly opposite the nudist camp was a small meadow with access to the lower pond. We were the only ones there. We undressed and went swimming. We didn't stay in the water long, but when we came out we found four men sitting on the spot where we had laid our clothes—all of them in their late twenties, certainly not rowdy teenagers. Ines stayed in the water, and I got out. But they wouldn't give me my clothes, they said my little Ines had to fetch them for me. They spoke very softly, almost as if they were friends of mine. They had removed our IDs and called me Friedrich the whole time. I didn't know what we should do. Ines came out of the water then, and they made comments and cracked dirty jokes at every step she took, every gesture, and just in general, and at first only handed over her velour pullover, followed then by her bra and so on. And her towel was the last item. Then they left. They'd been sitting on my things, but otherwise hadn't done anything with them. Our IDs were lying on top." Fred's fingernails had turned all white. "It doesn't sound very dramatic, because they never laid a hand on us. . . ."

At first I thought Fred was fighting back tears. But then he raised his hands, as if to indicate there was nothing more to say. Eventually, however, he did go on, even speaking a little faster than before. "I've always wished I could surgically remove those minutes, like some infected lesion, cauterize them—or start speaking a different language. I don't know, whatever. Of course Ines and I cursed them and made plans to go to the police, to take revenge. But once it had grown dark, Ines rode home. Maybe if we had spent the night together it would have saved our relationship. But maybe that was just no longer possible, at any rate it became less and less so from day to day. Just the way someone pronounced our names was all it took. The worst part was that it didn't have to be any particular word. Just a random remark, and we would be back at that woodland pond. But for me it was enough to know and to see that Ines was thinking of it too. I later blamed myself for not having hurled myself at those men. It would have been better to have taken a beating or for us to have ridden home naked. Anything would have been better than what did happen. But I was paralyzed with fear. Above all we didn't want things to get any worse. Fear—it's so disgusting."

Boris turned around to Elvira, maybe he was expecting some reaction from her, maybe he wanted to ask her something. Elvira's head was resting on Susanne's shoulder. Susanne could barely move a muscle but managed to carefully put a finger to her lips. When Boris offered to carry Elvira to bed, Susanne made a face. She evidently found it pleasant to have Elvira's head on her shoulder, was even a little proud of it, I think.

Ines and Pavel said they needed to be going. Boris nodded, but neither of them got to their feet. Everyone else likewise went on sitting there and looking at Elvira. The thought crossed my mind that if we left now, we would never see Elvira again.

I would have liked to have said something about Fred's story. I wanted to ask Boris if he remembered the brown water in those woodland ponds. I'd often gone swimming there myself. The bottom is very stony at that spot.

My recollection of that night at Boris's turns hazy after Fred's story, at least in terms of the contents and sequence of what was said. The mood, however, is just that much more present in my mind.

Fred, Lore, and Charlotte sat bent forward as if listening to a program on the radio. Now and then someone would reach out a hand for snacks or slices of baguette topped with tomatoes and cheese that Boris had brought in at some point.

A strange quiet had come over us. I'm intentionally avoiding the words "silence" or "hush," even if—or so it seems to me—almost nothing was said for a long while, or if so only sotto voce. I was relieved that the strange tension that had descended over everything with Elvira's showing up had now lifted. The stories had calmed Boris down as well. It bothered me that the storytelling had left me feeling good somehow.

I don't know of course what actually kept Ines and Pavel there. But I'm sure that Susanne, too—even if Elvira's head hadn't been resting on her shoulder—would never have considered leaving now.

I may well make myself an object of mockery when I admit that it made me think of strip mines being phased out, and suddenly—nobody knows just how—all sorts of stuff starts sprouting, as if it were umpteen million years ago, as if it were nothing for nature to start all over again. That's the feeling I had.

I didn't tell any stories myself. Nothing ever happens to me that could be shaped into some kind of narrative. I'm not an entertaining sort of guy, sad to say—which used to distress me. I wondered if I should contribute something I'd heard on the radio a couple of weeks before, an incident that kept running through my mind. I'd probably recognize the woman's voice. It was on Deutschlandfunk, an interview show plus classical music. The interviewee was an opera singer who had just given her farewell concert. I've forgotten her name, along with the whole interview really. Except for one question. The moderator wanted to know if it was possible to make new friends, real friends, friends for life, after the age of fifty. "Sure, why not?" the opera singer had exclaimed. The question had, as you could plainly hear, upset, almost outraged her. The moderator tried to explain her question, to which the singer then replied with a brusque, "No, I don't believe a word of it!" In the silence that followed you could hear the rustling of paper until both began speaking at once, fell silent again, and the moderator said, "Please, please, it's *your* turn!"

That's when the singer told about a friend she had come to know eighteen months earlier in Chicago, an American originally from Germany, who had come to the States as a child in the late forties. I think his name was Rüdiger, at any rate a name no American can pronounce. This Rüdiger had come up to her in a coffee shop after hearing her speak with a German accent. He had invited her to join him the next day to visit the Chicago Board of Trade, where he worked. She described how the shouting began with the ring of the bell at nine on the dot and how much physical stamina it took just to stand for hours in the amphitheaters of the pits.

"You were going to tell us about a friendship," the moderator said, breaking into the singer's account. She, however, was undaunted and plowed ahead. "And later that afternoon it was this man of all people who told me that socialism was the only real solution, that one should help the poor and take something from the rich, that industries essential to human life should be nationalized, because state industries were still better than private monopolies. And then he asked me," the singer said, "whether our way of life and the corrupt behavior that necessarily went with it wouldn't drag the whole world into the abyss. At first," the singer exclaimed, "I though he was joking, but he was in earnest, dead earnest. Nowadays I hate myself for thinking he was joking."

"And so it was because of his views," the moderator asked, "that you struck up a friendship with him?"

"He didn't say anything," the singer replied, "that we didn't think and say here thirty or forty years ago, not one thing. He just hadn't stopped saying it."

There was another brief pause, then the moderator asked her next question. But the singer didn't respond. Instead she asked, "Don't you think there will always be wars as long as someone is making money off them?"

The moderator tried a different question, but the singer insisted: "Don't you think that even here among us far too many people are making money off war?"

"That's something I'm not prepared to discuss with you now," the moderator said, and evidently signaled her director to play some music, so that all you heard was the singer's next, "Don't you think . . ." The music was followed by news, after which the interview continued without further incident.

I could have told about that. But it bore no relation to what had already been said. Besides which, recounting a radio show seemed a rather paltry contribution. I mention it, however, because I've asked myself a hundred times now what I would have done as the moderator. Probably have made the mistake of asking the singer about her American friend. Because what consequences should this Rüdiger have drawn from his views? Given up his job? Blown up the Board of Trade? Become a politician?

Mulling all this over, I fell asleep. I dreamed but no longer remember what about.

When I woke up, I winced—of course I found it unpleasant

to have dozed off like that. But no one, not even Susanne, appeared to have noticed. Lore was saying, "And there it lay, wet, slimy, smelly."

Boris, legs outstretched, head propped against the arm of his chair, had closed his eyes. Ines was lying on her back, her head in Pavel's lap, her legs dangling over one arm of the four-seater. Charlotte was sitting on the rug with legs crossed, elbows on her knees, head propped in her hands, a half full ashtray in front of her. Only Lore and Susanne still seemed wide awake. I later had Susanne tell me the story of the huge fish, which Lore had read about somewhere. But by then Susanne was likewise getting things mixed up.

I then watched how Susanne, following the model of Ines and Pavel, bedded Elvira's head in her lap without Elvira's ever waking up.

I nodded off again and woke up again just as Pavel started telling about a friend who had become acquainted with a young woman early last year, a woman not only of noble birth, but rich too. Her parents had bought back their ancestral estate, between Berlin and the Märkische Schweiz, and whipped it back into shape—a Bauhaus castle, as Pavel put it, surrounded by a huge park. "We knew the park, we had taken walks there, it's open to the public, with pavilions, ponds, meadows, and ancient trees. But whenever we got close to the house there would be signs, just barely taller than the grass, announcing, Private Property. You couldn't help dreaming about living in a palace like that. So we were strolling around, and suddenly saw a woman sitting in the pavilion up ahead. She was reading, she didn't even notice us. I could have approached closer, but I realized I was standing between two Private Property signs. I'm quite sure she wasn't reading Goethe's *Elective Affinities,* but no other book would have fit in so well. The most marvelous part was that the large meadow behind is on a low rise that blocks the view of what lies beyond it, so that it came to me that behind it must be the sea or at least a large lake, and the illusion didn't shatter until you were just a few yards before the adjoining field. When I later learned who my friend's new acquaintance was, I suddenly found myself believing in fate, but a fate that's been jimmied out of whack, as if there's been a mix-up, like dialing a wrong number, so to speak. . . ."

Ines smiled and said without opening her eyes, "I see, I see."

"I just mean," Pavel said, "that *we* belonged there, not Jürgen. His Elisabeth wasn't even the woman in the pavilion. Jürgen took us along one time, but the two of them were already on the verge of crisis. I played for them, on a Thürmer piano, but my mind wasn't on it, I kept observing myself doing the 'pianist routine.' From the third floor you could see not just the meadow with its pavilions, but the big field beyond it as well."

Pavel removed his shoes by pushing against the heels. I watched the motions his toes made inside his burgundy socks. He made no attempt at all to hide their sweat-stained soles. Boris's arms were dangling from the arm of the chair like flags in a dead calm. He was snoring softly. Susanne was asleep with one hand at Elvira's waist, her right arm along the back of the chair, her head thrown back, her mouth slightly open. It had been a long time since I had watched her sleep.

I tried to imagine what lay ahead for Elvira and Boris. I decided I would say something this time—I was going to tell him I'd like to see Elvira again.

I woke up at six on the dot. I was cold, my neck and shoulders ached. Susanne was smiling at me. Elvira and Boris were no longer in the room, I didn't see Charlotte either. Fred was lying on the rug, Lore beside me on the sofa. Ines was asleep in Pavel's lap. The window ahead of me had been tipped ajar, the floor lamp turned off, the Venetian blinds opened. A fly was crawling along one slat. Outside, a truck—it was either empty or pulling a trailer—was rumbling along over the cobblestones.

It may sound odd, but when I awoke I had a sense of pride, as if falling asleep in a sitting position with other people around were some sort of accomplishment. I was content, content and happy, as if I'd been given a gift I'd wanted my whole life long.

Susanne had closed her eyes again. I'm fairly certain that I didn't fall asleep again, and that what comes next was not a dream. I heard a helicopter, and then I spotted it between slats in the blinds. I slid down in my chair until I had the helicopter at the same level as the slat where the fly was crawling. The fly would move ahead just a bit, and then wait as if it needed to regain its strength. The helicopter, however, kept getting closer to it. I didn't need to make any more adjustments in my position. They collided, and then—I swear—the fly swallowed the helicopter. I waited for it to reemerge behind the fly or below the slat, as the laws of perspective dictated—but it never did. The helicopter had vanished. And only then did I notice that its noise had stopped as well—total silence, only our breathing, even the fly never moved from its spot.

Except for that last clause about the fly, my "little novella"—that was my subtitle—was now written, and I gave it to Susanne to read. If it ever got published, she said, even an impartial reader, who knew nothing more than what I had shared with him, would see through the whole thing from the start. I could spare myself the novelistic conclusion. Reality, she remarked, works very differently than in my stories. I asked her if she thought I might not even need to add anything, if the story might not already have come to its conclusion? If I didn't have a sense of that, she said, then I didn't need to torment myself by writing stories, there'd be no point in it, period.

Some say, yes, you're obligated to invent, it can't be any good otherwise. But I don't want to invent things. All that matters to me in this case is to be fair to Boris and that night. The subtitle was wrong, plain and simple. There are no novellas in everyday life. So I crossed out the subtitle, and will continue the way I planned from the start.

Although it was a Thursday, strangely enough no one seemed to be in a hurry. Boris, now in blue-and-white Adidas sweats, set the table and said that actually he hadn't invited us for breakfast too. When I joined him in the kitchen, he signaled for me to close the door. Leaning against the kitchen window, he asked, "Well, what do you think of her?"

"Wonderful, absolutely wonderful," I said.

"Except of course that she doesn't look at all like me."

"Why should she—"

"It wasn't what I had in mind, I can tell you," he interrupted, "for a girl like that to show up and say, 'Hi, Dad!' She doesn't look at all like me. I've demanded a blood test. Which has really pissed her mother off, and her, too, of course. But I want the test. How we'll take it from there is our business, but it needs to be clear-cut, don't you think?"

Boris went on talking for a while. He also said that if Elvira absolutely didn't want to live with him, he'd pay for a student pad of her own. The more he thought about it, the better he liked the idea of having a daughter.

I never explained to Boris about my—about our—misunderstanding. Perhaps he had intended it that way. That may well be. I congratulated him on having a daughter.

"We'll see, we'll see," he said. "Awful name. I would never have named her Elvira. But that's just like her, her mother, just like her!"

After his death Elvira took care of all the formalities. She had a funeral notice printed up and sent to everyone in his address book. There were about fifty people. We immediately recognized Elvira's mother, Elvira is her spitting image.

I found it a little inadequate that there was nothing except some music. Susanne said I should have spoken, I was his only friend, after all. But in fact we didn't know each other at all. I could have told them about that evening. But you don't do that sort of thing extemporaneously, at least I can't.

Last week we visited Elvira. She's going to put the apartment up for rent and pay off the mortgage that way. On the dining table was an old dark red tin box. On top of it was a black-and-white photograph. It was of my kindergarten class on monkey bars. Except for two little girls, everyone had risked climbing higher than I had. The next group was waiting in the background. Between my shoulders and the sandals of my friend Lutz Janke, someone had penned in a line with an arrow, pointing to the head of a rather tall boy. I asked if I could have the photograph, a request I realized was presumptuous the moment I made it. But Elvira had evidently expected it and was happy I asked, at any rate she smiled and with no hesitation gave me the photo.

One More Story

"He wouldn't even take the train if there were a nonstop flight from Budapest to Berlin on Sundays. That at least is what he said at the end of his interview with Katalin K., a Hungarian journalist, who had offered to help him buy his train ticket for Budapest—for Vienna–Budapest."

Perhaps a style modeled on a police report would best suit this story, an impersonal tone, sentences without a first-person narrator. The attentive reader would know right off that the real reason for the trip did not necessarily correspond to the reason provided by our traveler (for whom a name is easily found). The phrase, "that at least is what he said"—with emphasis on the verb—would clearly indicate that fact.

It is always tempting to switch from the first-person to the third-person. This third person ends up coming off a little shabbily, and the experience writes itself. But that won't work in this case, at least when it comes to the crucial turn of events—that is, when our traveler is sitting across from the woman, whose name could be Petra or Katja and whom (during their years together, or better, the years of his alliance with this Petra or Katja) he had called his wife. Or am I mistaken? Might it not possibly be more effective—at that critical juncture—to avoid any sort of commentary and to regard the first-person narrator strictly from the outside (that is, as our traveler) and thus subject him to the same scrutiny to which all other figures are exposed? I don't know.

I will nevertheless attempt to speak of myself and of how life shows a tendency to imitate literature.

On that Sunday, April 25, 2004—the last day, that is, of the Budapest Book Fair, where Germany had been the featured guest country—I had been struck by the possibly fruitful idea (depending on my mood I'm inclined to read frightful for fruitful, and vice versa) of making the trip to Vienna to present Petra with the manuscript of my story "Incident in Petersburg," in which the first-person narrator is mugged. That had in fact happened to me. I am convinced that the mugging could have occurred only because I had not been paying attention, because my mind had still been wandering in Vienna with Petra. I had flown from Vienna to St. Petersburg on the same day we had separated. In my story the "incident" became a kind of framework for my memories of Petra.

Of course I could have sent the story to her without commentary and waited to see what happened. But I thought it would be better—since Vienna was suddenly so close—to tell Petra face to face that for once, apart from a change of names (Petra or Katja), I had invented nothing.

I called her from Budapest—the same number, the same ring tone as back then—and left a message on her answering machine. When I returned to the hotel, I found a note with a check mark on the line "Please return call," above which stood the familiar number—which once again was answered only by a machine. I gave the date, time, and place of arrival, 12:20 p.m., West Station, and my time of departure, 3:45 p.m. I asked if it would be all right with her for us to meet at one o'clock, "just for an hour or so," and promised to pay for her lunch. I proposed we meet at the Museum Quarter, and concluded by saying my cell phone number was still the same. If Petra didn't appear, I planned to visit the Museum Quarter, which had first opened shortly after our separation.

Just buying my round-trip ticket on Friday made me feel like I was giving myself a present, treating myself to a luxury—even though it was a second-class ticket for which I had to fork over a mere thirty-four euros. It was strange to plan a trip on my own, to travel at no one's invitation, and pay for the ticket out of my own pocket.

Sunday-morning rain summarizes the view that Budapest offers me at the level of a car window. The images blur together, turning gray as the asphalt, which looks bubbly somehow. The radio startles me, sniveling, "and all the bells were tolling," the driver turns around and nods to me. "*Am Tag, als Conny Cramer starb, und alle Glocken klangen, am Tag, als Conny Cramer starb, und alle Freunde weinten um ihn, das war ein schwerer Tag. . . .*" I get it now—a German song, especially for me.

The car belongs to the hotel, the meter hasn't been turned on. As we pull up at Keleti pu., the sense I'm being well taken care of leaves me downright euphoric. I would never call the Keleti pu. East Station. The Keleti pu.—the last time I stood there was in the summer of 1989. Vacation trips to Budapest began and ended at the Keleti pu., marked the start and finish of hitchhiking tours to Bulgaria—a train station almost as familiar to me as the Neustädter in Dresden.

The driver and I say good-bye with a handshake. I have plenty of time and no baggage except a shoulder bag with a half-liter bottle of water, a book by István Örkény, my notebook, which I always carry with me and never use, the blue folder with the manuscript of "Incident in Petersburg," my wallet, and my passport. "I'm going to Vienna," I whisper as I climb the stairs to the main entrance and, once at the top, turn around as if I'm about to say good-bye for good. "I'm going to Vienna." A blue Michelin Man waves to me from a rooftop, blue is also the color of the Trabant in a row of parked cars, more than half of them made in Germany. And all the while I'm looking around—my hand pressed to my shoulder bag—there's not a beggar in sight, no one wants anything from me, not even a wino stumbles by. As far back as May 1979, the first time I left from here, loaded down with books from the GDR Cultural Center and S. Fischer pocketbooks from a shop on Váci-utca, I dreamed that I was a writer on his way to Vienna. For twenty-five years that had meant something very different. Or I could also say that twenty-five years ago it still had a very real meaning.

Vienna is not even listed on the posted schedule. But instead Dortmund—which never had a chance in its 3–0 loss to Leverkusen yesterday, and today Bremen has to beat Bochum in an away game, otherwise that blows any chance of the UEFA Cup too. I don't want to think about that and so buy a newspaper. You know what a train trip will be like within the first fifteen minutes, usually within a minute or two.

The train to Dortmund via Vienna is ready for boarding. I don't have a seat reservation. I'm choosy and inspect the cars both outside and in. When I finally find one without compartments, most seats are occupied. The unoccupied ones are either on the aisle, or the upholstery glistens with a fresh grease spot, or they're right next to the smoking section. There's always some reason why a seat is unoccupied or still available. I return to one where the heater has an especially loud rumble. The train fills up. I'm not someone people like to sit down next to. That's not a recent insight, but it still hurts even if I do breathe a sigh of relief whenever, after hesitating briefly, someone moves on.

I'm amazed at how soundlessly we pull out. But it isn't us at all, it's the Budapest–Moscow train. Or is it just switching tracks? I don't see anyone at the windows.

I unpack the blue folder with my "Incident in Petersburg" story, slip my cell phone into my breast pocket along with my ballpoint, and pick up my copy of *One-Minute Stories,* which had lain on my lap on the plane and on my nightstand in the hotel. I tug at the dark red ribbon marker, open to page 18, and as our train lurches punctually at 9:35, begin to read the story entitled "The Bow."

Even though as a train pulls out I usually panic at the thought that I've left my bag on the platform, I love riding trains. Just as you walk twice as fast on moving sidewalks at airports, I have the feeling I'm accomplishing more on a train than at home. In addition to all the reading and writing you get done, by successfully managing a change of place you easily triple the value of your daily output. And so I start to read, but am interrupted at once by bites of conscience, since I need to look through "Incident in Petersburg" and collect my thoughts about what I'm going to say to Petra three hours from now.

Beside me, on the other side of the aisle, is a French family. The parents smile, we exchange nods, the children are urged to say *bonjour,* which, however, neither the boy (curly hair) nor the girl (straight hair) does.

Green landscape outside and gardeners' yellow containers, walls of seven narrow concrete slabs. Home supplies—Praktiker, OBI, hp—Nissan (by next Sunday, Hungary will be in the EU), the Danube, low shores, new huge buildings, with observatories on the roofs, circus-tent roofs—of course they only look that way. Then blocks of apartments—best guess, Khrushchev era—green again, small houses. The sympathy people extend to young families. They scatter stuffed animals, comics, and a book by James Ellroy on each of their four seats and set off in the direction of the dining car just as we stop in Kelenföld. Then Shell, Honda, Plus, Kaiser's billboards lining the road. The buildings on the far side merging into the green. Perfect travel weather, IKEA, Stella Artois, Baumax.

I slip the ribbon marker back in, close *One-Minute Stories,* open the blue folder. I don't know what to tell Petra. I've been under way for sixteen minutes now. "Sixteen": Who was it that said "sixteen" so urgently? Suddenly I have the word "sixteen" in my ears but as if spoken by a foreigner, "sixteen" and "all the bells are tolling."

I read my story, this is work, no longer Sunday, no more freedom, no more independence. I've deliberately kept the tone unliterary, as if I myself have had to write up the police report that never got written.

"Saint Petersburg, December 1, 2000. I was in the city to join my translator Ada Beresina in presenting the Russian edition of *33 Moments of Happiness* at the Goethe-Institut and the university. For me it was a dream come true, because as I liked to boast during that week, my book was returning to its city and to the language of most of its characters. I was living in the Pension Turgenev on a side street off Upper Nevsky, not far from the Moika Hotel. I had exchanged money in a currency shop located below street level in an apartment house across from my own building, and so still had my passport. With wallet and passport in the inside breast pocket of my jacket and my little backpack slung over my shoulder, I strolled along the Neva, watched floes of ice passing in the water and thought of Vienna. . . .

"At the Marble Palace I left the Neva and crossed the Field of Mars, heading in the direction of the Nevsky. Standing around the Flame for the Unknown Soldier were several people I first took for soldiers. As I approached a young man said something to me. His body language was somehow servile—his gaze shifty, his face and hands grimy. He asked me the time. It was shortly after noon. He then asked me for money, he was hungry. I pulled out my wallet, gave him ten rubles, and moved on. Keeping to the right of the monument as I walked away, I noticed he called something over to the young men warming themselves at the Flame for the Unknown Soldier. In the next moment the pack was after me, half of them children. They were pleading, their hands clasped together as if in prayer, shouting, '*Kushat, kushat!*'—eat, eat. I didn't try to run away. After all, it was broad daylight, in the middle of St. Petersburg. Or maybe I didn't think that, maybe I was just embarrassed. Make a run for it? I probably guessed it would have been no use. Even as some high-pitched voices went on whining their '*Kushat, kushat!*' I could hear other low voices calling out to one another, agreeing on tactics. It was only then that I realized the situation I was in, and at the same time didn't want to believe it. I stopped in my tracks. Barely a moment later they had the better of me. The strongest of them had jumped me from behind and now held me in a clinch, pinning my arms to my body. . . .

"I bellowed like I've never bellowed before. I bellowed like an ox, twisting, tossing back and forth like a wild boar, like a bear attacked by a pack of dogs. They were truly everywhere. Tucking my body, I held tight to my backpack. All that my wrenching back and forth accomplished, however, was that my glasses fell off, and I thought: All I need! When I looked up my eyes met those of a woman hurrying toward me. Her shame and my shame—there's nothing more to say. A hand was thrust down into the breast pocket of my jacket, inching bit by bit for my wallet and passport. My jacket was buttoned, my coat, too, but no matter how loud I screamed and twisted and turned, the hand thrust forward, farther and farther, it wouldn't have taken much and . . ."

The conductor is wearing a round cap. Uniforms without billed caps can't be taken quite seriously. He smiles, lips like Belmondo's, I smile and hand him my ticket, which he signs off on. We're moving through Tatabanya now, an eagle painted on a rock face, some sort of hoist frame on a hill topped by massive ruins. The Danube on the other side almost makes up for it.

"Suddenly they let go of me, one after the other, I heard somebody cursing, the whole pack made themselves scarce. I got to my feet. Walking toward me was a man in a fur cap, a full net shopping bag in each hand. I reached for my wallet, checked to make sure I wasn't bleeding, and picked up my glasses. I was all right."

Here the real story begins, but the narrative flow starts to meander, since some explanations are needed for the reader to follow the miraculous turn that the incident is now supposed to take for me.

I had bellowed myself hoarse and at first could manage only a whisper, so my rescuer barely understood my thank-you, but traced his gloved forefinger along the vertical slit a knife had left on the right side of my coat. I asked him his name. "Gilles," he said, "I'm French." "Gilles?" I croaked in bewilderment.

Watteau's *Gilles* was the favorite painting of my deceased friend Helmar, to whom *33 Moments* is dedicated. The Russian edition is the only one in which his first name appears rather than just his initials. This is required information for anyone to understand why I was so thunderstruck by the name Gilles. On the day of my book's publication, I had been rescued in the middle of St. Petersburg by a Frenchman named Gilles, almost as if Helmar . . . But of course I didn't actually believe that.

Gilles insisted we look for a policeman. We found one outside the GAI station (the "State Auto Inspection," as the traffic police are called in Russia) next to the Marble Palace. We shoehorned ourselves into a GAI Lada and drove around a bit, but the kids, much to my great relief, had vanished into thin air. What would we have done with them anyway? The only items missing were a little dictionary and a lighter taken from an outside pocket of my backpack. They hadn't punched me or kicked me or pulled my hair. A gutsy Gilles had sufficed to drive them off. When I spotted the Russian Museum through the window of the Lada, I realized that what had happened to me was something I had already described. "Have you ever seen anything like it, in the middle of the street, and kids right behind, two of them, and another, on a line with them, across the way, watching doorways, and then another, just ahead, along the railing . . . Müller-Fritsch lay half on his back, half on his side, against the canal railing."

A few hours later as I was walking, escorted by a translator and an interpreter, through the pedestrian passage under the Nevsky that would take us from Sadko in the direction of Gostinny Dvor, I tossed some coins in the cap of a one-legged beggar, all the loose change I had in my pocket. I still recall how in some little nook of my heart I regarded this gesture—made more by way of overcoming my own inertia than of performing any sort of sacrifice—as an act of propitiation that would guard me from similar attacks in the future.

The beggar, however, called after me, in a tone of voice that didn't sound like a blessing. When I turned around he was already swinging his one good leg between his crutches. I still assumed this was purely accidental. But once he set to work hopping up the stairs of the underpass after me, there could be no doubt. I barely had time to pull the door of the taxi shut, and there was the rubber tip of his crutch pounding against the windowpane. "We'll walk," Ada said—the cabbie had demanded an outrageous fare. "We'll pay!" I cried, never taking my eyes off the rubber tip banging at the fogged-over window. At last the driver maneuvered toward the middle of the street. At the same moment I was convinced that—since this too resembled a scene in the book—I myself would now have to experience everything I had described in 33 *Moments of Happiness*. St. Petersburg was demanding its tribute for my stories. How could I ever have thought I would get away with it, and go unpunished for writing anything I wanted to write?

No sooner had we come to a stop at the end of a long line of traffic waiting for a light than Ada screamed. Flames were shooting out of the car to our left, its motor was burning. We ducked, I waited for the explosion. During those seconds I ran through the book in my mind. But nowhere had my fantasy gone so far as to set a car ablaze. It wasn't my fault, this fire had nothing to do with me—I was overcome with relief. The taxi pulled away, and when we stopped again we were at least thirty or forty meters from the burning car.

You might take them for paratroopers if it weren't for the "Border Guard" printed on their chests. I know what I have to do. Without a word the border guard assigned to me extends his hand for my passport, shifts his weight forward, and—with an imperceptible flick of the wrist of someone playing trumps—hands my passport back to me, as if he weren't the right official, as if he didn't even need to look at it. And now it's the French family's turn. "*Bonjour,*" the children say, the parents smile—it's printed on the backs of the border guards as well, yellow on blue, "Border Guard."

But what's become of the customs agents?

In Györ there is a long freight train waiting on a siding, with cars labeled, "We're doing the driving for Audi" or "We're doing the driving for VW," plus logos, brown and rusty as the cars themselves. A water tower in the background, UFO on its shaft. Customs really ought to be here by now.

I'll tell Petra that in my story "Incident in Petersburg" my fear of having to pay for what I had written is the mirror image of my desire to live with a poet, and that I confused my love for her poems with my love for her, just as she confused love . . .

The first time I saw you reading your poems, I will say, I fell . . . But then I've told her a hundred times now how when she read her poems her face took on an entirely different look, like that of a young girl, and that when, between poems, she talked about the situation out of which the next poem had arisen—both the organizers and the public loved her for these stories—you believed she had just awoken and was shaking off a dream. And I was certain that everyone who saw and heard her had to fall in love with her. And yet I won't confess to her this time either that I dreamed of being the intimate "you" in her poems. I didn't want dedications—dedications are like thirteen-year-olds who smoke. You'll see, I'll say, rebutting each of her objections, I haven't written anything that will hurt you. No, I won't say that. What I've written is that everyone will want to move into your apartment, with its old hardwood floors that would do any museum proud, they'll want to go strolling with you in Schönbrunn.

In my "Incident in Petersburg," the reminiscences awakened by the burning car are followed by a depiction of the scene that took place only twenty-four hours before. I was on the phone with my father, and while searching for pencil and paper to write down his telephone number in the rehab clinic, I wandered into Petra's room with its wide floorboards and old windowpanes ("can't find those anywhere but Vienna"). Petra looked up, reproachfully, angrily, because I had torn her away from her poem or because I still had on her bathrobe, which was much too small for me. I looked just as reproachfully back at her, because she needed to understand that I had to find a pencil quick, and because she managed to run around in nothing but baggy pants, sweat pants, gym pants, jogging pants—clothes even a lousy soap-opera scriptwriter can come up with if he wants to denigrate a character. Only someone aware of the increasingly long intervals between our meetings would understand these mutual reproaches. Petra and I were just no match for all the running around, the earning-your-daily-bread reading tours, not to mention the constant back-and-forth between Berlin and Vienna.

Why shouldn't I be able to write about this? What if a few people guess whom I mean by Petra or Katja? Take the statement that it's better to buy a chicken in Vienna than Berlin, since chickens in Vienna still have their claws on, and the claws tell you if a chicken has actually scratched around in a chicken yard—do I have to approve of such statements, even if they're yours? I don't claim you're to blame for my mugging. Of course, a person can always be a little to blame somehow.

Silence. As if someone has pulled the plug, the heater stops rumbling, all noises cease, the train starts to roll again, almost soundlessly, a few hundred meters, puts on the brakes—Hegyeshalom. Pansies in concrete buckets. Hegyeshalom, border station. Hegyeshalom! I close my eyes, picture myself at the end of the world, and finally I get it: There are no customs agents at Hegyeshalom anymore.

"It would probably be good for both of us," Petra said, "if we don't see each other for a while." That was the end, the separation, I understood at once. And I also understood how pointless it was to protest. She made our farewell so easy! No arguments, no recriminations, just this "don't see each other for a while." How drunk I was with this unexpected freedom, and how stunned that it was all over between us.

Our stop in Hegyeshalom—there are no customs agents now—lasts three minutes. The heater rumbles on again, the train pulls out, rolls over the border. The free son of a free country, I feel nothing, my soul does not soar in jubilation.

An hour later the EC 24 pulls into Vienna West Station, on time, platform 7. With a blue folder and an empty bottle in my shoulder bag, I wait until others have boarded. I wait until the platform is almost deserted. I know what it looks like when Petra—or would it be better to call her Katja after all—hurries toward me with long strides, breaks into a run for the last few yards, and raises her shoulders just before she hugs me.

At ten to one, I walk through the entrance building of the Museum Quarter, a passage that reminds me of hospitals and barracks and worse. Abandon all hope. As for what I'm going to say to Katja, I'm even less sure now than I was when I started out. Besides, I still have that song from the taxi running through my head—"And all the bells are scolding. . . . It was a lovely day. . . ." I know, it's not "scolding," or "lovely" either, but I can't help it.

In fact I feel ridiculous with my blue folder in my bag. Yes, I feel like an infant—as if I'm overtaxing my abilities to choose a destination myself, as if I can maintain my composure only if I've been invited, asked to give a performance, with follow-up questions. I'm standing in the middle of the courtyard of the Museum Quarter. I have no idea what there is to see here. My cell phone buzzes a message. For a brief moment I hope I'll be able to escape my meeting with Petra or Katja. T-Mobile bids me welcome to Austria.

When I look up I see Katja in the middle of the entrance. We smile and look to one side or at the ground, then our eyes meet again. She has short hair, her hands are in her coat pockets, she has gained weight. We kiss each other on the cheeks, like old friends. "*Servus,* my dear," she says. "You look tired."

Katja climbs a set of steps ahead of me, I follow and watch the hem of her coat above the hollows of her knees, her calves, the red spots on her heels left by her old-fashioned pumps. "Here?" she asks, as if I had made a suggestion. I nod. El Museo, it's almost empty, a kind of IKEA restaurant. Katja opens her coat, I reach to help her out of it. Katja is pregnant. She smiles. I congratulate her. I am seething with jealousy, there is no love in me. We sit down.

I want to ask her who the father is. I bend down and extract the blue folder from my bag. I feel like a subpoena server who is not about to be derailed by sociability.

"So why are you in Budapest?"

The waitress and waiter look like brother and sister filling in for their parents on Sunday. They are both pudgy in the same sort of way, she's a blond, his hair is black, his round head reminds me of a mole.

I hear myself say Esterházy.

"Oh, you mean Péter?" she says with a smile and lays a hand on her belly. So they know each other. I should have known. Of course they know each other. He's probably had her give him a massage. There is no love in me.

I hear myself say Kertész, I hear myself say Konrád and Nadás, when I actually ought to be dropping very different names, but I'm boasting, boasting nonstop, I'm insufferable. I'm digging a hole to jump into.

Katja is paging through the menu, I follow the movements of her eyes. I try to signal the waitress, but she's busy clearing tables. The mole appears. I point to Katja. She'd like an apple juice, an apple juice and water, no, nothing to eat, really nothing. I order a seafood salad, a white wine, and water. "Effervescent white, perhaps?" the mole asks with a smug Viennese lilt.

"It's very good," Katja said. Okay then, for all I care, effervescent white.

Once we've ordered we gaze at each other as if everything has already been said and we can leave now. I say that Vienna was suddenly just around the corner.

Yes, Katja says, Budapest is a just stone's throw away.

The mole arrives. I have to make another selection. This time I order the skewer of prawns for sixteen euros, the most expensive item on the menu.

Katja has now leaned back, one hand on the table. Her fingers move, she's actually drumming the tabletop. I make some remark, and it feels like I'm squeezing the last glob out of a tube of toothpaste.

Katja splays her fingers and examines her nails. For a moment it seems absurd to be this close to Katja and not be allowed to touch her.

"Are you two married?" I ask.

"For over a year now," she says. I would love to ask if she already knew him while we were together.

"Excuse me," she says, gets up and heads for the toilet. Two men observe her rear end. One of them turns around to me, our eyes meet.

Katja and I make small talk. She sips at her apple juice, I drink my effervescent white and say it's fine, a good recommendation. In Budapest, I say, the exchange rate is now 1 to 250, and can stay that way as far as I'm concerned. I say that in Café Eckermann an espresso—a really very good espresso with milk and mineral water—costs 240 forints.

A half hour later I wave the mole over. "It will be right out," he says. "Right out."

"I'm not an impatient guy," I say, "but I don't understand why just a skewer . . ." Except for the two men the restaurant is empty. I finish my effervescent white, reach for my glass of water.

"And?" the traveler asks, laying his left hand on the blue folder. "What are you working on right now?"

"Just translations," she says.

"And your new volume of poetry, when's it due out?"

She shrugs.

He sips at his water.

"I'm not writing," Katja says. "I haven't written for three years now." And after a pause: "Maybe I did something wrong, and this is my punishment." Suddenly Katja looks like she's about to read one of her poems.

"What are you supposed to have done wrong?" he asks.

"I don't know," she says. "Are you afraid I'll write something about us?"

"To be honest . . ." Our traveler smiles. Or is it more the face of a whiny little boy? And then it happens, maybe out of embarrassment, maybe out of weakness, maybe because he's putting all his trust in the power of confession. He admits that he boarded the train because of two stories, because of "Official Report" by Imre Kertész and "Life and Literature" by Péter Esterházy, which both describe a train trip from Budapest to Vienna—that is to say, in the case of Kertész, in the direction of Vienna. He admits that the fruitful idea of traveling two or three hours to Vienna arose out of the hope of assisting his own imagination and providing direction to the unflagging impetus of his creative spirit *(motus animi continuus)*, of affording it an opportunity to soar in jubilation. Just as Esterházy alludes to Kertész's story, he wanted to allude to both stories and produce something like a comparative drama of railroad stations. Each sentence of his models seemed to him as significant as an antiphon in a liturgy, so that, or so he believed, he needed only to insert, sentence by sentence, his own observations and memories in order to experience something of the world as it is today, of the changes of the last few years, yes, something about his own generation as well. For Kertész had elevated (or better: bumped up, boosted) the story of his customs experience to an interpretation of life itself. (Please, do take the time to read the reason why a customs agent confiscated his passport on April 16, 1991, ordering him to leave the train at the border station in Hegyeshalom.) He likewise wanted to confront this customs agent, to invoke within himself and as if in a vision—damn literature!—the official report of Imre Kertész. I close my eyes, our traveler wanted to write, and see myself at the end of the world and finally comprehend: It's this Hegyeshalom! For decades the Hegyeshalom of Imre Kertész, this wretched filthy Podunk, was seen as the symbolic way out—*in hoc signo vinces.* Hegyeshalom! I can still see him pointing to the crest of Svábhegy from his apartment balcony only yesterday evening. I still see him, he wanted to write, see his big, hunched, heavy figure, the anti–Michael Kolhaas, who does not seek his truth, because his truth has found him. I saw his sentences, each one by itself— big, hunched, heavy sentences—swaying inexorably toward the final naked insight. . . .

But the customs agents never showed up. Our stop in Hegyeshalom lasted three minutes. The train pulled out, rolled over the border, and he, the free son of a free country, experienced nothing, his soul did not soar in jubilation.

"Did you want to find out," Katja asks our traveler, "how deep the fear still sits?"

"But without customs agents—"

"You should have taken the train to Prague," Katja says, "from Dresden to Prague."

"Maybe," he says. "But I'm here now."

"So you didn't want to see me at all."

"Sure I did, of course, I wouldn't have made the trip if it weren't for you."

"No," Katja says, "I was just the pretext."

He looks at her. He lays his hand on hers. "I'm not sure, Katja—on my honor, I'm genuinely not sure."

"You're disappointed—no customs agents, no story."

"Yes," he says.

"No customs agent to demand you hand over your story."

He nods and leans back for the first time. "I even had the title," he says.

Katja smiles at him.

" 'One More Story,' " he whispers and looks like a little boy again.

"Well then just write a different story, leave out the customs agent."

With the gesture of a magician forced to take the stage at the most inauspicious moment, I remove the blue folder from the table and let it vanish into my bag.

"Do you have to go?"

"No," I say, and think: There is love in her. Then I get up and walk over to the counter. I wouldn't want those prawns now, even if they did show up. Accepting prawns after an hour's wait would be an act of self-abasement. "I'll pay for the effervescent white," I say, "two waters, and an apple juice." The mole immediately starts punching up the numbers. The waitress calls out, "Cancel the order, the whole thing," and says that the gentleman—to wit, me—doesn't need to pay for the drinks and that she's sorry, very sorry. I ask why even after an hour they were incapable of serving a skewer of prawns.

She says they had searched themselves silly but simply couldn't find the prawns.

"Maybe you're sold out," I say, as if it were in my interest to find a better excuse. "Not only is the seafood sold out, but also the prawns, prawns being after all a form of seafood."

"Yes," the waitress says. "That may well be, the gentleman is probably right."

Katja asks me if I can't stay a little longer, we could go for a walk.

"I've got a date this evening," I say. I smile, despite myself.

"Ah," Katja exclaims. "I can guess."

"Yes," I say, "I ran into Katalin again."

"I would like to have met her," Katja says.

She accompanies me to the subway entrance. I push her bike. As we stand there at the top of the stairs, I ask when the happy day is.

In August, Katja says, a boy. Leaning forward, we hug, but our tummies touch anyway.

I forget to validate my metro ticket. At the West Station I try to give it to the fellow selling the homeless people's newspaper, but he declines.

I buy some Leberkäse, oven-baked, 1.60 euros per hundred grams. It weighs a little more, so with bun and mustard, it comes to 2.90 euros.

Across from me at the entrance to the betting office, are two televisions—Michael Schumacher has just won his fourth Grand Prix in a row, exactly ten years after Senna's death. I buy another half-liter bottle of water. My shoulder bag now weighs exactly what it did when I left Budapest.

I'm on my way back to Budapest. I'm on my way to Budapest. Isn't that an act of independence and freedom—not leaving home, not returning home, but simply being under way?

I'm sitting on the right, facing the front of the train. I'm relieved and I'm discouraged. The Örkény is lying on my lap. I pull the little ribbon out, the book opens to page 18. I begin to read the one-minute story titled "The Bow." I'm tired. The Hungarian border guard comes through the train. They do their job quickly. Because the seats block my view of the passports of the travelers ahead of me, I have the impression the border guards are shaking hands with the passengers.

"Must go back Austria," says a border guard—beard and pointy nose—to a mop of gray hair one row ahead. "Go back!"

The mop of gray hair speaks softly, the border guard loudly. "Buy visa! No multi, Hungary fly, Budapest, go by train out, finish! Must go back. Really go back. Next train go back Austria."

The border guard—beard and pointy nose—makes sweeping gestures with his arms, his hand is the airplane on which the mop of gray hair flew to Budapest several days before. The mop of gray hair intends, as I understand it, to fly home tomorrow too. He took a little side trip to Vienna, and now they won't let him back in. "No multi visa. Must go back!"

The mop of gray hair stands up. A trim older gentleman in a pastel pink shirt. He is told to follow the border guard. He's ready to follow him, but the border guard plucks at the man's sleeve and mimics pulling on a coat. The mop of gray hair needs to take his baggage and jacket along. But he doesn't have any baggage or a jacket, just the Vienna guidebook in his hand. Moving toward the front of the train, the border guard and the mop of gray hair vanish from the car.

A hush falls over the car, the train pulls out, the train stops, the train starts picking up speed, we're departing on time, Hegyeshalom, 4:45 p.m. On the other track a milk train, its cars are red and white, with windows you can still pull down—the merry mood of the children, mothers, grandfathers makes it look as if the train has stopped for a picnic.

We're moving past the long platform, and then, for a brief moment, I spot two border guards and right afterward, there where the platform makes a dip so you can cross the tracks, stands the mop of gray hair, with his pink shirt and a Vienna travel guide in his hand, and right behind him at an angle, but in fact shoulder to shoulder, a border guard. The mop of gray hair stares at the train where he was sitting just now, as if trying to see what awaits him on the other side. You can't tell whether the border guard is holding him by his upper arm or not.

In Győr, with its modest but heavily rusted station sign, the border guard—the beard and pointy nose who tracked down the mop of gray hair—gets off and walks down the platform. He's dragging a bright shiny blue suitcase behind him. He waves to someone, he shouts, he laughs.

Our traveler—he's past being assigned a name now—presses his head to the window, but all he can see is the border guard disappearing from view. He asks himself why he even wants to see the person the border guard is hailing. He has no real interest in the border guard, any more than he has an interest in the man in the pink shirt. The man in the pink shirt will have some difficulties to deal with, maybe he'll have to postpone his flight. Then again, maybe the border guards in Hegyeshalom will help him.

Because their job isn't really travelers with Vienna guide books in hand—no, they're just bunglers, maybe even morons. The guards are there for other people, the ones we don't see, who aren't sitting on the train, who can only dream of sitting on a train like this, alone with a Vienna guide book, who perhaps have far more dreams of sitting on a train than our traveler ever did, although he's always dreamed of sitting on a train like this one.

The train departs from Győr. "We do the driving for Audi," "We do the driving for VW." The UFO on the shaft. The same conductor with the round cap from the trip to Vienna. He smiles when I pull out the envelope, with no ticket inside, *Vonnattal Európaba* apparently means "By train to Europe." In addition to the Eiffel Tower and two red London telephone booths, there are also pictures of the Hungarian Parliament and Schönbrunn Castle. He signs off on my ticket again, where all the information is in both Hungarian and German.

From the empty seat next to him our traveler picks up a leaflet entitled "Your Trip Plan," with an ad on the cover that proclaims: "April 23rd . . . World Day of the Book . . . Grand Sweepstakes." The pages of an open book, the two center ones reprehensibly folded inward to form a pink heart. He leafs through the accordion-fold brochure until he finally finds the end station for the EC 25 from Dortmund. He reads: Budapest Keleti pu., Arrival: 6:28 p.m. After 128 kilometers or one hour and twenty minutes our traveler will be in Budapest. From Keleti pu. there's a train at 7:10 p.m. for Kraków Główny, which arrives shortly after six o'clock the next morning, and at 7:15 there's one to Istanbul via Szolnok, Bucharest, Sofia, and Thessaloniki. This one arrives a day and a half later at 8:45 a.m. at Istanbul Sirkeci. Our traveler is amazed that the timetable gives thirteen minutes from Kelenföld to Budapest–Keleti pu., although the distance is listed as zero kilometers. But he doesn't let it upset him. On the contrary, the inconsistency pleases him. And all the bells are scolding. It was a lovely day.

Our traveler, until now neither happy nor sad, halfway, so to speak, between a lost story and a secret rendezvous, is experiencing a feeling about as illogical as the timetable. But he surrenders himself to the indomitable rise of jubilation in his soul, as if he has in fact crossed a border, escaped some ignominious fate, arrived at some grand decision. Our traveler is full of love, so that he cannot possibly read and closes the book by Örkény, shuts his eyes, and like some spoiled but content house pet cuddles his temple against the headrest.

Ingo Schulze was born in Dresden in 1962, studied classics at Jena University, and worked as a dramaturge and newspaper editor in Altenburg. For his first book, *33 Moments of Happiness*, published in 1995, he won various prizes, including the Aspekte Prize for Best Debut. In 1998 he won both the Berlin Literature Prize and the associated Johannes Bobrowski Medal for *Simple Stories*. In the same year, *The New Yorker* numbered him among the six best young European novelists, and the London *Observer* described him as one of the "twenty-one writers to look out for in the 21st century." In 2005 his novel *New Lives* was honored with the Peter Weiss Prize and the Premio Grinzane Cavour. In 2007 he won the Leipzig Book Fair Prize for *One More Story*, his second collection of stories. He is a member of the Academy of the Arts in Berlin and the German Academy for Language and Literature. His books have been translated into more than thirty languages. He lives in Berlin with his wife, Natalia, and their two daughters, Clara and Franziska.

A NOTE ABOUT THE TRANSLATOR

John E. Woods is the distinguished translator of many books—most notably Arno Schmidt's *Evening Edged in Gold*, for which he won both the American Book Award for translation and the PEN Translation Prize in 1981; Patrick Süskind's *Perfume*, for which he again won the PEN Translation Prize in 1987; Christoph Ransmayr's *The Terrors of Ice and Darkness, The Last World* (for which he was awarded the Schlegel-Tieck Prize in 1991), and *The Dog King*; Thomas Mann's *Buddenbrooks, The Magic Mountain* (for which, together with his translation of Arno Schmidt's *Nobodaddy's Children*, he was awarded the Helen and Kurt Wolff Prize in 1996), *Doctor Faustus*, and *Joseph and His Brothers*; and Ingo Schulze's *33 Moments of Happiness, Simple Stories*, and *New Lives*. In 2008 he was awarded the Goethe Medallion of the Goethe-Institut. He lives in Berlin.

A NOTE ON THE TYPE

This book was set in Minion, a typeface produced by the Adobe Corporation specifically for the Macintosh personal computer, and released in 1990. Designed by Robert Slimbach, Minion combines the classic characteristics of old style faces with the full complement of weights required for modern typesetting.

Composed by Creative Graphics,
Allentown, Pennsylvania
Printed and bound by R. R. Donnelley,
Harrisonburg, Virginia
Designed by Virginia Tan